LETTING RIP

& other stories

Susan Knight

ORIGINAL WRITING

ISBN : 978-1-909007-11-6

A CIP catalogue for this book is available from the National Library.

Published by Original Writing Ltd., Dublin, 2012.

Printed by Clondalkin Group, Glasnevin, Dublin 11

For Christine, a constant reader

About the Author

Susan Knight is the author of three novels, *The Invisible Woman*, *Grimaldi's Garden* and *Gomorrah*, in addition to a non-fiction book, *Where the Grass is Greener: Voices of Immigrant Women in Ireland*. She has received several prizes for her short stories and stage and radio plays, including the James Plunkett memorial award, the Bryan McMahon award and the premier award in RTE's P J O'Connor radio play competition. She lives in Dublin where she teaches creative writing and lectures on literature for the Shaw Trust.

CONTENTS

THE MEADOW

I am standing in the meadow watching him walk away. I am standing in the long grasses of the wide meadow. I want to call out to him. I want to will him to turn and look at me but he just continues to walk away, further and further.

The grasses are pale: bleached yellow, bloodless pink, dry green. They wave their seed heads, brushing my thighs. They undulate like the surface of the sea.

Turn, I call silently. Turn back to me. He walks away, along the straight path beside the meadow. I can see him seem to get smaller and smaller for there is no twist in the path. I can watch until he seems to disappear altogether, realising that I too will have disappeared. If he turns now he will see that I too have almost disappeared.

And what if I call out loud? What if he turns and waves goodbye? What if he turns and still fails to stop? How will I live with that?

If he turns now and sees the great sea of the meadow, its waves swirling and churning, perhaps he will think I have drowned. Perhaps he will think I was never there. That the form he thought was me, so carefully not looking, was just a scarecrow, just a sack stuffed with straw.

I'm a plain woman. I can't pretend otherwise. I can't pretend there was ever even in the nape of my neck a sweetness to draw a man back from an action he'd decided to pursue. My body was never that of a young girl, but always thick, my flesh coarse, my hair dry as straw. That's why I don't call out. Because I don't think it would make him stay. At least as things rest the answer to the question remains open. I stand in the meadow always, my arms stretched out to him as he walks away, his name screaming silently out of my throat.

That was long ago. And while my real self stands still in that eternal moment amid the long meadow grasses, my shadow moves through a series of automatic gestures in what people are pleased to call time. I marry a man from the village, a large, comfortable man who appreciates my aptitude for hard work more than my lack of feminine graces. Between the weary grind of work and the blessed absences of sleep we make five children. Then I curl up against his back, the two of us fitting together like pieces of a jigsaw puzzle. And when I place my hard hand on his soft, hairy belly, this is the best moment of all. This and those spent in a half-dream suckling the five babies, one after the other, so drunk on the sweet smell of their sweat that I almost forget that I'm not really there. That I am still standing in the wide meadow watching a young man swing away from me down a straight path of hard clay, without turning, the wind that lifts the grasses lifting his long dark hair.

Word reaches our village from time to time from the outside world. Word of wars fought and lost – for wars are always lost: how can even one death in battle be termed a victory? Word of uprisings and revolutions, cataclysmic accidents, acts of a God we are told loves us. Little touches the grind and sleep, grind and sleep of our lives. Word comes of him too but I laugh. I know his real self has never gone but is still eternally going. That the one who made it to the city is just a shadow, like me, like the me that laughs at the news of him.

Some of my children marry and have children of their own. One goes to the city and disappears there, one goes further and is killed in a battle some call a victory. My man dies suddenly in his bed and I awake beside a cold and stiffening corpse. I miss the comfort of him at night and I weep for it.

I am standing in the meadow. I am standing in the long grasses of the wide meadow watching him turn back to me. He is running towards me, his arms outstretched. They have told me that it is his son, so like him as he once was you can't tell the difference. But I know better. They say he died in the city and that his son is bringing his ashes home, to scatter on the meadow of grasses. It was his wish, they say. To bury his heart where he left his heart, where he would have stayed if the woman he loved had said just one word. If she had not indifferently watched him walk away from her. That's what they say the son said.

I am standing in the long grasses. The wind blows against me like kisses. He has turned towards my outstretched arms and is running back towards me. Always. Forever.

FLOWERING CHERRY

This morning I woke to find my husband Frank stone dead in the bed beside me.

I didn't scream, like they do in the films, not at first anyway. I just stared at him for a long time. Making sure, I suppose. But he was cold and no breath fluttered the little hairs in his nostrils.

After a while I went downstairs. I stepped outside in my night-dress, the pink one with teddy bears on it, and stood on the wet grass in my bare feet under the cherry tree.

The young fellow from number 43 passed on his way to work. I called out to him. Help me, or something. But either he pretended not to hear or he was wearing one of those iPod things. I suppose it distracts from the tedium of the journey.

So I just went on standing there until Missis from next door came out to fetch in her milk.

'Whatever are you doing, Eileen?' she asked. 'You'll catch your death.'

I don't quite remember what happened next but later I was in her kitchen drinking a cup of strong sweet tea. I noticed she'd got those pine-fronted presses in. They look nicer than mdf.

'That'll do you good,' she said, although I doubted it. I've always hated tea with milk and never take it strong. Sure enough, I had to run to the lavatory to throw up. Luckily they have a downstairs one, unlike us. Her husband's a builder and put it in himself. I noticed she has one of those air fresheners stuck to the wall that lets out little puffs on a regular basis. As a result, the room smelt sickly sweet, but better than sick, I suppose.

She was good about it, even though some of it went on the floor. Wouldn't let me mop it up and said it was a natural reaction. To the sudden death, she meant, not to the tea.

'How long have you been married anyway?' she asked.

'Thirty-seven years,' I said.

'That's more than half a lifetime.'

She's a nosy, managing kind of woman. I've never much cared for her but in this instance I was grateful. She called 999 and the ambulance came promptly and pronounced Frank dead, even though I knew that already. They reckoned it was a massive heart attack but had to wait for the doctor to confirm it. He wouldn't have known what hit him, they said, kindly enough. Terrible for you, though, they added.

I've been cleaning up. Well, clearing out. It keeps me busy and Missis next door approves. She's been telling everyone I'm in shock. To account for the fact that I haven't shed a single tear, I suppose.

'Let me know if there's anything I can do,' she says, but I don't need her. The undertakers are very helpful and have walked me through the whole business even though I wouldn't have had a clue about organising a funeral up to now. Padraig, my eldest, says I shouldn't have rushed into things and that he knows a firm would have done it for half the price but I told him I wasn't in the humour to shop around.

The funeral was well attended. I hadn't realised Frank was known to so many people. But then my daughter Gemma – back from Munich for the occasion – whispered 'ghouls' to me and, when I asked what she meant, she said the place was packed with ould ones whose idea of a fun way to spend a morning was to find some funeral and toddle along to it.

I didn't care much for the comments of the priest.

'Frank wasn't known to me personally,' he said, and then went on about what a wonderful husband and father he was. That was all rubbish. I mean, how could he know? Gemma and Padraig were in floods of tears but I still couldn't. Not even at the graveside in that bitter wind. I kept thinking about the cherry tree and how now it wouldn't have to be cut down.

Padraig and Shirley, his wife, came round this afternoon.

'What ever are you doing, mam?' asked Padraig. 'Can't it wait?'

'I'm collecting it up for the Vincent de Paul,' I said.

'But that's all good food. You can eat that.'

It was tinned stuff, the sort Frank liked, the sort his mam used to make for him. Tinned peas and peaches and rice pudding, oxtail soup and lamb stew and steak and kidney pie. I never liked any of it and wasn't about to start now. Frank always harped on about how I didn't eat properly. At least I won't have to listen to that any more.

Actually, earlier on I had been watching one of those cookery programmes, the one with the pretty girl who's a vegetarian. I've never been comfortable with meat, so I thought, I'd like to try that. I'll probably buy her book, the one they advertised at the end of the programme.

'If you want any of it, help yourself,' I said to Padraig.

He picked up the spaghetti hoops.

'The kiddies would eat this,' he said, 'wouldn't they, Shirl?'

The upshot was he took everything except the rice pudding, so not much for Vincent de Paul after all. Padraig also went through Frank's things and picked out his good suit, not the one he was buried in of course, but the grey with the navy stripe. Also a couple of pairs of shoes. Now that's what I call ghoulish – wearing dead men's clothes – but Padraig said it would help keep his dad's spirit alive.

'Oh and those shirts look hardly worn, mam. Might as well take them as well.'

After they'd gone I cooked myself some dhal with lentils, onions and spices I got down at that new oriental shop. I even stirred a bit of natural yoghurt into it, the way your one on television advised. Then I took the phone off the hook and curled up on the couch to eat it. I could hear Frank saying furniture isn't for feet. It is now, I thought.

I've been taking driving lessons. I mean it's stupid having the car sitting outside the house, rusting away. Padraig said he'd take it off my hands – it would do nicely as a little runaround for Shirley – but I said I'd like to see if I could manage it first.

'Won't be easy at your age, mam,' he said. 'And by the way the house stinks like an Indian takeaway.'

Missis next door knows this old fellow, Sidney, who gives lessons. His car's a Golf and mine a Fiesta but I suppose the principles are the same.

Sidney's a widower, he tells me.

'Life's just not the same, is it,' he says.

'It certainly isn't,' I reply.

'Anyway, you'll soon get the hang of it,' he says, probably referring to the driving.

I've been admiring the cherry tree. I remember when we planted it, how years later the kids used to climb up into the branches. Padraig won't let his now. He says it's too dangerous.

'What would happen if they fall? Would your insurance cover that, mam?'

In fact he's been on at me to have it cut down.

'Isn't that what dad planned to do?' he asked.

'I'm sick of the sight of the bloody thing,' Frank used to say. 'No use to anyone. It doesn't even have fruit you can eat.'

Padraig was still rabbiting on about it.

'You wouldn't know yourself, mam,' he said. 'It would make the front room much brighter. I know this fellow would do it for you cheap and take the wood away after.'

But I love that tree. And now the spring's here it will be flowering soon, a mass of snowy white blossom.

I'm shy to say this, since it's very personal, but I think I had an orgasm last night. I'm not sure because I've never had one before. Frank liked to get the business over quickly and I couldn't do anything about it myself, not while we shared a bed.

Anyhow, I'd been curled up on the couch, drinking a glass of bacardi and coke and watching one of those adult channels you can get on digital. It was quite explicit and I was about to turn it off when they started on about masturbation. Seemingly some comedian had quipped 'don't knock it: it's sex with someone I love' which I thought was quite funny. So anyway I tried it out and I must say it was very enjoyable. I'll certainly do it again sometime.

I think I'm going to give up the driving lessons. With Sidney at least. He keeps on about the loneliness of the single life and how there's a lot to be said for companionship in the autumn of our days. When I think about it now I should have put him straight at once and told him that if I ever wanted a new relationship, it wouldn't be with a seventy-two-year-old midget without a tooth of his own in his head. I know that because his false sets keep slipping.

Then this morning Missis next door called over to me while I was hanging out the washing.

'I hear you're getting on very well with Sidney,' she said, and winked.

He lives in some miserable old person's flat and probably has an eye on my house.

In fact, I reckon I might sell the car after all. If there's one thing to be said for Frank, he kept it in good order, and his mechanic, Andy, has already told me he could find a buyer at a fair price if I was interested. Then I could take a holiday on the proceeds and not feel I was dipping into my capital. There's a very nice looking Mediterranean cruise in one of the brochures I picked up recently that's not expensive at all when you consider what they provide. I've always wanted to go abroad, further than North Wales, I mean. I could always go and visit Gemma – she's forever inviting me – but her partner Helmut is a sneering sort of a person, too much like Frank for my liking.

I won't tell Padraig about my plans just yet. I'm not sure if he meant to offer me any money for the car but I don't think it would be anything like what Andy can get. Andy's a nice man. A widower too, by coincidence, and very well preserved.

Today I parked rather skilfully under the cherry tree, which arches out a bit over the road. It's covered in tight buds now, about to burst into flower. Almost the best time, like a promise. I was plucking up courage to tell Sidney I was stopping the lessons, when he cut in.

'You know something, Eileen,' he said. 'If I was living here, first thing I'd do is chop down that yoke. There must be an awful mess on the car when the leaves and that fall down all over it.'

I know his car is his pride and joy, but for me that was the clincher. I told him rather abruptly that it didn't matter because I was selling the car. I'm afraid he took it badly. He seemed to suggest that I'd led him on and wasted his time. Although at €30 per lesson, he didn't do too badly out of me.

I'm sitting in the tree. I don't think anyone noticed me climb up – it was easier than I'd thought – and no one can see me now unless they look really hard. The leaves are thick and through them the sun is flickering camouflage patterns on my skin. A soft breeze is stirring the blossoms, for the buds have fully opened at last. My lovely flowering cherry is all dressed up just like a girl at her debs, ready set for a new and amazing life.

Miss Fonseca And The Nemesis

Miss Fonseca was a sensitive soul. She only had to hear of bunny rabbits being used to test cosmetics or come upon pictures of neglected puppies or kittens, to burn with outrage. Such enormities even inspired her to compose poems subsequently read out in her booming voice at the writers' group of which she was a member. On these occasions her eyes would goggle through thick glasses daring anyone (a certain sarcastic individual in particular) to criticise or suggest she had fallen short in her sensibilities. In addition, she regularly wrote poems to commemorate disasters like the twin towers attack or famine in Africa or the tsunami that killed hundreds of thousands of people and devastated communities. A particularly successful example she considered to be her *Threnody on the Assassination of President John Fitzgerald Kennedy.* She had been a schoolgirl playing camogie that day, returning home in a muck sweat to find her family bunched round the wireless, and a skilful image (even if she said so herself) linked the two events. In fact, she put herself forward in all her lyrical fragments in order to express in rigid metre and unflinching rhyme (Miss Fonseca despised, vociferously and often, the laziness of free verse, a source of contention between herself and the sarcastic individual) the deep emotions such events stirred in her formidable bosom.

'I am,' she would often announce to her audience, 'an open wound that cannot heal. I suffer,' she added, 'the pains of this sad sad world.'

She was, in short, a lady of exquisite feelings.

But while Miss Fonseca's poet's soul bled into words bemoaning starving black babies or those terrified children displaced by obscure wars or acts of God in countries you didn't know where to find on the map, it has to be admitted that her emotions were not aroused in the same way by youngsters closer to home. Not to beat about the bush, she couldn't stand them, snotty babies that everyone else was oohing and ahhing over or commenting on with indulgent smiles on their faces, 'I think little Cyril has done a jobbie.' Disgusting, in Miss Fonseca's humble opinion and not something to be talked about in polite company. And children just got worse as they grew into loud screaming toddlers and later into the young ruffians who kicked their footballs among her hydrangeas or knocked on her door and ran away before she could answer. And this dislike, loathing even, of hers was all the more unfortunate because Miss Fonseca was a national school teacher.

Her class consisted of the eleven to twelve age group, the last year before the children moved on to secondary school, on the verge of or verging over into puberty when things, Miss Fonseca considered, went from bad to worse. And there was always one, at least one, that she couldn't abide beyond all the rest. In this year of Our Lord 2011, the child in question was George Wiggins.

Now Miss Fonseca wasn't a small woman. In fact she prided herself on what she considered her statuesque build, despising the current fashion for stick-insect figures. Large-breasted, broad-hipped, she yet possessed a flattish stomach (for her age) and strong but shapely legs. Not that anyone ever saw her legs above mid-calf except when she went swimming once a week, up and down the pool for thirty lengths, slow and stately in a breast stroke that kept her rubber-helmeted head of short grey hair well out of the water. George Wiggins, in contrast was a lardy blubbery boy with breasts that undulated disgustingly under his PE vest and wide soft hips that bulged over the waistband of his shorts. His hair resembled soiled straw, he had pale eyes and wet pink lips and every time Miss Fonseca caught sight of him she had to suppress a shudder of revulsion.

In a just world, Miss Fonseca reckoned, George Wiggins would be the butt of the class bullies, for his shape, his looks and his stupidity – he was so far from being an A student as to have fallen off the end of the alphabet. But it was an unjust world, as Miss Fonseca knew only too well, and George Wiggins was popular. Observe a cluster of boys laughing their heads off and George Wiggins would be at the heart of it. Or there he'd be leading a troupe off to mischief, climbing on the roof of the bicycle shed or kicking balls where it was prohibited to kick balls, or writing graffiti on the outside of the girls' lavatory, VIV BINNS STINKS, EMMA PAGE HAS BIG TITS, ALVA MAC IS A LEZZER, with additional obscene if anatomically incorrect illustrations, including girls with oversized breasts and penises. Not that George Wiggins had ever been caught drawing these. It was just that Miss Fonseca knew in her heart of hearts that he was one of those responsible. In short, as she frequently concluded to herself as well as forcefully to her colleagues in the staff-room, the boy was a tragic waste of space, a blot on the landscape, a carbuncle on the face of society.

Having for many years cared for aged and, truth to tell, rather trying parents now deceased, Miss Fonseca lived alone, the way she liked it in the family home, a small corner terraced house on a road near to a large sports ground. This meant that on Saturdays and Sundays during the season, her road was barred to traffic, guards standing at each end to prevent cars of non-residents entering and parking. Her neighbour, Mrs Gannon, a woman of extreme fertility with many grown-up children, as well as the three that still lived in the house, complained bitterly of the difficulties they experienced when trying to visit her, which Miss Fonseca reckoned, was every single weekend. Passes had to be got, to enable them to drive up with their spawn.

'Imagine that. In a so-called free world. We might as well be living under Hitler,' Mrs Gannon would remark over the front garden fence to Miss Fonseca weeding around her hydrangeas.

'Mm,' Miss Fonseca would answer, privately rejoicing in the peace resulting from the absence of passing traffic. But she was reluctant to express this thought to Mrs Gannon yet again. The woman never listened anyway. Miss Fonseca for her part had few if any visitors to her home, the way she liked it, so wasn't incommoded by the traffic ban. Actually, to state that Miss

Fonseca lived alone was not strictly true. Her life companion was a large white cat, with a consistently supercilious expression on his face. He would turn this to the world through the glass of either the front downstairs window or the front upstairs window, whenever Miss Fonseca was out, be it at work or at mass or shopping or attending the various groups of which she was a member. Snowball, for such was the creature's name, was greatly indulged by Miss Fonseca. No tinned food for him, no dry pellets, only fish fillets or chicken breast prepared with a gourmet's zeal by his adoring owner. One might even surmise she did this to appease the animal, to make up for her frequent absences, for whenever Miss Fonseca turned the key in the lock to return home, she would find Snowball standing in the hall regarding her with a reproachful gaze, only then to turn and walk in stately fashion away from her in the direction of the kitchen as if to say 'Wherever have you been? I'm starving near to death.'

Later, after he had been fed and petted to excess, he would forgive her and sit on her lap if she was trying to read, or across her shoulders and face if she was trying to rest, or move under her feet if she was trying to complete her household chores. But Miss Fonseca didn't mind. Snowball was merely displaying his devotion to her. It would perhaps be needless to add that he shared her bed.

It was one of those sporting Saturdays when traffic was banned from their street and Mrs Gannon was as usual giving out about it while minding two exceptionally scruffy-looking grandchildren, with mud and chocolate on their cheeks and green snot under their noses. Miss Fonseca was trying to ignore the mindless babble of her neighbour and the ear-piercing shrieks of the spawn while admiring the colour and size of her hydrangeas. They were truly splendid this year. Great balls of blue and pink and purple. Mrs Gannon of course failed to comment on or even notice them. The woman had no soul.

Snowball meanwhile was lying on Miss Fonseca's daisy-and-dandelion-free lawn, eyeing a robin that had rashly landed nearby.

'He'd love to get his claws into that, I reckon,' Mrs Gannon opined.

'Not at all,' Miss Fonseca replied, 'Snowball wouldn't hurt a fly.'

'Hmm,' said Mrs Gannon. 'Well, he oughtta. I mean, it's in his nature to hunt, isn't it.'

Miss Fonseca didn't feel the need to grace that remark with a riposte.

'Still and all,' Mrs Gannon went on, 'you'd love to know what's going through his mind, bless him, wouldn't you.'

Miss Fonseca smiled graciously. After all, hadn't she so often thought the same thing.

'Bet he's thinking I just fancy a nice bite of bird.' And Mrs Gannon guffawed with merriment, her red face redder than ever, her small eyes squeezed tight with mirth. 'A nice bite of bird.'

The two grandchildren laughed too. Then the smaller one poked its tongue out at Miss Fonseca.

'Here, Adrian,' said Mrs Gannon. 'Cut that out. That's rude, that is.'

But the child just laughed some more and poked its tongue out again. And so did its sibling.

The little tykes! Good God, Miss Fonseca thought, what I have to endure.

And then, just as she thought things couldn't get any worse, they did.

'Hiya, Miss.' A loathsomely familiar voice spoke over her garden wall. 'Howaya!'

It couldn't be, but it was, as she finally registered. George Wiggins, out of school uniform and weirdly got up, together with a larger facsimile of himself.

'This where you live then?' the boy continued but, before Miss Fonseca could reply, he went on. 'We're almost neighbours so we are. We live over there,' waving a fat hand vaguely in the direction of the corporation flats. That figured, she thought grimly. The sort he was. Then he added, gratuitously, for how could it possibly be of interest to her, 'me n me brother are going to the match.'

'Really,' Miss Fonseca replied coldly. That explained the fact that the child had green, white and orange face-paint crudely applied across his large cheeks and forehead, no doubt to mimic the national flag. She was vaguely aware that the match was a big one: Ireland versus some other country. Progress to some cup or other depended on the home team doing well.

George was fingering the petals of a purple hydrangea which was blooming over the wall. She longed to shout 'Stop that this instant!' but recollected in time that she didn't possess here the authority she held over her class. Also, the older brother, a boy of about sixteen, with a sprouting growth of gingery hair and pus-filled spots around his chin, was watching her with eyes that held an expression in them that wasn't pleasant. She was suddenly uncomfortably conscious that he too had passed through her hands in years gone by. Wiggins... Wiggins...? Hadn't there been a Frank, or maybe a Charles.

Meanwhile Snowball had approached, had jumped on the wall. George left off mauling the hydrangeas to pet the cat with his grubby hands. He would soil Snowball's pristine fur. Again Miss Fonseca wanted to instruct him to desist but refrained. After all if the boy liked cats, he couldn't be as bad as all that.

'This your mog, miss?' George asked and when she reluctantly nodded, added, 'he's some bleedin monster, in't he? What you think, Jase?'

Jason Wiggins. Yes, she remembered now, only too well. Or at least, had a vague sense of a boy who had once been the bane of her life.

'He's a big brute all right.' Jason spat on the ground and stared at Snowball, who stared balefully back. 'A big fuckin brute. Pardon me French, miss.'

He sneaked a look up at her as if to sneer you can't do anything to me now.

There was a pause.

'Well, enjoy your match,' Miss Fonseca said briskly, pulling up a clump of chickweed which had insinuated itself among the night-scented stock.

'Cheers,' said George.

Jason was again gazing at the cat, which finally, imperiously, turned away its head.

'Ha! See that,' he said to his brother. 'I stared the fuckin bleeder out.'

Later, when the shouts and roars from the sports ground became too much to bear, Miss Fonseca went up to her bedroom at the back of the house, inserted wax plugs in her ears to block out both the match noises and the nearer yells and shrieks and laughter of her neighbours and lay down with Snowball to have a rest. Recently she had been in the habit of taking a short nap in the afternoons after she came home from school and found herself, as she informed other staff members, reinvigorated as a result. This time she fell into a deep sleep that lasted, she was aghast to observe when she finally woke up and checked her watch, for nearly three hours. Her head was throbbing and she jumped up in a panic. The match would be long over!

To explain this seemingly excessive consternation, it should be explained that it was customary on such days for her to make a point of standing in her garden with a severe expression on her face as the crowds shuffled by in their sports shirts. (How absurd, she always mused, for people whose bulging bellies indicated they never took any exercise of any sort to wear such gear.) Unless she monitored them in this way, they would chuck their plastic bottles or crisp packets or sweet wrappers over her wall. Sometimes, as she had observed in the dusk after evening matches, they would even bold as brass go into someone's garden and urinate.

She raced down the stairs to find what horrors had been perpetrated while her eagle eye was closed and was almost disappointed to find nothing more than a few cigarette butts, which she adroitly scooped into a plastic bag without actually having to touch them. It was after she had accomplished this task that she realised Snowball was nowhere to be seen. She went upstairs again but not only was he not lying in his customary position on the duvet but the spot was cold. He evidently hadn't been there for some considerable period.

It wasn't time to panic yet. Sometimes, very occasionally, Snowball availed of the cat flap – he was almost too big to fit through it these days – to go into the back garden to lie in the sun and watch the birds. Miss Fonseca went into the back garden. There was a high concrete wall all around it so that she was at least spared the view, if not the noise, of Mrs Gannon's descendants, who even now were rampaging around the place.

No obvious sign of her pet. She peered under bushes, around the decking where she sometimes sat and drank tea with a good book. (The overly-friendly young man who installed it had suggested its suitability for barbecues and Miss Fonseca had shuddered. Did she really look like the sort of woman who went in for that sort of thing?) She even checked in the shed. Nothing. She contemplated standing on a chair to look over the wall and see if Snowball had somehow got into the neighbours' garden or at least ask if they had seen him. But she anticipated the blank faces that would mock her concern and she put the chair back on the decking.

First, she decided, she should hunt through the house properly, systematically. She recalled only too well that nearly tragic occasion years before when she had pulled out the drawer under the bed that held her linen to remove some clean sheets when the doorbell rang. She had rushed down only to find a collector for some allegedly good cause. 'I only give to certain charities and never at the door,' she had stated before the person could launch into their prepared spiel. Although the collector had looked at her sceptically, this was nothing less than the truth. She supported three animal charities: pet rescue, the donkey sanctuary and an organisation devoted to neutering stray cats and dogs.

Vowing to place a notice on her door – which she had subsequently accomplished: it read NO SALESMEN, HAWKERS, CANVASSERS OR RELIGIOUS CALLERS, (the last in the light of the two women from the Jehovah's Witnesses who didn't seem able to take no for an answer, pressing their tackily printed newsletter on her. 'Just read this,' they had urged, even expecting her to pay for the thing, until she slammed the door in their faces) – she had returned upstairs, absentmindedly pushing the drawer closed, without noticing that Snowball, considerably smaller than he was today, had climbed in to snuggle among the soft fabrics. It was only several hours later and after an increasingly distraught search that she had heard his outraged mewing and rescued him.

She now looked in the same drawer, but no Snowball. It was in any case hardly likely that a cat of his supreme intelligence would make the same mistake again. She hunted in every conceivable place. No Snowball. She went down to make his dinner, leaving the back door open. The smell would no doubt lure him in. While the salmon was poaching, she called his name out across the garden. After a while she heard an echo, 'Snowball, Snowball' in high-pitched voices. It was Mrs Gannon's grandchildren, copying her, making fun of her. How right she had been not to ask them if they had seen her cat.

Dinner time came and went. The salmon was cool enough to eat but no sign of the intended consumer. As for herself, under the circumstances and unusually for one who had a healthy appetite, she couldn't eat a thing. The night was drawing in and with it a heavy shower of rain that had been forecast, coming in from the West. And poor Snowball out in that! Miss Fonseca was distracted with anxiety. At last, not knowing what else to do, she ventured next door, ringing the bell that sounded out 'La Cucaracha'.

Mr Gannon, a person she avoided as much as possible, opened the door in his vest, his drinker's face leering out at her.

In answer to her question he shouted back into the house, 'Neighbour wants a snowball!'

Mrs Gannon then bustled out. From the smell of her breath, she had been drinking too and it took a while for Miss Fonseca to make her meaning clear.

'Oh, the cat is it? No love, haven't had sight nor sound of him since this afternoon.' She paused. 'I just hope one of them vivisectionalists hasn't got a hold of him.'

Miss Fonseca looked at her wildly. Whatever was the woman on about?

'They cruise around seemingly and pick animals off the street to experiment on them. I seen it on TV.'

Miss Fonseca let out a strangled cry.

'Now, now, dear. I don't reckon that's happened to your'n. Probably just gone walkabout. Looking for a lady friend, like.' She winked. 'Know what I mean.'

Typical of these people, Miss Fonseca thought. Sex on the brain.

'That's impossible,' she replied coldly. 'Snowball's been neutered.' But then her sudden access of *sang froid* deserted her again and she choked with emotion.

Mrs Gannon looked up at her neighbour, grey hair spiky from where agitated fingers had repeatedly run through it, the mad eyes, as she later described them, that seemed to pop out through the lenses of those thick glasses.

'Why dontcher come in and have a beer, calm you down, pet,' she said, moving aside to let the other in. The hall beyond was strewn with children's toys.

'No... I couldn't... I couldn't,' Miss Fonseca burbled. 'Not while Snowball is out in this... Heaven knows what might happen to him, the poor little thing. Oh God, whatever would I do without him!' Big tears welled out of her eyes and sploshed down her cheeks.

'Take it easy, love. Take it easy. It's only a cat.'

Only a cat! Miss Fonseca leapt away from her neighbour as if whipped by the words and raced back down the path. Only a cat! Only a cat! How could she say that? What did she know about it?

Mrs Gannon watched her go, shook her head and closed the door.

Till three in the morning, Miss Fonseca wandered the streets, searching for her pet and calling his name. (Her desperate voice even entered people's dreams and on waking they puzzled over visions of snow in summer.) Home again at last, she rang the guards, only to be answered by a weary and unhelpful officer, who fobbed her off. When this is over, she thought with a brief return of her customary astringency, complaints will be made to the proper authorities. After all, it's my taxes pay his wages.

She tried to sleep but vision of Snowball in dire distress rose before her eyes. Could it be that the vivisectionists had really captured him? At four in the morning it seemed only too likely. She imagined him stretched out on a table, pinned down, unable to move, a surgically-masked man in a white coat brandishing a hypodermic needle over him, scalpels to hand. She could almost hear the terrified mewing. Snowball! She would never see him again.

As dawn rose she fell again into a heavy sleep, crowded by frightful dreams she wouldn't remember in the morning except as a sickening sense of dread. A bell finally roused her. She looked at her watch. It was eleven already and she had missed morning mass. Gradually she realised it wasn't the church chimes sounding out but her own doorbell. She jumped out of bed as she was (she was still dressed, though mightily dishevelled) and ran down the stairs. She threw open the door and stared in horror mixed with relief at what she saw. For there on the threshold stood her nemesis, George Wiggins, gripping with difficulty a lump of something large, wet and luridly coloured that at the sight of her leapt out of the boy's arms, screeching with rage. Snowball! But Snowball as she had never seen him. Someone had defaced his beautiful white fur with orange and green stripes. The same orange and green that the day before had adorned George Wiggins's face. Someone had cruelly perpetrated this obscenity on Snowball's pure white fur and inflicted unspeakable suffering on her poor dumb pet. George Wiggins, no doubt about it, now returned to gloat over her distress.

'You!' she yelled and seized him by his shoulders. 'You!' She shook him violently. 'You depraved animal! You fat, ugly abomination! What have you done to my poor Snowball?'

The boy tried to speak but she knocked him hard across the face. Then seized him by the throat, throttling him until his eyes bulged and he gasped for breath.

'You lowest of the low, to torture a poor defenceless creature. You... you abomination.'

She pulled him by the hair, him screaming from the pain of it (no more than he deserved), across the garden, intending to fling him out the gate.

Suddenly she realised she had an audience. A large audience. The Gannons, just returned from mass, in their Sunday best (Mrs Gannon, as Miss Fonseca automatically registered, wearing one of her ridiculous hat) were standing in a body, grim-faced watching her. Other neighbours, people she seldom saw, were suddenly all around. My God, even the individual from the poetry group, a sarcastic smile on his face. Wherever had he come from? She loosened her grip and thrust the boy away from her. George Wiggins fell sideways, heavy as a sack of potatoes.

'Here,' Mr Gannon said. 'You leave that boy alone. He was only bringing yer fuckin cat back.'

Her Nemesis, suddenly small and pathetic, hunched among the broken hydrangeas where he had fallen. There was blood coming from his lip where her hand had cut across his mouth. Everyone looked from her to him.

'I found it this morning over in the bushes,' he whimpered. 'I thought it was a mascot, for the match. With all that paint on it, like. Then I saw it was your'n. It scratched me when I tried to pick it up.' He held out his podgy hands, criss-crossed with the thin red marks of his martyrdom. 'I didn't do nothing to it, miss, I only picked it up. I only wanted to bring it back. Honest...' He burst into tears.

'That's child-abuse, that is,' one woman said. 'Shocking. Someone should call the guards.'

'She's a teacher, isn't she? Shouldn't be allowed near kids.'

'Poor little chap, only wanted to help.'

'Ugly old bitch.'

'But... But...' Miss Fonseca suddenly realised that she had made a mistake. Surely they would understand that. Under the circumstances. A mistake anyone might have made and one she was ready to acknowledge.

She even said it. 'It was a mistake,' she said.

But even with all those people watching her and muttering, the sarcastic individual smiling in a nasty way, George Wiggins still sobbing among the wreckage of her hydrangeas and an angry-looking stout couple, who would turn out to be his parents, marching purposefully towards her led by the boy Jason, Miss Fonseca was as yet unable to comprehend just how huge, how irrevocable, how world-shattering that mistake had been. But later she would. Indeed she would.

TIGER

Just now is the best time of day here. While the sun is gentle, glancing off the waves out in the bay, sparkling with promise. While the hills behind the town are blue with mist, before the sun turns hostile and burns them yellow and glares off the whitewash on the walls of the houses, and makes the street, the sand, too hot to bear in your bare feet.

It's the best time of day but Sylvie always sleeps through it, rolling out of bed at noon, her pink silk pyjamas stuck to the sweat of her big brown body.

'Up with the lark again,' she'll say to me, stretching languorously. As if she knows. Perhaps she does. Perhaps she sees me in her dreams, prowling about the house liked a caged cat.

Back home I could never have imagined the thirsting heat of midday here, sucking the moisture from everything, the land, the trees, plants, from me. At least it stays cooler here in this house, this room. The north-facing window that looks out over the bay won't let the sun stare in, even without blinds. Some of the house is even cold. The stone floor in the kitchen will be chill now. But even later, when the sun is high, I shiver down there: it's dark and musty, like a tomb. Up here, though, the fleshy plants, the pet parakeet raucously complaining, make me think I'm in some sort of jungle. An imagined place, like in a picture by Henri Rousseau. And Sylvie the dreamer about to be pounced on by a tiger.

When I arrived – how many weeks ago now? –I could tell that she was astonished to see me. But her face soon broke into a wide smile, teeth shining welcome.

'Margaret!' she said. 'You are 'ere.' That very slight lack of an aitch the only signal that English isn't her first language.

'Madagascar,' she had told me that first time we spoke, in the club after class. 'That's my country. Very far away.' And laughed. She always laughs a lot.

She could talk to anyone. Secure in herself. That's what struck me at once, with envy, since I am one who mumbles and shuffles and tries never to catch anyone's eye. And it wasn't just me: everyone was transfixed by her, the hugeness of her. From her mane of hair (a rich shade of red) to that tight top low-cut over swelling breasts, that leather skirt hardly covering massive thighs. But mostly it was her personality – warming as a glass of sweet dark rum – that drew us to her. Even Dorothy, who has been heard to express resentment at the number of black people in Ireland.

She was a newcomer to our class. There's a group of us have been trying to learn Spanish for years. Other people join and leave, but for a small core it is part of our lives. We don't learn much because Candelas, our elderly teacher, spends the hour recounting her colourful life, mostly in English but occasionally throwing in a Spanish word or two to justify her wages. She grew up in a noble household. Her parents were *francistos* – meaning that they supported General Franco – and her elder brother was killed in the civil war by accursed reds, *los rojos malditos*. Every time she recounts this episode, her eyes, usually hard and bright like jet beads, fill with tears that overflow down crumbling cheeks. As a girl, she tells us, she was sent to Ireland to learn English, staying in a good convent boarding school. 'I decided to become a nun, *una religiosa*,' she told us. But, after several years, she was ravished by the convent gardener, a man with soil under his fingernails. 'They threw me out,' she said of the nuns. 'I became an artist's model: *el modelo de un pintor*.' The start – shaking her head with its dyed black hair dragged back into a thin bun – of yet more troubles.

You can imagine how riveted we were by her tales: our band of spinsters and elderly bachelors, widows and orphans, whose lives had been circumscribed by habit and tradition.

Actually, I blame Candelas for landing me here. If she hadn't opened a window on another world, I would probably have stayed put.

Sylvie shook up the class. Shook up Candelas, who soon stopped joining us after our Spanish hour, for her customary cognac. I fear that our teacher, like Dorothy, disliked *las negras*.

Sylvie has her stories too. Like Candelas she comes from a privileged background. Her father is a diplomat.

'Money no object,' Dorothy would mutter, sniffing Sylvie's expensive perfume, squinting at her diamond necklace, stroking her fur coat, watching out the window as Sylvie sped off in her yellow convertible to some party.

As for me, I fell in love. No, that gives the wrong impression. I felt warmed by her, as if all my life up to that moment I had been chilled, huddled up in a fruitless attempt to stave off the shivers. She is like sunshine. Not the pitiless midday heat of this place but the joyful morning light that she never sees.

Where is she? I have been watching the clock and it is already past noon.

She told me of her plans: to open a chain of beauticians across Ireland, *Chez Sylvie*. But over the six months she spent in the country she concluded that Ireland wasn't the right place.

'This eternal damp,' she said, 'puts out my fire.' And threw back her great head and laughed, quivering all over.

The next idea she had was to go to France.

'Home from home,' she said, French being her first language. Madagascar imbued, apparently, with Gallic culture.

To go to Provence to study how perfume was made. And eventually open up her own perfumery.

'What do you think? It would be fun?'

'So you are leaving us,' I said, envisaging her striding through fields of lavender.

I must have looked sad, because Sylvie said to me, 'But Margaret, you can come too. Why not?' And laughed and kissed my cheek.

I sat at work, in front of my monitor with its dreary lists of figures, and thought, why not indeed? What is there to hold me here? However, Sylvie didn't go to France in the end, but much further, to this place. The home of an elderly family friend who had gone away, maybe forever. It had been suggested that Sylvie should caretake. And feed the parakeet and water the plants. So she said, why not for a bit? It would be fun.

Sylvie, it struck me then, was like some exotic butterfly flitting from flower to flower, while I was an ant, working, scurrying, storing. And for what?

'It is great here,' she wrote in expansive script over the back of a postcard. 'You should come. We would have such fun. Kisses.' Followed by three xs. I ran my fingers over them and then over my lips.

I pondered. It seemed crazy at first, but then less so. There was still time to change my life. I even had a little money from my late parents' investments. I sent a reply accepting the invitation and then another indicating my arrival time. There was no answer but she had already warned me that she was a terrible correspondent. She smiled when she opened the door, but I could tell she was astonished to see me.

That was weeks ago and now I stand here shivering in the kitchen. I am preparing Sylvie's hot chocolate, to take up to her. I imagine how pleased she will be at my thoughtfulness. Maybe she will even stroke my hand the way she did last night, after she came in smelling of perfume and wine and men.

Carefully holding the brimming mug, I climb the wooden stairs that creak with old age. On the second floor, the parakeet upbraids me. I don't go near it any more. The day I arrived, enchanted with the pure whiteness of its plumage, I went to stroke it. It bit my finger, drawing blood that fell on its breast in two dark drops. Then, as I cried out, it stared at me with malicious bead-black eyes that reminded me of Candelas. Now, instead, I pause briefly to look past it, through the window at the light that has changed, the sun glaring straight down on the terracotta roofs of the town, a dazzle off the white walls, shadows like spilled ink. I see the chair draped with the green silk jacket Sylvie was wearing last night when she came in, her bag, the fashion magazine she picked up briefly when I started to ask her about her evening. The magazine that she dropped, telling me she was too tired. Going laughing towards the creaking stairs to bed. Smelling of wine and perfume and men.

I climb a second flight to the landing where the door to Sylvie's room and mine face another like polite acquaintances. I tap lightly on Sylvie's door and it swings open just a little. I tap again. I lean my head forward. Can I hear her breathing in her sleep? The way I have so many times, trying to match my own breaths to hers and giving up because she breathes so much more deeply than I ever could. I inhale the perfume that fills her room, heavy and mixed with sweat. I push the door wide open. The bed is empty. But how could she have got up without me noticing? I call her name. I cross to the bathroom but already know she won't be there.

Now I am panicking. I have remembered with terror bits of the dream I had last night. The prowling tiger, circling its prey. Pouncing. Blood. 'Sylvie,' I call down the stairs, 'Sylvie!'

'Sylvie,' the parakeet mocks me.

Maybe she has gone for an early swim. She often suggests it: 'Tomorrow, my darling, we will get up with the lark and go down to the sea.'

She is concerned because I don't go out any more.

I tell her the sun affects my skin and brings it up in lumps. But that doesn't excuse the nights.

That first evening we went down to the shore. We paddled and cooled ourselves by splashing each other, clothes and all. We laughed so much, soaked as we were. I have never felt so alive. But then she wanted to go to the bar and drink wine.

'All the friends will be there.'

Dark men with white teeth gleaming in the candlelight. Women in vivid silk dresses who laughed in their own language. And me, sitting at the edge, clutching a glass of red liquid that glinted as I swirled it round.

One of the men danced with me but I trod on his feet. And when he touched my breast, I pushed him away. I didn't come here for that, I told him. He just shrugged and hissed something in low tones. I never went out again. But she did. Every night. Even though I begged her to stay in with me, she never would.

'I am young,' she said once. Was it only last night? 'I want to live my life. You are an old woman already, Margaret. Old in your head. A shrivelled old woman. Do you even know what it is to love?'

Out she flounced. I waited in the velvety dark of the jungle for her to return. I caught her scent, her stink.

'When are you going to leave?' she had asked. 'When are you going to fuck off?'

'Sylvie!' I call, but my voice echoes in the emptiness. And now I remember everything, the dream that was not a dream.

When they come round to ask their questions, as they will, I'll tell them it is she who has left The butterfly has flitted off again. They will look in the presses and find nothing of hers, only dresses that fit the owner of the house. I have tried them on, and they fit me, too. Widow's weeds to hang on a scarecrow frame.

I'll say Sylvie asked me to stay and keep an eye on things. Then, once they stop calling, I'll wring the parakeet's neck. I know how to do it, after all.

I take her silk jacket. Later I'll place it under my pillow. That way I can smell her perfume all night. Her bag will have to go downstairs. Along with everything else. Into that cellar I found under the flagstones of the kitchen floor. I'll do that in a minute. Meanwhile I flip open the magazine and glance through it but it has no interest for me. Instead I stare out through the window, at the setting sun turning the waves blood red. I finger the diamonds at my neck. They were still warm when I put them on last night but now chill like frozen tears. I shiver and know that nothing will ever warm me again.

THE GATEKEEPER

All things considered, Knuss was satisfied with the way he had conducted himself. He had inclined his head respectfully when the director was speaking to him. He had replied 'Yes, sir' and 'No, sir' as appropriate. Nothing he had said or done could have been faulted in any way.

He knew, moreover, that this apparent compliance had made the director uneasy.

If the director had said, 'Knuss, these are your orders. Obey them,' and slapped the papers down in front of him, in duplicate or triplicate, with the proper stamp from a higher authority, then he would have bowed to the inevitable. But the director had done no such thing. Instead he had cajoled, tried to persuade. He had behaved, in short, like the weak man he was. Like all his predecessors. Directors, from Knuss's long observation, came and went with rapidity. For them the job was just a stepping stone or, rather, a rung on a ladder that reached up and up, the sky, as the saying goes, the limit.

And that was how he knew the director would not make a stand on this particular issue. No less than Knuss himself, the director was hopeful that the whole miserable business would simply fizzle out, but imagined this would be achieved if Knuss gave way. Knuss himself was determined to stand firm. From experience he knew something the director failed to understand as he shinned up his ladder: you had to have someone holding firm at the bottom, or the whole lot would topple over.

So while directors moved on up, going who knew where, Knuss stayed where he was, feet on the ground, doing what he had to do. Knuss, and so many like him. Despised by the ignorant, he knew his to be a noble calling. He even belonged to an association, the Most Honourable and Ancient Guild of

Gatekeepers, and attended monthly meetings. On such occasions all members wore the olive green uniform that marked them out, with its gilt buckles and trim and matching peaked cap adorned with the emblem of the association: crossed keys. For many years indeed, Knuss had proudly worn his uniform to work. Then one day a predecessor of the present director had summoned him, endeavouring to explain that times had changed, that we were now living in a new, less formal age, in short that Knuss's uniform gave out the wrong impression. He had been barred – in triplicate – from wearing his uniform to work and since that black day it had hung in his wardrobe, brought out only for the monthly lodge meetings.

Knuss looked forward to these. They were convivial and yet dignified occasions, with speeches from the chairman, secretary and treasurer, followed, when the formalities were over, by mugs of beer and savoury snacks prepared by members' wives in rotation. The potato pasties, sausage rolls and cabbage dumplings his own wife, Berta, had provided on more than one occasion always merited gratifying expressions of satisfaction from his peers. This, too, was the moment when members were encouraged to exchange anecdotes about their experiences, uplifting, amusing or shocking. And then there was the annual parade, always an inspiring day. A marching band led members from all over the country in a procession, each lodge proudly holding aloft its banner, to visit the stations of the cross in one or other of the regional centres. For the guild, unlike so many other sections of modern society, never forgot to Whom they owed their final allegiance. Part of the initiation ceremony even included a solemn pledge to serve the God of their forebears and to carry out His orders at all costs. The procession over, the marchers retired to some local hall for the traditional feast of spit-roasted pig and copious quantities of the local beer. As a rule, Knuss partook only moderately of both food and drink but on such occasions he permitted himself to let his hair down, as the saying goes. This year the procession was to be held in his own town, and he swelled with pride at the prospect.

And now too, he himself would have an anecdote to impart to his fellow gatekeepers, a rare occurrence since he was guardian to a small museum, housed in an old church and consisting of objects of ecclesiastical art. It was not exactly on the main tourist trail and had few visitors, most of those moving deferentially and swiftly past the exhibits and perhaps purchasing a postcard or two from him on the way out. The only excitement was when someone tried to cross the line into the museum without paying. Although this was an invisible line, stretching from the gatekeeper's booth to the edge of the screen which partly concealed the church from the visitors, for Knuss it plainly existed and he was ever ready to leap up and chide interlopers, driving them back out over the line until they paid up. Which some did, while others shrugged their shoulders, perhaps muttering curses, and strode off.

Otherwise the only irritant in a quiet and some might say boringly uneventful occupation was when people tried to see into the museum by peering round the screen and not bothering then to pay the nominal entrance money. Some even took photographs through the small gaps Knuss had been unable fully to block off. There was nothing he could do about it except to give such people stern looks, but it always put him in a bad humour if it happened more than once or twice on a given day.

Then suddenly there had been this intrusion into his domain. Whose idea it was, he did not know. They would never bother to inform such as him. No doubt it was the bright idea of one of those hanging off that infamous ladder. One of those who went around spending good public money on something they were pleased to call art but which, in Knuss's humble opinion, hardly merited the title of garbage. For one thing, either it was something you could not hang on your wall, or something you would never want to. Knuss knew what art should be like, these wooden saints for one thing, these ancient chalices, these dignified Madonnas. But failing that, a nice picture with cows in a field, or flowers in a vase, or a harbour scene with boats. Something to make you feel good about life. Not to confuse you or make you ill. When she was much younger his own wife, Berta, had painted several still lives of fruit and some picturesque scenes of mountains copied from postcards. Indeed, several of them adorned the walls of his house, along with a family heirloom, the portrait of his grandfather, the old man severe in a black suit and snowy cravat. At first Berta used to complain that grandfather was always watching her and making her nervous. But surely, Knuss explained patiently, that was the skill of the artist: to paint so that the eyes followed you. Knuss betted none of these modern so-called artists could achieve as much. Anyway, Berta seldom complained any more so she must have come round to his way of thinking. Even though once in a while she might drop and break some domestic article and mutter that grandfather was giving her that look again.

But what had been foisted upon him here was something different. A foreigner, who 'painted with sound', as the director explained it.

Knuss had never heard anything so foolish in his life. And then, when he finally got to hear this so-called sound painting, well, what was he supposed to think, what was it supposed to be? Music for Knuss was something you danced to, sang to or best of all marched to with your peers. It was played on an instrument: a trombone or a piano or an accordion or something. These weird echoey sounds came out of a computing machine.

'It is a painting in sound of this very museum,' the director had explained.

'Is that so, sir?' Knuss had said, his eyes on the ground. If he had looked up and encountered the blank gaze of Mrs Krumphandl, who customarily supervised the upper gallery, he was sure that, despite his best efforts to contain it, his scorn would have snorted itself out through his nose.

The sound-painter was standing next to the director. He was a tall foreign-looking individual, whose hair stood on end as if he had just been subjected to a strong electric current. He said something indecipherable, no doubt in his own language.

'It is to play constantly in a loop,' the director explained. 'You just switch it on in the morning and switch it off at night. Mr Brandes will now demonstrate.'

Knuss watched the procedure with a sour face. These foreigners who thought they could swan in with their alien ways and change the way the world was ordered!

'Now you try.'

You switched it on. You switched it off. It was simple. Of course, thought Knuss to himself, the simplest thing would be not to switch it on at all.

Which was what had got him into all the trouble. The summons to see the director. After the foreigner and his pals had started turning up at unexpected moments only to find peace reigning as it had always done in the museum, Knuss at his post and Mrs Krumphandl knitting upstairs.

The peace had then been disrupted by the angry shouts of the foreigner who furthermore wanted his pals to be admitted without paying the entrance fee. Knuss had never heard of such a thing. There was the invisible line to think of. There were the rules.

He had explained to the director – the foreigner sitting there angrily, his hair more electric than ever – that those weird sounds all day gave him a headache. Knuss would have liked Mrs Krumphandl to back him up but she, in the way of women, was intimidated by the director and even more by the foreigner and just lowered her eyes.

'It is a great honour, Knuss,' the director had smiled ingratiatingly, 'for Mr Brandes to have brought his installation here to our town. There is a huge interest in his work world wide. A man like Mr Brandes would be welcome to exhibit his piece anywhere.'

Then let him go anywhere, Knuss thought. Anywhere else.

'I understand,' he had said, inclining his head.

The director had smiled again and shook his hand, had shaken the foreigner's hand. Knuss, however, did not offer, nor was offered, to shake the foreigner's hand. And he had continued not to switch on the machine unless someone paid their money and asked specifically to hear it. In fact, to be precise, it was not he who switched it on at all. It had been placed in a small side room upstairs, and so when necessary – for he could not be expected to leave his post – he would call to Mrs Krumphandl, who would lumber up out of her seat (first putting down her knitting) and go off to wrestle with the computing machine. They then had to endure the weird sounds for as long as the visitor wandered about, pretending to be interested. And when the visitor left, Mrs Krumphandl got up again at a signal from Knuss, and switched it off again.

What a pity it would be, Knuss often thought, grinning to himself, if she should accidentally – because women like Mrs Krumphandl, and indeed his own wife Berta, had such a limited understanding of such technical things – if she should accidentally wipe it off.

Yes, indeed, all this would be something to tell his fellow gatekeepers at the next lodge meeting. He anticipated gleefully how they would make expressions of outrage in support of his stand.

The only previous occasion when he had been in a position to tell any sort of anecdote was after some woman had dashed into the lavatory just at closing time. He had rung the bell and called out but still she failed to emerge. He recalled the nods and sly smiles of his fellows when he described this. Finally he had been forced (Mrs Krumphandl having left for the day) to bang on the door. The woman had rushed out in some kind of a state, pushing past him without a word of apology, and Knuss had at last been able to start locking up.

Almost instantly the woman had returned, tapping on the glass door to attract his attention. Knuss had indicated by pointing at his watch that it was already well past closing time. The woman had persisted and when he opened the door a crack, she told him that she had left her handbag in the lavatory.

'You may collect it in the morning. We open at ten,' Knuss had said. The woman irritated him with her nervous manner, her dishevelled appearance. It would do her good, he thought to himself, to live with the consequences of her lack of self-discipline for a few hours. And he shut and locked the door.

He had retrieved the bag from the lavatory. It was a battered object, just what he would have expected. He did not look inside though he surmised it possibly contained cigarettes or drugs or something of the sort. He placed it on his desk where the woman, still looking hungrily through the door, could observe it.

'I don't understand,' Berta had said when he explained it to her at the supper table. 'Why didn't you just give it back to her?'

She looked at him with her freckled white face that always reminded him of a dish of milk pudding sprinkled with nutmeg, and he was overcome with a realisation of the impossible gulf between them. She could not understand the mysterious calling that he, the gatekeeper, had. To make sure the rules were kept. To keep hold at all costs of the bottom of the ladder. The preservation of society as we know it depending on him and his ilk.

'At least,' he said, 'it wasn't a baby.'

Berta turned her face up to him from the macaroni and cheese that she was eating.

'A baby?' she asked.

And then he told her of the experience of a colleague of his when some woman – it was inevitably a woman in these instances – had actually gone off leaving her baby behind.

'It was in a chariot by one door and the woman just flew out of another. Closing time, d'you see.'

Berta was blinking those pale eyes of hers very rapidly.

'And he kept the baby until the morning?'

'No, of course not!' How absurd women were! 'In this case he bent the rules and gave the baby back. But it was an extreme case. An exception.'

'A baby!' Berta said with longing in her voice.

Now Knuss remembered why he had not told her this story before. Her dream, and one of which Knuss approved, was to have borne children. But it had never happened. Something they both had to endure in their different ways. In fact, to tell the honest truth, Knuss was somewhat relieved. He would have put up with a child if it had proved necessary to do so. He would have behaved properly and even on occasion envisaged himself instructing the infant in the ways of the world. And yet how disruptive these noisy creatures could be. He was sure he could have made a better job at enforcing discipline than some of the fathers who visited the museum, but on the whole he was content that God had not sent them any offspring.

For Berta it was different. Women, he understood, needed children to make them feel complete. To give purpose to what were often purposeless lives. There was Mrs Krumphandl, a mother and a grandmother, knitting endlessly for her family. One garment after another. At least not staring blankly into space.

In the first few years of their marriage, Berta had endured the demands of the marriage bed in the expectation that what occurred there would lead to a child. When this failed to happen, Knuss saw how she turned away. Physical relations between them were infrequent, but still at times he was overcome with a great need. On one such occasion, he had suddenly become aware that although his wife's broad white body lay still and resigned, her face was turned to one side as if expecting a slap.

Knuss had been startled. Never, never would he hit a woman. But there she was, as if expecting it. He had groaned and rolled off her and she had pulled down her nightdress. Since then, he had not felt the need, or if he did he relieved it in other ways.

Now the day of the parade was nearly upon them and he, Knuss, had been appointed to march with the ceremonial emblem of crossed keys. It was a great honour, as he informed Berta. And yet there seemed to be a conspiracy to spoil it for him. Once again he was summoned to the director's office, forced to leave the museum in the far from competent hands of Mrs Krumphandl, forced to leave the weird music sounding out.

Once again, the electrified artist stood arms folded, a grim expression on his face. And next to him his own director's immediate superior, a man who represented the provincial authority.

'Knuss,' the director said, attempting a stern tone, 'You have persistently ignored instructions regarding Mr Brandes's installation.'

Head bent. 'Yes, sir.'

'Is that all you have to say?' This from the superior.

'I'm sorry sir, but...' Knuss looked up.

'But what?'

Knuss took a deep breath. Now or never.

'It's not appropriate, sir. It's not what people who come to the museum expect.'

'Oh really! And who are you to decide this?'

I am the man who is there day in day out, while you are off treating foreigners to unmerited hospitality, while you are lining your pockets with my taxes and plotting your next step up the ladder.

But Knuss said nothing of this and bent his head again.

'Any further insubordination will be severely punished, do you understand?'

Knuss nodded, 'Yes sir.' But he kept his face down because he was smiling. It was not for these people to discipline him. He was employed by a different department of the civil service. All they could do was to recommend a certain course of action which he was sure his guild would oppose with all the strength and influence at their command.

'So we'll hear no more of your opinions as to what is or is not appropriate for the museum.'

'No sir.'

And you'll hear weird music there, Knuss thought, over my dead body, as the saying goes.

The foreigner had uttered not a word. What was the point when no one could understand him except the director?

Now he turned on his heel and flung himself out the door.

'He is threatening to write a letter to the Minister in the capital,' the superior informed Knuss. 'It could be very embarrassing for us.'

For you. Not for me. But Knuss pretended to look chagrined.

'It's only for a few more days, Knuss.' That cajoling tone again from the director.

Until the next time, Knuss thought. A wearing away at the base of things. The thin end, as the saying goes, of the wedge. He at least would not let it happen while it was in his power to prevent it. Never.

The officials drove away in their large cars. Knuss then gestured to Mrs Krumphandl, and peace, except for the distant clack clack of her knitting needles, filled the vault of the old church once more.

The next three days passed silently, except for the occasional visit from one of the foreigner's spies. An architect who lived in a weird house on the outskirts of town exploded a flash in front of Knuss's face before running off. A photograph. Mrs Krumphandl was concerned, but Knuss laughed off her foolish worries. She failed to understand that he was untouchable because he was right.

Finally the foreigner arrived to dismantle his equipment. It happened that Knuss was out taking his lunch break at the time, not because he feared a confrontation – he would have relished his victory – but because he had after all to eat. When he arrived back Mrs Krumphandl was placidly casting off.

'That's that then,' he said to her, and smiled.

On the morning of the parade, he removed his uniform from the plastic packaging placed around it by the dry cleaners. There was a faint chemical smell off it, not wholly unpleasant.

Berta polished the already gleaming buttons, the big black boots, while Knuss lay in a hot tub. He washed his newly cropped hair, he soaped his armpits, his feet, his crotch. Then he showered himself with cold water. No time for idle needs.

From the skin out his clothes were freshly laundered. Whatever else you might say about Berta, she was efficient at her duties. He checked himself in the long mirror in the bedroom and was satisfied.

He was, however, taken aback to learn that Berta did not intend to come and observe the parade, his great moment. It was not right, he told her, even if she felt unwell. It was the least she could do. All the other wives would be there for certain. Doing the done thing. If she stayed away his colleagues would be asking questions, raising eyebrows, nudging each other knowingly. Suddenly, her anxious puddingy face infuriated him and he raised his voice even more.

'Please yourself,' he said finally, turning away.

The procession wound through the town. It was a smallish place, so the number of onlookers was limited. And many folk had joined the parade, through the square, along the main street, up the hill, past the few last houses, the way of the cross. Knuss marched in the first line behind the brass band, holding aloft the emblem of the guild. What matter if his arms ached? It was the greatest honour of his life.

He looked out for Berta's brown felt hat, in the hope that his words had touched her conscience and made her change her mind. But the only woman he recognised was Mrs Krumphandl, surrounded by equally foolish-looking people of varying ages, members, no doubt, of her extended family. She waved at him and he gave a curt nod of recognition.

Now they were passing the architect's odd-looking house. The large glass pane in the sharply sloping roof had been explained to him as a solar panel, to collect heat from the sun and save energy. Knuss thought it was, as the saying goes, an eyesore. It certainly made his eyes sore just looking at it and he could not understand why the authorities allowed such a thing to be built when traditional architecture had served the people of the town since time immemorial.

And see how everyone's eyes were drawn from the way of the cross to the monstrosity. Knuss tried not to look but took a quick peek. It really was ugly, a carbuncle. Several of the inmates were standing on some sort of low concrete ledge, an unrailed balcony, drinking, laughing. Raising their glasses towards the parade in a no doubt mocking toast. Such people had no respect for the good old ways.

Then Knuss looked again and nearly dropped the crossed keys. That startling hair was unmistakable. Right beside the architect stood his enemy, the foreign sound painter, laughing and mocking with the others. Knuss glared at him. The man frowned. Recognised him.

Suddenly the foreigner leapt right off the ledge and came running across the grass. Towards him. Towards Knuss. There was no doubt about it. And there was no dignified means of escape. The man pushed through the marching band, the trombones, the cymbals, the kettledrums. He charged into Knuss, knocking him to the ground and pummelling him. Instinctively, to defend himself, Knuss cracked the emblem of crossed keys on the man's head, but it broke in two pieces. Not gold at all. Nor even brass.

Now someone was pulling the foreigner off him and then the architect started explaining something before leading the man back up to his house. Knuss got to his feet, still shaking, and resumed his position at the head of the procession, trying to hold the emblem together so that the break would not be apparent.

But people were regarding at him in a strange way. Fellow members dropped their eyes when he looked at them in appeal. They moved away from him. Shrank back. Suddenly he realised the full horror of what had just happened. He had used the sacred emblem crudely as a weapon instead of defending it at all costs against the attacker. He had not only broken the crossed keys, he had broken his oath. He had brought shame to the Guild.

His face was wet and dark drops were spattering his uniform, blood from his nose, tears from his eyes. Mrs Krumphandl came forward out of the crowd with a large blond son. In soft tones she offered to help him home, but Knuss refused. The last thing he needed was pity from such as Mrs Krumphandl. Spoilt. Everything was spoilt. Nothing would ever be the same again. He scuttled off down the hill by himself, back to his house. The procession was longer than he expected, endless, and everyone turned to look at him.

No sign of Berta in the kitchen. He ran to the bathroom and splashed water over his face. His nose was swollen and there was a lump over his eye. It would be black by morning. Soap stung his eyes, burnt his nose. His hand failed to locate any towels. Wherever did Berta keep them? The linen cupboard, of course. Everything in order here at least. Blinded, he pulled out a drawer at random and rummaged for something to wipe himself. He pressed the cloth to his face and dried his eyes. It was only then that he realised that what he was holding, spattered in blood, was too small for a towel. He stared at the square of soft white cloth, which resembled nothing more than a baby's nappy. He pulled more and more items out of the drawer: more nappies, tiny rose pink and sky blue and lemon yellow garments, little knitted jackets, little suits, bonnets, mittens that would fit over one of his thumbs, bootees tied with ribbon. The drawer was stuffed full of them. He gazed at them stupidly.

'Berta!' he called. But there was no answer. He ran into the main bedroom. No one. Silence.

At last he went to the spare bedroom. This would have been the children's room, if there had ever been any children. Berta lay stretched out on the white sheets of the bed in a clean nightdress. There was a half empty glass of water beside her and an empty bottle of sleeping tablets. Knuss looked at her in shock. Then threw himself on top of her. He thought she was still breathing but she didn't respond to his shouts. And when he shook her, she just slumped back.

They told him later that his early return had saved her life.

By now, of course, word had spread in this small town about the foreigner's attack, the shameful way that he, Knuss, had fled from the parade.

The doctor smiled.

'Every cloud has a silver lining, as the saying goes,' she said.

Later Knuss wondered about that. He looked into his heart and wondered which alternative he would have chosen, if God had asked him first. Then he looked deeper and started to wonder about the very nature of the choice and the road that had brought him to the point where he now found himself. He wondered about Berta, too, perhaps for the very first time.

But when he sat down beside his wife's bed and took her hand, she turned her face away from him, as if expecting a slap.

JEALOUSY

Me in a hat! Imagine it! I haven't worn a hat since that black floppy thing I bought years ago in an Amsterdam flea market.

The invitation is on hand-made paper sealed with red wax and stamped with a crest. I show it to Astor, who throws back his head and laughs.

'Not only that,' I say. 'They haven't invited you.'

He stops laughing now.

'What a shame,' I say. 'You'd look great in a dress suit.'

It's my nephew's wedding, my brother's only son (there are however a rake of girls). My brother is a millionaire – the source of his loot is actually a bit dubious – and he likes to put on a flashy show. But not inviting Astor is mean-spirited and I tell my brother as much. Later, my sister-in-law Jennifer, the snobby one with the big hair and make-up lashed on like Polyfilla, phones me to say that of course Astor will be welcome to the afters, but the reception is strictly for family members.

'He might feel uncomfortable,' she says, and I wonder if she's prejudiced. Astor is very dark, Argentinean, even though his ancestry is Italian.

'If you marry me,' he says, 'we wouldn't have all this trouble.' Here we go again, I think.

My revenge on Jennifer is the hat. Astor helps me with it. We buy the basic model, a bashed up felt job, in Oxfam and sew things on to it – bright feathers and beads and flowers and dead birds. Astor attaches it to my hair – my wild Irish hair, as he calls it, all matted red curls – with a jewelled hat pin.

'Ouch!' I say.

Actually, I'm very fond of my nephew, Eoin, and even more of his fat girlfriend, Molly. So I take off the dead birds before the service. Astor flutters his dark lashes at me. I wish he wouldn't do that when I am supposed to be in a rush.

The upshot is that I am late. Also that the church door slams loudly behind me just as the rake of daughters are launching into song. Everyone, especially Jennifer, turns round to stare at me. Her glare visibly turns into outrage at the sight of my hat. But I don't falter. I smile self-deprecatingly and sit down at the back. Next to Jennifer's kleptomaniac brother, Tighe. (When he was sent to jail and his picture was in the papers, Jennifer informed all and sundry that he was in that section of Mountjoy reserved for the better class of criminal: embezzlers, forgers and tax evaders).

'Love the hat,' whispers Tighe as the rake of daughters aim with varying success at the high notes. 'Where's Astor?'

'Banned.'

The service takes its usual meandering course. Eoin and Molly promise to love each other forever and all that rubbish, and sign something to that effect. The Catholics take communion, Jennifer leading the way like a battering ram charging the walls of unbelief. Then suddenly it's over and the bride and groom walk down the aisle to the accompaniment of the theme from *The Godfather*.

'Am I hearing things?' I ask Tighe.

Fond as I am of Molly, I have to concede that the dress she has chosen does nothing for her. She looks like a large portion of cream-filled meringue. But Eoin is licking his lips at her like crazy, so I suppose that's what matters.

The reception is in some fancy hotel with a golf course instead of gardens. We perch by the eighteenth hole and pop chocolate-covered strawberries into our mouths and guzzle champagne while those five inexhaustible daughters sing a medley of songs. Although 'The Way We Were' and 'I Never Promised You a Rose Garden' seem strangely inappropriate to me. Maybe the girls are bitching because none of them has yet found a steady beau. We move into the bar, because a group of golfers want access to the course without the risk of knocking cold some vision in pastel. I sense already that it's a mistake to keep pouring champagne down my throat but can't stop. I feel like I'm drinking for two.

They've seated me for dinner between a banker and a dentist. Both of them take one look at my hat and turn to the people on the other side of them. To counter boredom, I consider flicking the prawns from my cocktail at the mountainous cleavage of the banker's wife opposite me but instead catch the amused eye of Tighe across the room. Turns out, there's an empty seat at his table, so I stand up (as best I can), smile sweetly and say, 'I'm going to be awfully rude and abandon you.' Then I wobble across to Tighe. The banker's wife actually turns round in her seat to stare at me. Maybe she was hoping to make me her new best friend.

Astor peeks in during the dessert. There's a book going round, organised by Tighe, to guess how long the speeches will take. Five euro a bet and winner takes all. I refuse to participate due to an uncharitable suspicion that Tighe will somehow manage to pocket the takings. Instead, I go over to Astor, who is looking gorgeous in his orange silk shirt and tight black trousers.

'It's safe to come in,' I say. 'Everyone's legless.'

Even Jennifer is grinning foolishly by now, her Philip Treacy creation askew on her big hair and her lavender tulle all puckered.

There's a band. Not bad, in fact, and seemingly able to turn their nimble fingers to anything. We jive and shimmy and line dance and cling. At a certain point, Astor has a word with the concertina player. I can guess what's coming next and sure enough, after a short discussion, the band hits a significant chord and launches into 'Jealousy.' Astor extends his right hand to me. God, I wish I was as svelte and beautiful as he is, as young. I wish I could carry off a tight dress with a slit up to my forehead, but I'm built like a typical colleen, sturdy collops and all. It doesn't matter because when Astor looks into my eyes, I know I'm beautiful. I toss my hat off (minding the bejewelled pin) and sashay towards him. No wobbling now. Some of the others shuffle courageously to the melody but they soon stop and stare as Astor throws me back until my hair brushes the floor. Then we slowly circle each other in the mating ritual that is the tango.

When it's over, I'm exhausted. People smile or frown. A few clap. Jennifer glares. My brother raises his brandy glass and puffs on his Cuban cigar.

Astor pulls me out through the French windows. There's a sort of balcony here overlooking a rose garden I didn't know existed. The air is balmy and a fingernail of moon scratches at the stars.

'Did you arrange this on purpose?' I ask.

'*Querida*!' he says, and pulls out a little velvet box.

I dread what's coming next.

'Open it.'

Of course, it's a ring. Rather a nice one actually, a tiny ruby clutched by tendrils of thin gold.

'I won't marry you, Astor,' I say for the nth time.

'No... I suppose you want this Tiger.'

Tiger? Tighe! What!

'I see how you look at him. How he look at you. How you laugh together.'

Jealousy! Was that why he requested that particular number? We soon start shouting at each other and then I storm off to the bar to drink daiquiris. 'Why not marry Astor?' Molly asked me once. 'You adore each other.' I suppose I'm afraid that, once wed, he'd want me to start producing a rake of babies, while he goes off tangoing with someone else.

I pick up the box which I forgot to fling back in Astor's face, and rub its soft blue velvet. I discover that tears have welled up in my eyes and are spilling down my cheeks. Probably carrying with them little train tracks of mascara.

'Is it that bad?'

Oh, no! It's Molly's horny Uncle Bob.

'Weddings always make me sad,' I say.

'I know what you mean,' he replies gloomily. He has been married for twenty-seven years to Eileen.

Then Bob buys me a drink and starts to chat me up. His leg rubs against mine. Surreptitiously, I slip the ruby on to the fourth finger of my left hand and pick up my glass.

'Well, it'll be me next,' I say.

'At long last! Who's the lucky man?' His leg is still rubbing mine. I hope Astor comes and gives him a puck on that big red nose. 'Not the Dago, surely!'

If I still had the hat pin, I'd ram it into some tender part of him.

Luckily Eileen arrives and scoops him up, looking at me as if I'm something she's stepped in.

Several daiquiris later and I can no longer move. Life is terrible. Astor has disappeared. Whatever will I do if he's gone for good! It's at this low point that Molly finds me.

'Thank God someone's conscious,' she says. 'Come. I need you.'

We step over prostrate bodies. I notice vaguely that the accordion player seems to be in a compromising position with the banker's wife, both, however, comatose.

Molly leads me to the bridal suite where Eoin lies fully clothed across the bed, snoring.

'I can't get my dress off,' she tells me. 'And he's no use.'

My fingers clumsy with alcohol, I finally release her stays. Molly bursts out of her dress like risen bread dough.

'Phew,' she says. 'That's a relief. Where's Astor?'

'Don't know.'

'Where are you sleeping?'

'Don't know.'

'Have you a room here?'

'No.'

So that's how I end up in bed with Molly and Eoin on their wedding night, her in the middle as a large, soft buffer. But I'm restless despite the drink. For one thing, there's something uncomfortable under my head. When I look beneath the pillow, I find a large knife.

'It's a kukri,' Molly explains. 'Eoin picked it up in Thailand. Likes to have it by him in case of thieves in the night.'

It's difficult to sleep after that. I imagine any sudden movement on my part and I'll wake up to find my head neatly detached from the rest of me. But I must have dozed off eventually because I am woken by golden light cascading through a crack in the curtains. I get up and don't get dressed because I already am.

I go downstairs. Mysteriously, most of the bodies have been removed in the night but there's still no sign of Astor. I go through the deserted ballroom, stale with smoke and spilled drink. I fling open the French windows and breathe scented air. Suddenly I glimpse a splash of orange down among the rose beds. Oh, these passionate Latins! Evidently in a fit of despair Astor has flung himself from the balcony! I clamber down to find if he is dead, grazing my leg on the rough stone. But my love is sleeping peacefully on a wooden bench, a petal stuck to his dew-damp cheek, my hat on his chest.

'Astor,' I breathe and kiss his forehead.

'*Querida*!' waking up.

He touches the ring still on my finger.

'I refuse to wear white,' I tell him. 'It'll have to be turquoise, or emerald or ruby red.'

'And we'll have many babies,' he smiles.

What can I say? What would you say? Whatever rubbish is usually said on such occasions.

We climb back into the ballroom and dance a tango to the strains of an imaginary orchestra.

BLIP

Every morning Charles Schmidt woke up a fairly fine figure of a man but by evening he had shrunk to less than half his original size.

Sometimes he tried to pinpoint the exact moment when this had started happening, and whether it was an overnight phenomenon or if it had crept up on him gradually. After much hard thought, he recalled a tightening sensation he had started experiencing following a dream in which his lovely young wife had been transformed into a feather duster. Not a duster of ordinary feathers, let it be said, but a concoction of flamingo pink that one would hesitate to defile with the greyness of dust.

He had woken that fateful morning with his hands grasping her ankles, trying to swing her up to the pelmets, always notoriously hard to keep clean. The withering look she had turned on him on that occasion had produced a muscular spasm of gigantic proportions. It was thereafter, he was pretty sure in retrospect that the daily shrinkages had begun although he lacked absolute proof of the correlation. All he knew was that the midget that slid between the sheets of the marital bed at midnight awoke at seven in the morning restored to a respectable height of five foot ten inches and a slim but manly girth (trouser size thirty four), facing the innocently slumbering face of his attractive young wife.

Perhaps after all there was no connection. Perhaps it was his job as a lowly computer programmer that drained more than his self-respect from him each day. He had expected more when he joined the company all those years before: he had certainly thought to rise rapidly in the organisation, to shoot upwards like a cork from a bottle of champagne. That's how the position had been sold to him. But others had passed him out while he still wrestled daily with bits and bytes. He supposed his beautiful wife must be disappointed: she had surely imagined that she would be married to middle-management by now, with all the perks that went with the position (regular tickets to the circus, to the corporate hospitality box, no less; a complimentary purple three-door-hatch-back with white wall tyres, acquired as part of a job lot but no less desirable for that, an emblem of the high-achievers; a puppy from one of the litters endlessly propagated by the boss's pair of shih tzu – if you didn't have one, you were nobody).

Even before the shrinkages, Charles had felt small, answerable to higher-ups for his every move. And now his immediate boss – younger than himself, though balder – was starting to look askance at him for his frequent trips to the men's room where, in the privacy of the cubicle, he had to tighten his belt notch by notch and roll up his trouser legs. The odd thing was that nobody – not his boss, nor his colleagues, nor even his own delightful wife – remarked on the phenomenon. At least, not to his face. Not even when he had to place a telephone directory on his chair before sitting down in order to be able to see the keyboard on his desk or the invariably tasty meal on the dining room table.

The other aspect of the matter that troubled Charles was that, day by day, week by week, he seemed to be shrinking more. One more notch on the belt. One more roll-up of the trousers. One more telephone directory.

Then he had another startling dream: that his delectable wife had turned into a washing-machine. Only this time, when he came home from work, he was appalled to find that his dream had come true. There she stood, encased in stainless steel, merrily stuffing his soiled shirts into the open door of her belly.

After that Charles was never sure what he would find on his return. One day his wife was an electric cooker, whipping out a perfect spinach and ricotta soufflé from her innards and presenting it to him the moment he entered the house. Another time she was crawling around the floor, gobbling balls of fluff, old bus tickets and cake crumbs, transformed into a vacuum cleaner. On yet another occasion, she was a cappuccino machine with hot milk frothing from her mouth. Bad enough as all this was, it was made worse by the fact that when she returned to her own shape – which she did invariably each night while Charles was wrapped in slumber recovering his own manly dimensions – she shed her domestic appliances like snake skins so that they started to make the house very crowded indeed. At first Charles, before setting out for work and while still at full strength, would carry them out to the shed in the garden. This was unsatisfactory, however, as the shed – not large to start with and already stuffed with garden implements: a hover mower, a strimmer, shears, a rake and so on – soon filled up. Then Charles in exasperation took to simply chucking the washing-up machine or microwave oven or steam press or whatever into the garden itself, on the neat lawn and herbaceous borders, the rose bushes and blooming lilac bushes, even into the goldfish pond, startling the carp, until the place started to resemble nothing less than a junk yard. Charles expected a visit from the local neighbourhood watch and tidy districts committee any day and dreaded what he would have to say to them.

'You know,' he finally remarked to his wife one evening, as a plastic cup filled with tea from her automatic spout at the same time as her alarm went off, 'things are going a bit far. I can't help feeling that you've become a tiddly-bit over-domesticated.'

The steam suddenly stopped as she clicked off. Charles feared he had gone too far, as indeed he had. From that moment his charming wife stopped turning into household appliances, which was a good thing, of course. The disadvantage was that she no longer did anything at all around the house, so that when Charles – no taller than two foot four inches at this stage – came home from work, it was to find no more delectable dinners awaiting him. And while he got hungrier and hungrier and even started to notice with increasing dismay that he was failing to return to his full manly stature each night, his wife got fatter and fatter until she was too large even to clamber up the stairs to the marital bed. She would just flop in an armchair and stare at him with eyes like wet pebbles. Finally she got too big for the chair and took to the couch.

What she ate was a mystery to Charles since she never went out, being too big to fit through the front door, and there was never any food in the house. Then he noticed that the rooms were starting to look emptier and once he even caught sight of screws and washers on the floor around his bloated wife's gigantic ankles. He had his suspicions confirmed when, peering through the crack between a half-open door and its frame he caught her snacking on a toaster. So that was it: she was eating her way cannibal-like through the appliances. After one nerve-wracking occasion when she made a lunge for him – there apparently not being anything else edible within reach – he made sure that there was always some household object handy for her, hauling them with increasing difficulty back in from the garden and shed.

There came at last the sorry evening when, weak with hunger and reduced to a height of no more that one foot ten and a half inches, Charles Schmidt could do no more. He pulled himself up the stairs, entered the bedroom, climbed on to the marital bed by means of a previously knotted sheet and then, exhausted with so much effort, lay down and died.

The house shook. Charles's once virtually fat-free wife quivered like a huge rhubarb mousse. She hiccupped and a flat iron flew from between her lips. She hiccupped again and an electric kettle shot out. She started to laugh – not a laugh of malice or triumph but one of sheer, innocent joy, like a child's – and between laughter and hiccups gradually all the appliances she had ever eaten piled up beside her on the floor, the last of all being a duster, with pink feathers as if plucked from the tail of a flamingo. Finally, when she was her old self again – her name was Julie, by the way, née Bunch – she telephoned a gentleman of her acquaintance in the second-hand appliance business, who called round with his van and promptly gave her a rather large cash payment for every single one of her regurgitated objects, not omitting those piled up in the shed and garden. He even complimented her on the up-to-the-minute, state-of-the-art quality of the merchandise, to which she simply replied with a winning smile, as she shoved the bundles of fifties into her handbag. Then she shut up the house, taking only a small travelling bag in which she had placed a change of underwear and a red tee-shirt bearing the iconic face of Che Guevara. She opened the front door, took a deep breath of fresh spring air, and set off whistling down the street to enjoy a well-earned break in the sun.

And if you're looking for a moral, there is none, nor ever was, nor ever will be. And if you're wondering whether Julie lived happily ever after, maybe she did and maybe she didn't, but that's another story.

FOR EVER AND EVER

The old man blinked. The only sign that he was conscious or even alive. Otherwise, in the full heat of the day, he was motionless, like a lizard on a rock, his skin the same knobbed and gnarled texture, and as dark as a dried tobacco leaf.

'They're coming.'

That was Enrico, his son-in-law, somewhere to his left. Priding himself on catching the sound of the engine before anyone else, peering up the road to get the first glimpse. Enrico, as eager as ever to grasp the dollars from the hands of the gaping tourists, although he was elderly himself now, with a heart that raced and skipped and even sometimes stopped for seconds at a time. At such moments, Enrico would turn grey, death brushing his face with her soft lips. Time, the old man thought without emotion, for his son-in-law to prepare himself to meet his ancestors, instead of greedily continuing to heap up worldly goods.

'Get up!' Enrico was urging, but the old man only sat still and blinked.

'It you they've come to see. Don't disappoint them.'

Slowly slowly the old man pushed himself to his skinny legs. Enrico thrust the two sticks into his hands and the old man started his perilous wander down the street. This walk he'd had to do several times a day for forty years, near enough, ever since the tourists started coming. Forty years ago, and he was an old man even then, or at least, that's how he was known.

He kept blurry eyes fixed to the ground, muttering a prayer to the *orisha* that he would not fall. He could still just about see enough not to stray off the path and anyway he knew that Enrico was behind him, ready to put him straight if necessary.

And now he could hear the bus himself, its low growl as it crept down the hill into the village.

Miguel from his spot behind the bar heard the bus, too. He looked back into the darkness where five shadows were lolling in the comparative cool, took a deep breath and called out, 'Music!' The shadows stretched long limbs lazily. Then, as if indifferent, moved slowly over to their instruments, guitar, mandolin, claves, drums, maracas.

Meanwhile Miguel was busy. The thirty or so glasses lined up in front of him already contained sprigs of mint that he had pounded with sugar for the *mojitos*. He dropped three or four ice cubes into each glass, going along the rows with a practiced speed. Next he upended the bottle of white rum and put a small measure in each glass. Then the lime juice. Finally, just as the first tourists came through the door, he filled each glass to the brim with soda water.

'Welcome,' he smiled warmly, to the accompaniment of a popular tune. But then he saw that these were elderly Germans, which was bad news. They weren't known to be generous tippers and often left the musicians complaining. Once there had even been a nasty scene when a tourist tried to take back his money and he'd had to intervene. Miguel sighed. Life could be hard. Through the window he was at least relieved to see the old man shuffling along on cue. Such an old man, but still with a certain dignity. Which was more, Miguel thought, than could be said for the clown stumbling behind him.

The tourists were sipping their drinks and exclaiming at the photographs of fishermen on the walls of the bar and at the life-size bronze head of the great writer on its plinth and at the huge stuffed marlin in its case, which legend (and only legend) had it that the great writer himself had caught. But Miguel could see that they were puzzled. Why had they been brought here? They had thought there would be more. Even the drink, supposedly one of the great writer's favourites, was a disappointment to them and laid aside by many before they had finished.

Miguel judged his moment, pointing out the door.

'That's the old man from the story,' he said. 'The one in the photograph there with the great writer.'

They all turned to look and of course the old man was summoned into the bar and made to sit down on a seat where they could stare him, so very old he was. Enrico bustled about as usual, unashamedly collecting money from the tourists. When he had stuffed enough into his pockets even to satisfy himself, he would call on the old man to speak. Miguel had observed this circus often enough. It was the same as ever.

Or not quite the same. Even after Enrico had given the signal, the old man sat still and silent, as if in a trance.

'How old is he, anyway?' one woman asked. She was thin, with skin as white and crisp as paper. In her seventies, her lips tight and lined as if they had been sewn together and only recently cut apart

'More than one hundred years, maybe already one hundred and three,' replied Miguel. And the tourists oohed at the dinosaur and started popping their cameras.

A thick-necked bald man, bursting purple as an over-ripe plum, was staring down into the old man's face aggressively, as if challenging him. 'What was he like then, the writer?' As if he really cared. Miguel doubted whether he or any of them had ever read a word of any of the books.

The old man stayed silent and gradually the questions trailed off. Everyone watched him, Enrico with concern. He'd have to give the money back if there was no performance.

But finally the old man started to speak, his voice low and harsh. Miguel, a one-time teacher of languages in the university, translated the story. How the writer used to moor his boat in the village, at the pier they could see for themselves if they cared to take just a short walk. How the old man himself, much younger then, of course, had frequently gone fishing with the writer – casting a significant glance in the direction of the marlin. How his own solitary battle with the sea one unforgettable day and night, had given the great writer the inspiration for a prize-winning story.

'He was a great man, a good man,' the old man chanted. 'I will never forget his goodness to me. Even in the dark days, he never let me or mine go hungry.'

And Miguel saw how Enrico grinned as his fat fingers closed over the wad of dollar bills in his pocket.

The old man had been feeling strange all day. It was as if the words he uttered came from a place beside him and not from his own mouth. He knew the lines well enough – he had been reciting the same ones for forty years – and could think of other things even as he spoke. Of Josefa, his long dead wife, with her flat face and flat body, like a tortilla. Of his four children, all dead now, too. Of the wide flat waters, glistening turquoise in the hard tropical sun, that could change in a moment into churning swells under riven black clouds. As they had on that day when the great writer had clung to the mast of the boat screaming, 'I can't die yet. Save me. I'm a genius.' That was the day, he, an old man – though strong and younger then – had muttered promises to the sea and to the god of the storm until they relented and let them sail home. No one more surprised than he to learn later how the great writer had turned the episode into a famous story, writing his own inglorious part out of it.

By now the old man had finished his recitation and was answering a few questions, always the same questions, even though Enrico told the tourists that he was tired and should be left in peace. Gradually, their curiosity sated, most of them moved off, some to listen to the music, some to have another *mojito*, some to wander down to see where the great writer's boat had once been moored. There was nothing else in the village to keep them and they would soon be gone, like all the others. Blown in and blown out again, torn up scraps of paper. But slowly the old man basking in his pool of stillness became aware that another old old man was sitting beside him, smoking a cigar and watching him.

'What you said, that's all balls,' the German muttered in coarse Spanish with a guttural accent. 'I met him, too. He was a shit.'

The old man grinned suddenly, a crocodile smile.

'Buy me a drink,' he said. 'But don't let on who it's for.'

'One of these?' The German indicated his barely-sipped *mojito*.

'No,' the old man grimaced. 'That's a woman's drink. *Reserva* and ice.'

The German crossed to the bar and placed his order. Miguel glanced sharply at the old man, who, however, was staring into space. The barman shrugged. It was a sale. What did it matter to him who drank it? With any luck he'd soon be gone from this god-forsaken place, like the tourists, never to return. He served the two drinks, rich amber liquid flowing over ice in long-stemmed glasses. Enrico, talking animatedly to a group of tourists, trying to hit them for a few more dollars no doubt, was too busy to notice a thing.

As soon as the German returned to his table, the old man grabbed his glass by the stem and swallowed its contents in a single gulp. He flicked a pale tongue over dry lips.

'Yes, *mein Herr*, you are absolutely right. He was a shit.'

The old man felt exhilarated as the forbidden alcohol charged through his veins. Another drink appeared in front of his blurry eyes. The German had pushed his own glass across to him.

'I'm not allowed,' the old man said, as he gulped it down. Then he started to talk again.

He stayed in the bar after the tourists left. The music had stopped and the singers had flopped back into the cavernous dark, smoking cheap cigarillos and counting their takings – not bad after all for half-an-hour's work. Miguel stood rinsing out the glasses. The old man still felt invigorated . He could see! He could hear! After the two drinks, everything suddenly had become sharper: sound and sight and taste. He could for example make out every detail of a stocky man sat slumped at the bar, a sea green shirt stretched taut across the muscles of a wide back, a grizzle of grey hair.

And if he could see and hear, then perhaps he could also remember? For someone who was making a living off his memories, he didn't after all recall very much. The fiction had blurred into the reality, just as tourists thought the story the great writer had written was about him, the old man, and not just a sum of inky markings on a page. The tale he told every day on cue might be true and it mightn't. He couldn't say any more than that. Or else he'd told it so often that it had become the truth. Until the moment when another old man came along and ripped the pretty fabrication apart with a word and then gave him dark rum so that he also could see and hear clearly.

The writer was indeed a shit. The old man knew that much, at least. Perhaps a great shit. Maybe the greatest the old man had ever met, even including Enrico. One minute he'd insult your mother, the next he'd want to kiss you. Then you'd say something and he'd swing a punch. Not that he'd ever connected with the old man. He needed the old man and knew it. He'd wept on his shoulder many a time, and not just after swallowing a skinful of rum. But even if he claimed you were his best friend, it made no difference. He'd still sleep with your flat-bodied wife, your three lovely daughters, even maybe your curly-haired son. And think nothing of it. He was a genius, right? A genius could do anything. Make love to anyone. Kill anything, kill anyone. Even kill himself. What a shit!

One more drink would make all the difference, but the old man was sure Miguel wouldn't give it to him. After all, wasn't he the goose that laid the golden eggs around these parts, even if he got precious little benefit for it. Enrico claimed that he was putting the money away safe for harder times, but the old man knew Enrico had got himself another woman and even a new child, since his first wife, the old man's daughter, had died. Did the fool think he was too deaf and blind to know that much? That no one would say anything to him? Enrico was tight-fisted and gave the old man little more than his dinner, mixed beans and rice – Moors and Christians – and fried pork with plantain on Sundays. For a quiet life, the old man said nothing. But it wasn't good enough. The old man couldn't even get a drink when he wanted one. Never mind a cigarette. Then there was that long walk, long for him at least, back up the village street to his tiny house. After collecting the money, Enrico always left him to fend for himself. He wouldn't attempt it yet. Not yet. Maybe in a moment he'd even get up and go to the bar and ask Miguel face to face for a glass of rum. On account. Dare Miguel to refuse him.

The old man sat for a long time, blinking rarely. Then his eyes closed where he sat and ah, he could feel again the battle with the sea, ah, the great waves lashing over him, the blinding whip of salt water across his eyes, the bitter taste in his mouth, the water pouring into him and the man shouting, 'Save me, I'm a genius!' He felt again how with a huge effort of will he'd coughed out the waves of water and how he'd risen up as big as the mast of the boat itself and bargained with the god of the sea for the life of the man. He remembered how the god had said, If I save him, you will never die. And he'd agreed, because after all, it's a great thing for a young man to live for ever. But now he knew the bitter edge of the bargain, how cruel it is for an old man never to hope for the release of death.

He suddenly opened his eyes wide and the blurry veil was ripped apart. So that when the stocky man slumped over the bar turned at last to look at him, the old man recognised who it was had come back, beard crusty with vomit, eyes red with despair, raising the gun to his mouth and shooting himself, again and again. And the old man knew at last what kind of a bargain he'd struck and with whom.

Note: In Cuba, the Hemingway tourist trail includes Cojímar, a fishing village near Havana where the writer used to moor his yacht, the Pilar. Gregorio Fuentes, Hemingway's fishing guide and skipper, who is said by some to have inspired the tale, 'The Old Man and the Sea', lived there until his death at the age of 104 in 2002, and would reminisce to tourists for a fee, collected by his grandson. This story is not about Gregorio in any biographical sense, nor about Hemingway, but is an imaginative recreation, inky markings on a white page.

THE OPTIMIST

Eh, Snegurochka, how d'you define an optimist?'
Achil was sniggering. Evidently this was a joke.
'I don't know,' I said.

'An optimist is someone who sets the alarm clock for midnight on New Year's Eve, wakes up, drinks a toast and then goes back to sleep again.'

Achil was convulsed with laughter. I tittered politely. I didn't get it. Must be a cultural thing, I thought, a Russian thing.

There was a lot I didn't get back then in the seventies. Tied up with self-consciousness, looking in rather than out. With the selfishness of the morbidly shy, relating everything to myself. Above all, I didn't get Russia, Leningrad, that upside down society, that unreal city shimmering on a marsh, on ice, always about to sink or evaporate into air.

Achil had sought me out several months earlier, when I had arrived in the city port with my two big cases and clutching a handbag containing the book someone had sent him, along with a letter which I had concealed in the lining. This someone was a mutual acquaintance. One of the people he had picked up along the way. Because, as I was to discover, Achil was a relentless finder, a collector of all sorts including people and, after all, there weren't that many of us, Westerners in Russia, in those paranoid Brezhnev years.

I had been told, cloak and dagger style, that he would be waiting. And I was trembling in case the secret police were waiting too. To strip search me and find the letter.

'You are Alison?'

I turned and saw him for the first time. With some surprise, it must be said. Given the elegance and culture of our mutual acquaintance, this was an unlikely looking contact. Tall, skinny and ungainly, with spikes of straw sticking out from under a rabbit fur hat. A pallid Slav face, eyes the colour of a wintry northern sky. A character, it seemed to me, straight out of Dostoevsky (I was studying Russian literature at the time and had come to this city to find out about white nights and holy fools and students who murdered old women with axes), one of those shabby individuals who attach themselves to the unwilling or indifferent heroes, running after them in the street, in the gutter, catching at their sleeves, trying to ingratiate themselves by performing useful little services.

Achil worked in a bookshop, a sales assistant. An insignificant person, you might think. You might indeed think that, coming from Western Europe, with its clear-cut assignation of social roles and class demarcations. But Achil was in fact a man of importance. A fixer. I discovered this the first time he asked me where I wanted to go: the opera, the ballet, the theatre? Whatever it was, he could arrange it: all I had to do was turn up on the night. Turn up outside Dom Knigi, for instance, the large bookshop on Nevsky Prospekt where he didn't work (he was in a small place near the Kirov). But the Dom was handy for a rendezvous. Unmissable.

I would blow down the windy street, a bit late as usual, and he would emerge from some dark doorway and sweep me round the corner to the concert hall or across the road to the Pushkin theatre or down into the Metro to travel to some other mysterious place. Nodding and smiling at the fat women who barricaded the doors, murmuring some mystical mantra that would cause their fierce faces to break into smiles and let us through.

'How's Mamma?' one or two would call.

Achil would mutter a reply and rush on to the director's office, pulling me after him into some room where a man, nearly always a man, sat behind a desk.

'Here's the book you wanted, Sergei Ivanich,' he might say, and lay a volume on the desk. Something apparently impossible to get hold of normally. This was his ace card. The director would pick up the book and riffle through the pages, sighing with pleasure.

Then there would be more smiles all round and a bare glance at me. I'd follow Achil out again into the theatre. We'd go to an empty box or he would push me in with other people or we'd wait until the lights went down for the start of the performance and he'd race to the front and squeeze me between some heavily powdered woman, some thick-set dark-suited man. Mostly he wouldn't stay himself, but whirl out murmuring a message I didn't catch. Sometimes he would disappear for good but more often he would be waiting for me in the mirrored lobby during the break, with a slice of bread and caviar or sausage or fake cream cake and a glass of Russian champagne. He never let me pay.

'Last year such clever men,' he used to smile through crooked yellow teeth. 'And this year such beautiful women.'

I wasn't beautiful but I suppose I was pretty enough: small and slightly plump, with long blonde hair. All that Russian winter I wore a pungent and dirty white Afghan coat – skin side out – the fashion for the young of Western Europe then but shocking to old babushkas who, as I passed, seized the ripped sleeve where fur poked out, hissing, 'You must sew this up, young woman.' Achil nicknamed me Snegurochka, after the snowflake maiden who assists Father Frost – the Soviet Union's blue and secular Santa Claus – to give presents to the children at New Year.

My Russian was poor, which perhaps accounted for the fact that so often I had no idea what was going on around me. Often I didn't know what I was going to see and sometimes ended up at some play where actors declaimed and strode and wept and left me no wiser. But more often it was the ballet with fragile Giselles or Odettes, productions repeated over decades. Achil had it in his head that I was mad about ballet, perhaps because of that acquaintance back home, a balletomane who tried to come over every two years for the Kirov and Bolshoi. In fact I found classical ballet tedious. Only the high leaps of the male lead, thigh muscles rippling under pale tights, or the expectation that at any moment he might drop the prima ballerina when she threw herself at him, raised my interest.

But I enjoyed the glitter, the spectacle. The sight of Russians at play, guzzling culture along with the greasy snacks in the interval. The endearing availability of toothpaste and brushes or soap, precious commodities, beside champagne at the theatre bar. Above all, I liked rushing out into the frosty night after night, over the little bridges of the canals, the rearing horses of the bridge across the Fontanka, the long bridge over the Neva leading from the Winter Palace to Vasilevsky island, rushing with a sense of expectation and possibility while my co-students huddled in our dreary hostel drinking themselves senseless with vodka and cheap wine (of course, I often joined in that activity, too).

'Come and meet Mamma,' Achil suggested after a few weeks.

They lived in a distant suburb in one room of a communal apartment. Once opulent houses divided up among the citizenry. Achil and his Mamma had built a wall against intrusive neighbours with shelves of books and artefacts, many of them gifts from Achil's acquaintances in the West. Some of the books were in English or German or French or Italian, although to my knowledge Achil understood none of these languages and I never actually saw him reading. Prints from Greek mythology hung on the wall: Perseus holding up the head of Medusa with its wriggling snakes, Theseus slaying the Minotaur, Paris presenting the golden apple to Aphrodite, others I didn't recognise. A curtain of heavy brocade divided Mamma's bed from the rest of the room (Achil pulled out the sofa-bed each night for himself).

'At last,' Mamma said, advancing on me. 'I've heard so much.'

My first and abiding impression was of a large spider. All in black, with a swollen body and stick arms and legs encased in leggings, tiny feet in ballet shoes, a small white head with watchful eyes. She took the bottle of Bols I brought her, as instructed by Achil, and stashed it away. She was ailing, and apparently never went out. Her movements were slow and she sighed as if every one of them gave her pain.

There were vinegary edibles on the table, shredded cabbage, salad with potatoes and beetroot, salted cucumbers, cheap sausage. Black bread. Biscuits that tasted of sawdust. Sweet wine.

For some reason she called her son Alexei. Later I figured that the more prosaic name was his own but that, dreaming of Greek heroes, he had appropriated that of one of his favourites.

But if he was a dreamer, he was also pragmatic. He hinted broadly at the things Mamma liked, only available in hard currency shops. Bols and tinned Danish hams and French cheeses and amaretto biscuits that she soaked in wine and then sucked. I could see how deprived they were from the food they served, always the same. But I was poor too, with only a meagre student allowance. Achil, like all Russians, thought we Westerners were loaded. I suddenly realised (it took me longer than it should have done but, as I said, I didn't get it, I was naive, I thought he was in love with me) that the treats to the theatre, like the books he brought to the directors, were the currency of barter and as such would have to be paid for in kind. I couldn't afford the price – in fact it would have cost me a lot less than a bottle of Bols to buy a theatre ticket myself – and made excuses not to go so often to the shows.

After six months I returned home. Achil heaped me with presents, books and old postcards of Dostoevsky, of Chalyapin as Boris Godunov, of scenes from long forgotten plays, charming nevertheless.

'When you come back,' he said, 'you must bring...' And he pressed a paper into my hand with the name of some drug on it, unobtainable in Russia that might help Mamma's mysterious condition. 'Also, some Bols.' And he winked. He asked nothing for himself but soon after I got back, I went to a museum where they had an exhibition of Trojan myth, history and archaeology, with ancient statues and vases and memorabilia of the archaeologist Schliemann among others. There was a fine postcard of a statue of Achilles, which I bought and sent to my friend.

He sent me back a view of the Winter Palace. 'Do not forget us' it read.

I had of course made other friends in Russia in the six months while I was there. Most closely with Anya, an intense young woman who worked in the library where I was doing my research. She would stand on the staircase for hours talking about literature and cinema and art. All Western, she despised most native products. It didn't seem to matter that she took so much time off from working. They were overstaffed anyway in this country where no one was unemployed and there was little to do. As long as you clocked in and out regularly, no one made a fuss. I even smuggled her into the hostel where she met the other students and made friends with them, too. After we all left, someone denounced her to the KGB and she had to explain herself.

'They told me you were spies,' she informed me much later. 'That you climbed to the top of high buildings to send information to the CIA. So I made myself appear naive and stupid. I told them we only drank toasts to international friendship.'

Deciding that she wasn't dangerous, they merely sent her as a warning to pick potatoes for the summer.

Then there was a man I had met in a café one day, who wanted to practise his English so much he ended up holding a party for our entire group in his mother's apartment while she was away in Georgia. I think she must have been a party functionary, something important anyway. Hers was a well-appointed separate apartment with several rooms and heavy wooden furniture. Tasteful if somewhat indigestible decor.

This Sasha had a good line in jokes: Brezhnev is giving a speech on Channel one, so Vanya turns to Channel Two. There he finds Brezhnev giving a speech, so he turns to Channel Three. The same thing and so on. When he finally gets to Channel Seven the KGB officer looks out at him and says, 'Ha, caught you.'

Or this one: A Russian was asked how, if he were going abroad, he would travel, by air, rail, car whatever. 'The question doesn't arise,' the Russian said. 'I have no plans to travel.' 'No, but imagine that if you were, how would you go?' 'I wouldn't,' the Russian replies. 'I wouldn't be allowed.' 'Yes but just imagine that you finally got permission, how do you think you would travel then.' 'In that case,' the Russian said finally, 'I'd go in a tank.'

One day as we walked beside the river, Sasha proposed marriage to me. It could have been a romantic moment – the pale pinks and greens and blues and yellows of the imperial palaces and forts, the frozen river, the cold bright sun – but it wasn't. He explained that he simply wanted a passport out of there: the arrangement would be strictly business. I mumbled that I would think about it and quietly dropped the subject. I think maybe he proposed to several others in the group, too. Finally several years later, Anya told me that Sasha had discovered a 'tiny little drop' of Jewish blood and got out without our help.

Dima was a ballet dancer (introduced to me by Achil), a small elfin man in his thirties, who surrounded himself with motherly middle-aged women and who claimed to have been best friends with Rudolf Nureyev before he defected. 'That's why I can never travel abroad with the company,' as he explained, 'in case I run off to join him.' Or maybe, I thought, he just wasn't good enough, or too short. (Before I left he gave me a message for Nureyev – God knows how he thought I would deliver it – to send over a mid-season overcoat, 'Italian design, if possible'). Over the years I would usually meet up with him whenever I was in the city, with a slightly guilty conscience regarding the overcoat. But nothing was ever said and Dima was always snappily dressed. (I came to the conclusion that Russians asked everyone for everything in the hope that some day someone would deliver.)

Much later, during perestroika, my elegant and cultured – and incidentally gay – acquaintance in London informed me that Dima had been killed under mysterious circumstances, strangled, it was said, in his bed. I thought of the last time I had seen him. A small man in black leather trousers and a striped tee-shirt dancing with dumpy Lyuba in the room of his communal apartment while the rest of us laughed and clapped in time to the music. (Lyuba, cuddlesome and motherly, who once warned me off friendship with someone 'because he is a Jew', turned out also to have been working for the KGB. Just because you're paranoid it doesn't mean that people aren't out to get you.)

But this is all in the future and is mentioned just to indicate that I knew people other than Achil in that city of mists and miasmas. In fact, it became almost a ritual for me to return for New Year every three or four years to visit my friends, taking one of those cheap tours that combined flight and hotel. Achil eventually lost his job in the bookshop. I don't know why although the reason was probably muttered at me. Maybe he had appropriated several books too many. Not done a favour for someone he should have. One year I returned to find him selling lottery tickets in an underpass of Nevsky Prospekt. A nasty dark and smelly place, subject in this winter weather to icy blasts straight from Siberia.

I had the regulation Bols for Mamma and as I approached through the sleet in my fake fur, Achil smiled a wide smile.

'Snegurochka!'

His teeth were black with decay, his pale skin streaked with green, his clothes the same as ever but ragged with time. He told me to meet him at Dom Knigi at six (some things never change) and we would go and see Mamma.

'How is she?' I asked.

'You will see.'

I nearly didn't go. I nearly accompanied my tour group to the circus. Then I remembered the performing hippopotamus I had seen on a previous trip, the beast tearing panic-stricken round the ring while the crowd hooted with laughter. On balance, Achil and his Mamma were preferable.

I stocked up with Danish tinned ham and Swiss chocolate from the Beriozka hard currency shop at the hotel and for my own sake added a bottle of good Georgian wine (I was richer now, with a job at a publishing house and a husband who played French horn in an orchestra), thinking I would need it to get through the night. Then I walked down Nevsky to my rendezvous. The snow was several feet deep but the pavements were clear for pedestrians, the good work of the army of old women who still plied their spades and besoms.

He was there, a darker shadow in the doorway. I'd almost been hoping he wouldn't turn up although I knew of course that he would. At least in the dim light his appearance wasn't so shocking. But then we got on a tram and the cold light showed him up even worse than in the underpass.

'Life's hard?' I asked sympathetically.

He shrugged. 'Normal,' he said. An optimist, you see.

Apparently he could still get me tickets if I wanted. The network was still in place although I couldn't imagine what he traded these days. A winning ticket on the lottery was surely beyond even his ingenuity.

The room, the books, Mamma, everything was the same. I had never supplied the drugs she needed for her condition. I had made some half-hearted enquiries back home only sternly to be told (this was before the Internet supplied anything to anyone, at a price) that such medication was only available on prescription. But maybe Mamma had got it anyway. She looked no worse than before, as much of an arachnid as ever.

She however was less sanguine about life under Gorbachev than her son.

'Everything is falling apart. Who knows what will happen.' Shaking her head as with slow painful movements she secreted the gifts, the Bols, the ham, the chocolate, the good Georgian wine. We sat down to the same old vinegary zakuski, the same dusty biscuits, the same sweet port and drank a toast to the New Year.

Then suddenly it all changed. I was sitting in my garden on a sunny summer day, playing with the children and the dog, half-listening to the radio, when I heard the news that tanks were in the streets of Moscow, Gorbachev had been arrested, Boris Yeltsin was making his final heroic stand in the White House. Everyone cheered his bravery at standing firm. (Later Shevardnadze was to comment drily that Yeltsin had in fact been stretched out on the White House floor, too blind drunk to leave.) I managed to phone my librarian friend, now living in the centre of the city with her second husband – I had visited them for the previous New Year. They lived with a view of the pond which featured in Bulgakov's *The Master and Margarita*. She told me they were too terrified to go out.

But as everyone now knows, the forces of reactionary communism were soon to be defeated and the Soviet Union was to fall into the avid hands of crass capitalism and criminals. Fortunes were made by anyone willing to take chances and a mutant breed arose, the 'new' Russians, with their flashy consumerism and of course new jokes to go with them:

Two New Russians are on a plane. 'I paid a million dollars for this watch,' says one. The other looks at him pityingly and displays his own timepiece. 'I paid two million for this,' he states with satisfaction.

The following year I returned to St Petersburg, as Leningrad had officially been renamed. With some dread I notified Achil of my arrival. It was five years since I had seen him and we had only exchanged occasional greetings in the meantime.

He turned up at my hotel. I was drinking a coffee in the bar and wondering at the high new tariffs. A sharp-suited guy approached me, bright blue glazed tie with a gilt clip, black patent shoes with tassels, straw hair slicked back.

'Achil?' I wondered. Could it be?

He smiled. Dazzling with whiter than white porcelain.

'Snegurochka!'

'You look great. How's Mamma?'

'Come and see.'

No more trams for him. We took a cab but I insisted on paying, shocked at the dollar price.

I almost expected a new apartment, too, but either Mamma couldn't be moved or his new wealth wasn't that great. Or maybe he was just careful. The same scenes from Greek mythology decked the walls but they were curling at the edges, browned now with damp spots. The books looked the same, and as untouched as ever. At least the spread on the table was different, sturgeon and caviar, Parma ham, French cheeses, vinegary salads but of a superior quality, better wine but still tooth-achingly sweet.

Mamma herself wore her usual clinging black outfit. Maybe her belly was more bloated, her arms and legs even more spindly. Her thin hair was tied back tightly. Oil black hair. At least I was pretty sure by now that it was dyed. One concession to vanity.

I showed photographs of my family, my husband and two daughters. Mamma, whose sleeping area was festooned with sentimental pictures of kittens and puppies, was more interested in my dog, Fiddler.

'What a darling! What breed is he?'

That's another thing I had finally learned, the brand snobbishness, the jeans you brought over had to be Levis or Wranglers, dogs had to be pedigree.

'He's just a mutt, a mongrel.'

'Oh well...' and Mamma looked at my beloved Fiddler with a pitying expression on her face.

Achil wasn't interested in any of it, not husband, daughters or dog. He seemed preoccupied. The phone kept ringing, causing him to leap up and murmur intensely into it, facing away from us.

I asked him, current phone conversation over, about his job.

He looked shifty.

'I still sell lottery tickets only now from an office.' Refusing to elaborate.

It was a strained evening. Mamma was the same but Achil and I had moved off in different directions. I felt that his point had been made the moment he came up to me with that dazzling smile in the hotel. Now we had nothing to say to each other. When I asked about theatre, ballet, opera, he just shrugged.

'He has no time,' Mamma said as the phone rang again. 'Such a busy boy.'

A boy in his late forties.

I never saw either of them again.

My elegant acquaintance, now a distinguished old queen, told me what happened. He had been over once more for the ballet for old time's sake more than pleasure. It wasn't the way it used to be, he said. The companies were experimental, 'detrimental' as he said. He personally preferred it the way it had always been done, like a museum exhibit, while understanding that the dancers might prefer change. 'I suppose I'm just an old fogey,' he smiled in his charming way. Anyhow, on his return to the hotel after some particularly painful spectacle, he found an urgent message from Mamma. He took a cab to the apartment where on that mid-winter night she was waiting for him, 'in the street'. He paused to let this amazing intelligence sink in. In the room he found Achil bleeding on the couch, badly beaten.

'The most heart-rending sight of all,' he said, 'were the teeth.'

Those dazzling dentures broken to shards.

'It seemed symbolic.'

Apparently Achil had been doing little jobs for the mafia but then tried to branch out independently, albeit in a small way. They had decided to teach him a lesson. To learn his place.

'Knowing Achil, he'll bounce back,' my friend said.

I meant to get in touch. I really did. But life got in the way. The elegant friend died suddenly of a heart attack, breaking that particular thread of communication. My children got married, started to have families. I sent a Christmas card once, Christmas having been reinstated in Russia, but got no reply. Nevertheless, every New Year I raise a glass and wonder if the optimist has set his alarm to wake him up for the toast. Or if, despairing at last, he simply rolls over in bed and sinks back into blessed oblivion.

At least I understand it now. Actually, I think it's quite a good joke.

LIKE SHE SAID

The cheek of her, criticising me! Like I said to her, What do you know about it, missus? I mean, it's not as if she has any children of her own. Adopted don't count, do they.

Coming to think of it now, she always was the first to call round complaining and whining. Celine broke Rebecca's toy. Celine scratched Rebecca's face. Celine called Rebecca a dirty bastard. I said to her, what do you expect? They're just kids. I'm sure Rebecca gives as good as she gets. Anyway, it was no good her getting on her high horse. After all, like I said to her that time, it's a fact of life. According to the dictionary definition, missus, Rebecca is just that: a bastard. Otherwise she'd be home in Romania with her mam and dad, wouldn't she. That shut her up quick, I can tell you. She turned all cool with me after that. But like I said, there's no denying the truth. Hadn't she and Liam gone over and got her in some orphanage there, oh, years ago now of course, when Rebecca was a baby. Well, we all knew about those orphanages from TV, the sort of places they were and the sort of kiddies they had in them. Like I said to Jim at the time, I'd be scared bringing something like that into the house. I mean you wouldn't know, would you. They say AIDS is rife in those countries never mind anything else. And even if the kiddie looked all right, looks all right now except for that dark skin – goes near black in the summer, she does, you'd take her for a coloured – there might be all sorts of what Philip calls 'genetic mutations'.

So for her to stand there and tell me I only had myself to blame when Celine went to the bad, well, that was the last straw. Now when I see her, I just ignore her, like she doesn't exist. Even if she speaks I just act like I don't hear her. She'll get the message.

Not that Celine has never caused me worry. I can't say that. Ever since she got her flowers she's been an antichrist. But before that she was the sweetest little thing. You should have seen her then. Like a doll. I used to love dressing her up, buying all those frilly frocks, white ankle socks with lace round the tops, patent leather shoes with silvery buckles. Long golden ringlets, she had too that I curled myself. Not like that shaved look she has now. As for all those piercings… You'll get blood poisoning, I told her, or worse. How do you know the equipment was sterile? She just gave me one of her looks.

But coming to think of it, even in those early days she had a wicked streak. Used to tell me so-and-so had torn her dress or thrown dirt at her when all the time she was climbing trees and crawling through hedges and generally behaving like a knacker. I had to take the wooden spoon to her many times, I can tell you. And even then your one next door – I used to be quite pally with her in those days, popping into each other's houses for a coffee, treating ourselves to a couple of cream slices or chocolate eclairs – that one saw me smack Celine after she'd been bold and said, wasn't there another way? I soon put her straight. Spare the rod and spoil the child, I said. Just goes to show how she had no idea. No maternal instinct, you see. That's not something you can buy in Romania. No, like I told her, it never was any good talking to Celine. Hadn't I tried that over and over? She'd just look at you with those blue eyes and swear black was white.

Philip, now, he was a different sort from the start. Never wanted to be out rough-housing. Preferred to stay in. A nicely behaved boy. I never had to take the wooden spoon to him, not once. He's too quiet, Jim's mother used to say, God rest her, but I said, what's wrong with that. If all the boys stayed in with their mams and watched TV or read books, there wouldn't be any wars. There was no answer to that, so she tried a different tack. He's too fat, she'd say. Or, he'll ruin his eyes. Or, why doesn't he speak up and look anyone in the face? That's just his way, I told her. He's shy. He's sly, she said, that's what I think. Well, mother, I told her, I don't want to know what you think and neither does Jim. Oh doesn't he, says she. We'll see about that. The long and the short of it was there was a falling out and she didn't come visiting much after that. Jim and the kids went to hers, which suited me fine except that I couldn't help wondering what poison she was feeding them about me. Anyway, didn't she drop dead one evening watching 'You're a Star', so that was that. Lovely funeral mind you, although I could have told that priest a thing or two about his precious Violet that he didn't mention in his eulogy.

Anyway I hope wherever she is now, she can see how Philip turned out. He's a credit to you, missus, Father Declan told me the other day. Not many sons of his age would come with their mothers to mass. Not many sons come to mass full stop, he added. Maybe he has a vocation. Well, I nipped that one in the bud on Philip's behalf. Philip has a good job in IT, I told him. I mean I know they're worried that the only place vocations are going up is in Africa and we'll soon have to bring all these coloureds over here to be priests and how will that go down with the congregations? But leave my Philip out of it. He's doing very nicely thank you. We even converted the attic so he could have it as an office, although I'm worried every time he climbs up that ladder. It seems so flimsy and him such a big boy. On the other hand, it's great he can work from home. I can connect up with anyone anywhere in the world, he tells me. Jim says it's unhealthy and tries to get Philip to go to the pub with him but I reckon, no harm keeping out of those places. If more boys stayed home instead of going to pubs there wouldn't be all this violence and antisocial behaviour. That's what I said to Jim and he replied, I need a drink, and laughed in that nasty way of his.

But getting back to Celine. I mean, it's a terrible thing to have to say about your own child but I've finally washed my hands of her. There's only so much a mother can take. Like I told the juvenile liaison officer that time Celine was fourteen and he came round after she and her friends were found in the park rotten drunk on vodka. I've tried, I said, as God is my witness.

I told him what Mrs Molloy from number six said to me, that I was a saint to have put up with Celine for so long and that if it was her daughter she'd have sent her to the industrial school long since. Of course, on the one hand I didn't appreciate Mrs Molloy sticking her beaky nose into my business but she hit the nail on the head, that time. But this latest is the last straw. Of course, Celine maintains she wouldn't come back if I paid her, which like I said, I have no intention of doing, young woman. Wait till she comes crying to her mam. We'll see then.

Philip has rigged up this surveillance device, don't ask me how. He's set up these cameras so that you can watch the house even when you're not in it. Well, you can if you have the proper equipment like he has. One of those laptops. I have to laugh. Other fellows go for lap dancers but my Philip prefers his laptop. It's our little joke. Only Jim doesn't think it's funny. Better for him if he went for lap dancers, says he. Whatever that's supposed to mean. So anyway, yesterday Philip and I went into town, him with his laptop, and we treated ourselves to lunch in Smiths. I just settled for the chicken vegetable soup but Philip had the full shebang, lasagne, beans and chips, if you please. God bless your appetite, I told him as he finished up with chocolate fudge cake and ice cream.

Anyway, then he said to me, I can go wireless here. Let's see what's happening at home shall we, and turned on the laptop. He fiddled about a bit and then said, what do you think of that? I couldn't believe it: there was our house in black and white, seen from different viewpoints, flashing one after the other. Philip laughed his head off at the look on my face. It's a surprise, mam, he said. It certainly is, I said. Does that mean anyone can look at our house any time they like? No, he said, only when you put in the necessary passwords. He explained to me it's not a video but a series of still images. A security measure so you can see if anyone's robbing the house while you're away. We looked at it for a while but nothing much happened. The postman called and Carmel Crowley's young one passed with their big dog, the one I complained about to the guards because it should be wearing a muzzle and isn't. They assured me they'd have a word but I noticed it still wasn't muzzled. This could be useful, I said to Philip. So he showed me how to save an image.

That one next door – not the one with the adopted daughter, the other side – called over the back fence later, when we were both hanging out our washing. First thing she said, looks like the rain will hold off for a bit, please God. Yes, I said. It does. I noticed her sheets and towels looked very worn. Then she got down to the real business of the conversation, which was to ask after Celine and I said I didn't know. Of course, your one couldn't wait to tell me the latest: hadn't she seen her that very morning in the supermarket looking about to pop. You'd think the least Celine would do in her condition is have the decency to stay out of the neighbourhood.

Later when Philip came down for dinner – I heated up a nice steak and kidney pie I got from Dunne's Stores – he could see I was upset so I told him what your one had said. Well, you can hold your head up again, mam, he said. Celine's married. She's what! I said. Married, he said. I went to the wedding. Well, you could have blown me over. Seemingly it was some kind of pagan ceremony, involving leaping over a bonfire. It can't be legal, I said. Oh yes, Philip replied, they did all the necessary in that regard.

I was hurt he hadn't told me before but he said Celine had asked him not to because she knew I wouldn't like it. Well, true enough I didn't. Where, I asked, did they have the reception? On the Hill of Tara, if you please. Wait 'til your father hears about this, I said. Philip didn't say anything and avoided catching my eye. Or does he know already? It didn't really surprise me – Celine always was her daddy's pet. Philip mumbled with his mouth full. Was he there too, I asked. I must have been shouting because Philip got all upset and had to take one of his tablets and then he went up to his office and pulled the ladder up behind him.

All very well, I thought, but who's the victim here. Your only daughter gets married and you're the last one to hear about it. I ate the face off Jim when he came in later smelling of booze. Oh, is that the way the land lies, says he, and walks straight out again. I put his steak and kidney in the bin.

Philip has moved out. Something of a bombshell, as you can imagine. I'm thirty-three, mam, he said. Yes, but are you able to look after yourself, I said. Who'll wash your shirts and socks now? Who'll cook your dinner? I can manage, he said. Or else I can bring my washing over for you to do. This was a joke, apparently. Funny that, I've never known Philip to make a joke before. It's an apartment, seemingly, not even a proper house. Rented. That's just money down the drain, I told him. It suits my needs, Philip said. And it'll be quiet. I suppose that's a reference to the rows Jim and I have been having recently. Mostly over Celine and Jim's drinking. Like I told him, if you'd stayed home more we wouldn't be in this situation today. What situation, Jim said, anyhow you never made me welcome in my own home. Thirty-seven years married and that's what he comes out with. You're not even interested in your first grandchild, he said. Let Celine come over here and apologise, I said, and then I'll show an interest. Maybe you should apologise to her, said Jim and slams the door on his way out. I think he spends a lot of time over at Celine's now the baby's born. That or down the pub. It's a girl, seemingly. Philip said they called her Pearl. Sounds common to me and not Christian.

Rebecca graduated from that college she was at and they had some noisy party in the back. I was thinking to myself that if it went on after eleven I'd call the guards but by then they'd gone into the house. I couldn't really hear anything through the walls, so I left it.

Went over to Philip's. Not much of place. Not even that clean. He said he doesn't notice. All sorts of funny pictures on the walls. A friend of his is an artist, he said. What friend, I asked. I didn't know you had any friends. Apparently it's this girl he met at Celine's wedding. Isis. What class of a name is that, I asked. Doesn't sound Christian to me. No, mam, that's the name she's taken, Philip said. Anyway, she's responsible for the pictures. What are they supposed to be, I asked. They're abstract, he said. You can make of them what you like. Well, I don't make anything of them, I said. He gave me my dinner. Something he cooked himself if you please. Lots of near raw vegetables. No meat. What do you call this, I asked him. Stir fry, he said. Seemingly, this Isis one told Philip he's been doing everything wrong all his life, eating wrong and so on. She's a vegan, Philip said, but he's not ready for that yet. I said, you want to watch it, Philip. I've met that sort of girl before. Just wants to get some innocent into her clutches. Well, maybe I want to get into her clutches, mam, said Philip. More noodles? I said, I could murder some egg and chips.

He'd set up his laptop before dinner and we looked at the house while we were eating. Nothing much happening there. Later I washed his socks.

Came over to Philip's this afternoon after another shouting match with Jim, but Philip was on his way out. Sorry, mam, he said, but Isis is having a barbecue. I brought you a nice bit of steak, I said, and some oven chips. I thought we could eat together. Not today, he said, I promised Isis I'd be there. Well, don't drink too much, I told him. Isis doesn't drink, he said. She's into karma. What's that, I asked. Some prohibited substance, I suppose. You be careful or I'll report your precious Isis to the proper authorities. He got quite narky, which isn't like him at all. I'm off, he said. You can show yourself out, mother. Well, I had a little look around but there was nothing to be found. I don't think Philip keeps a diary or anything like that. At least, I've never been able to find one. Not like Celine, only hers was in some sort of a code.

I cleaned up a bit. Tidied a few things away. See, I didn't feel like going straight home after I'd told Jim I'd be out for the evening sampling Philip's cooking and enjoying intelligent conversation for a change. So I turned on the laptop to watch the house for a bit, the way Philip had shown me, one still shot after another. And there in the garden was Jim and Celine and some skinny fellow with long hair that must be the husband. And this little tot. Could have been a boy or a girl for all I knew, tee shirt and dungarees. And Jim picks her up and throws her up in the air and the little one is laughing. I can see quite clearly.

They are all laughing. And now your one from next door comes out and she's laughing too. And because I know how to do it, I freeze the image and stare at it for a long time.

POSTPARTUM

This is nice. Isn't this nice?'
They were sitting at an outdoor café, under a parasol that sheltered them from the harsh sun. Every few moments Lottie checked on the baby in his buggy, to make sure he was still in the shade too, still asleep, still alive.

'Yes,' she replied, looking out over the little harbour, the boats bobbing, the turquoise wavelets dancing and sparkling . 'Yes,' she replied indifferently. 'It's very nice.'

Then she smiled too brightly at her husband. Andrew meant well. He was doing his best. This holiday an attempt to drag her up from the pit of depression that she had fallen into after Sam was born. This resort he had so carefully selected because it was advertised as perfect for relaxation, a quiet town on the Mediterranean, no noisy young people with their nightclubs that stayed open till morning, their beach parties. Actually, thought Lottie, a bit of noise might be welcome to distract Andrew from watching her all the time with that solicitous expression on his face and to relieve the stultifying boredom of days spent on the beach or wandering through the little streets behind the harbour. Picturesque? Yes, certainly. There were the postcards to prove it, postcards she had dragged out a couple of hours buying and writing until she ran through her list of friends and relations and had to rack her brains to think of anyone else she might conceivably send one to, along with a neatly scripted banal message, just to fill her brain with trivia for a while longer, to distract from the horrible black void.

Sam was a lovely baby. No doubt about it. People stopped all the time to ooh and aah at him, his little hands curled up like rosebuds, the smile that lit up his face, the mop of black hair astonishing in its abundance for a nine-month-old. And as well as being handsome, he was quiet and good. It wasn't Sam who kept her awake at night. He slept soundly while she tossed restless with anxiety. She couldn't blame him for the exhaustion that hit her on waking, that washed over her all day long. Except that he was too quiet: one reason she couldn't sleep was for thinking he had stopped breathing, so she kept jumping up to check, putting her hand next to his mouth to feel the tickle of his breath, or watching the almost imperceptible rise and fall of his tiny body.

Lottie was an elderly first time mother. That's what they had told her at the hospital.

'I'm only thirty-eight, for God's sake!'

'Exactly,' the nurse had smiled back. 'That, I'm afraid, classes you as over the hill, like footballers or tennis players.'

Lottie hadn't smiled back. She had got offended and then panicky as the nurse reeled off the greater risks associated with pregnancies later in life.

'Of course, an older mother has advantages too.' The nurse smiled that briskly professional smile again. 'Greater maturity and so on. Don't worry, we'll keep a special eye on you, to make sure everything goes smoothly.'

Between the antenatal visits, the ultrasounds, and her sister-in-law telling her dire stories about the complications and abnormalities she'd heard about in births to women over thirty-five, Lottie spent an uncomfortable nine months, not helped by almost constant nausea, excruciating back pain, an ugly outbreak of varicose veins and a terrifying bleeding from her backside that the reception nurse informed her publicly and loudly was piles, adding 'suppositories will clear them up in no time.'

Sam had been a planned baby. Once Andrew and Lottie found themselves sufficiently comfortably off, with a house in a child-friendly suburb surrounded by couples like themselves, a large garden and a park in front of the house perfect for safe play when baby grew up a little, they decided they were ready to start a family. The neighbourhood children kicked footballs or cycled their bikes along the paths or played hide and go seek behind the trees. It seemed idyllic and Andrew and Lottie couldn't wait to be part of it. Weeks into the pregnancy and she tried to remember that warm anticipatory glow in the mornings while leaning over the lavatory trying to be sick, or performing the gentle but tedious yoga exercises she was told could help her backache.

She forgot about it again through the long and unbelievably painful labour, the forceps delivery they assured her was in the baby's interest.

'Baby is in distress,' they told her and Andrew held her hand while they cut her open to make Sam's passage easier, and then he let go at the astonishing sight of the little purple baby-shaped bundle they pulled out of her.

It was at the moment when Sam started to howl, while the doctor was sewing her up again, that Lottie realised fully for the first time that the lump in her belly was in fact a new person, a being totally dependent on her for its survival. The weight of responsibility terrified her. She reached for Andrew but he wasn't there any more.

Now he put his hand over hers.

'Everything will be fine,' he said.

She tried that bright smile again but it came out as twist of the lips as she blinked back tears.

'I know,' she said, knowing nothing of the sort.

'Do you want another coffee?'

'No, thank you.'

She was back on the caffeine now that she had stopped the breast-feeding she had been encouraged to do for the baby's better health and to help her bond with him. She had needed no help with that at least. Lottie wasn't the sort of mother who rejected her offspring. On the contrary, she felt an agonising closeness, as if he were still part of her, only partly ripped away, the wound continuing to bleed.

'Will we go for a walk then?' Andrew asked.

'Yes, that would be nice.'

They wandered back to the main square with its ancient church, souvenir shops, lively cafes. They had already visited the church, cool and dark within, perfumed with incense, candles flickering in front of virgins and saints and suffering Jesuses. Lottie had even lit a candle before a Madonna and Child, not because she was religious, but out of superstition. Now they crossed to the middle of the square, to a white marble fountain, with some sort of goddess or sea nymph rising from the top, holding a large urn from which water gushed, while attendant cherubs hung over the rim with scallop shells to catch the falling drops. The guide book told them it was considered one of the jewels of the resort, but Lottie didn't care for it, its cold whiteness, the sneer on the mouth of the nymph, the fat limbs of the cherubs.

On this day, a small market had been set up on one side of the square. They went over to see what was on offer: shiny vegetables and fruits, huge tomatoes, plum-dark aubergines, peppers not only red, yellow or green, but orange and purple and combinations of all these, short plump cucumbers, oranges, giant lemons, 'a feast of colour', as Andrew said, smiling.

'Beautiful, beautiful...'

Lottie spun round to find a woman leaning right over Sam in the buggy. Her hand even touching him.

'Beautiful baby...'

'Please don't!' Lottie said. 'He's asleep.'

The woman looked up smiling. She was middle-aged, with sloe-black eyes, leathery skin and several gold teeth. Greasy greying hair scraped back in a bun. Her hand, still next to Sam's cheek, was tobacco-brown against his pearly whiteness. Lottie pulled her away, the sudden movement waking Sam, who started to cry.

'Look what you've done!' Lottie screeched at the woman. 'Go away!'

The woman shrugged and smirked and backed off.

Sam was howling now and people were looking. Lottie undid his straps and lifted him out of the buggy to comfort him.

'She didn't mean any harm,' Andrew said.

'How do you know? Anyway she was fingering him with her dirty disease-ridden hands...'

'Calm down, Lottie!'

Didn't Andrew know anything? Instead of taking her side, backing her up, supporting her, he always made out that she was overreacting. But babies were stolen all the time on holiday. There was that famous case where the kidnappers had even entered the child's bedroom to steal her. It was thought they had been stalking the family for some time and took advantage of the brief absence of the parents. That wouldn't happen to Lottie. She wouldn't let herself be separated from Sam for an instant, but now apparently even that wasn't enough: she couldn't turn her back in case someone reached forward and whipped him out of the buggy while she wasn't looking. From now on, she resolved to carry him in her arms and let Andrew raise his eyes to heaven all he liked.

Sam was snuffling in misery.

'Would you get his bottle?' she asked Andrew. He rooted it out of the bag hanging on the back of the buggy. Lottie went back to the fountain and sat on its edge to feed him, her back to the sun and her body shielding Sam from its power.

'While you're doing that, I'll just check go and out the market,' Andrew said. 'They have some of those olives we like.'

He walked off. Lottie thought she noticed a lightness to his step, as if he was glad to be getting away from them even just for a few minutes.

Sam was sucking contentedly. People passed, smiling at them. Lottie smiled back, more relaxed. Maybe some of the old women were thinking she should still be breast-feeding and actually she had been sorry to stop, but the public health nurse had reckoned the baby wasn't getting enough nutrients, so suggested a bottle supplement. Soon afterwards, Sam had rejected the nipple, no doubt finding the teat less hard work. Nevertheless, feeding him was still a dreamy joy.

Suddenly she spotted the woman who had interfered with Sam earlier, standing across the square staring at them. When the woman realised that Lottie had seen her, she gave a friendly nod. Lottie turned away. When after a few minutes she checked again, the woman was still there, staring. Lottie started to get frightened, then angry. What right had she? What did she want? And where was Andrew when she needed him?

She cast her gaze over the multi-coloured throng at the market but couldn't spot Andrew's dark hair among so many, his paler face, his light blue tee-shirt. She took a deep breath and looked down at Sam, intent on the job in hand, warm, maybe slightly too warm, the sweet odour of baby sweat rising from him. She put her hand up inside his vest. Yes, he was roasting, abnormally, it seemed to her. Maybe he was sick.

She looked again for Andrew. In vain. How could he do this to her? And the woman still staring.

Lottie got up abruptly, and held Sam up against her shoulder. She had to find Andrew and never mind that the bottle was still half full, the baby still hungry. She held him, awkwardly pushing the buggy at the same time.

But there was no sign of Andrew in the market. She approached the olive seller but her command of the local language was almost non-existent. Please and thank-you and coffee, beer or wine, and the bill. That was about it. The olive seller, though friendly, clearly hadn't a notion what she was asking him. She looked round again, in case Andrew had been distracted by other stalls but he wasn't there. Andrew wasn't there.

Turning once more, she almost jumped out of her skin. Right behind, almost touching her, stood the woman, her gold teeth glinting as she smiled, her hands moving as she gabbled something in her language.

'Leave us alone,' Lottie said. 'Go away.'

She strode off. They couldn't stay here. They would go back to the hotel. Andrew would eventually find them there.

She set off down the narrow little street that wound towards the hotel, holding Sam tight and pushing the buggy over the cobblestones. The baby was fretting, clearly thirsty, wanting more bottle.

'When we get home, pet,' she told him. 'It will be cooler there. I'll give you some water.'

But she soon realised she had taken the wrong street. Instead of going back – not that, never – she cut through an even narrower, darker alleyway, figuring that was the direction she should have taken in the first place. It wound round, eventually bursting out into a little square Lottie had certainly never seen before. An old woman sat fanning herself under a tree that was covered in heavy red flowers, but when Lottie approached her and said the name of the hotel, the old woman just shook her head. Never mind, Lottie was fairly sure this was the right way. If she kept going eventually she must surely cut into the street she should have taken in the first place.

But would she even recognise it? The guide book, stowed in Andrew's shoulder bag, wherever he happened now to be, had kept referring to the resort's picturesque maze of back streets. It was a maze, certainly, the picturesque nature of which she was in no state to appreciate. And no one to ask except that stupid old woman. Of course, that was because it was the afternoon siesta, when the sun burnt down at its fiercest and wise locals took refuge in the cooler interiors of their stone houses instead of pacing the burning streets.

She arrived at a canal, and recognised it as the waterway running beside the ancient building that was their hotel. With relief, Lottie started up it in the direction that had to be away from the sea.

The bank was overgrown and the path rough with broken paving stones. It was hard to push the buggy, and stalks of grass whipped back at her bare legs as she passed. The canal water was murky, and long strands of green weeds trailed just under the surface. A sickeningly rotten smell rose from it.

Lottie suddenly doubted that this was in fact the right canal, seeming now to recall from that same map she had glanced at incuriously when Andrew showed it to her, that several waterways radiated through the town to the sea. She decided to retrace her steps after all and turned abruptly, only to gasp aloud with horror. Fifty yards behind her, the woman with the gold teeth was hurrying to catch up. And now Lottie no longer had the crowd to protect her.

The woman shouted something that sounded threatening. Knowing she had to get away at all costs, Lottie started to run, abandoning the buggy, holding Sam tight, pursued by the woman's calls. She ran, stumbling over the broken path, the baby now sensing her panic, screaming in her ear. She ran, checking back from time to time to see was the woman still behind her. Yes, but further back, her voice fainter. Certain now that the woman was intent on snatching Sam, Lottie didn't dare slacken her pace, and ran on even though she was gasping from the effort, her arms and the hands that held the baby slippery with sweat.

Then ahead, beyond some sort of lock gate, on the other side of the canal, she saw a man fishing. Thank God. All she had to do was cross the lock to him. The woman wouldn't dare do anything to them then. They were saved.

Lottie screamed. She screamed and screamed. Every waking moment she remembered how it had been, trying to cross the narrow ledge of the lock gate, slippery with green weed, trying to hurry, aware that the woman was again closing the gap. How, hurrying, she had lost her footing on the wet weed and tumbled into the murky water. Losing hold of Sam, losing him. Trying to see where he was in the dark, her lungs bursting to stop the water flooding into her. Looking for him and not seeing him, peering up through the murk at the wavy faces of people staring down. Surfacing with empty arms and screaming, 'Where's Sam? Where's my baby?'

Sometimes Andrew sat beside her hospital bed, despair on his face.

'Why didn't you wait for me?' he said once. 'I just popped into the church. I just wanted a moment to myself. Why didn't you wait?'

But he had abandoned her. He had left her alone to protect Sam, and instead... Lottie started to scream again. A nurse came and injected sleep into her, a dreamless deathlike sleep from which she would wake unhealed.

She was alone. She looked beside her, expecting to see the little cot where Sam was sleeping, one arm flung out to the side, his chest rising and falling with the tiny breaths that proved he was still alive.

Then she remembered. He wasn't. He was drowned dead. His tiny body fished out of the water after she had been pulled to safety by the fisherman.

Lottie didn't scream any more. She stared out of the hospital window at the glare of the sun on stone. And later when they brought her food, she wouldn't eat unless someone fed her, encouraging her to open her mouth, which she did automatically. She didn't even scream when the nurse came to give her another injection, and she saw that it was the woman with the gold teeth, smiling at her.

'It'll be over soon,' the woman said, pushing the needle into her arm.

And as Lottie started to sink down into oblivion, she could see, as through murky water, the wavy face of the woman and Andrew both, staring down at her. And then there was nothing.

GILDA

This isn't a ghost story. Or if it is, you'll have to revise your notion of what is meant by a ghost. In optics, for example, it refers to a bright spot or secondary image produced by a defect in a lens.

The story begins when Eleanor went on a cruise to Leningrad for the ballet in the days when the ballet was worth going for. No, actually, to be precise, the real start was long before that when Eleanor was small, the lonely daughter of parents who were proud of the fact that they kept themselves to themselves. The two of them only children as well, with no extended family network, no aunts to squash Eleanor to stupendous bosoms, no uncles smelling comfortably of pipe tobacco, no cousins to play hide and go seek with in the far recesses of the house. Not that the house was rambling in any way: poky would be a more appropriate description, three up two down with a spare box bedroom that never held guests and stayed spare until Eleanor's father decided to move in there by himself for some reason. But it was in that poky house during long silent afternoons that Eleanor learnt to fall back on her own resources.

She was a solitary child without however being anti-social, for, although she never met up with them outside, at school she had a network of quite close friends. Unlike Mildred Smart who never spoke to anyone unless it was unavoidable, whose milky eyes slipped past your face while she whispered her message or answer to the rare question posed. Mildred wasn't particularly disliked or picked on, just ignored, and it was with a puzzled shrug that most people greeted the news of her suicide. As for Eleanor, she felt uneasily guilty about it, not quite sure why.

Little of this is relevant to the present account, except to show the sort of person Eleanor was, self-sufficient, sensitive.

She was quite adventurous, too, taking this cruise to Leningrad by herself when to go there was still to venture behind the iron curtain and tourists had to be briefed on how to avoid sexual blackmail. At least, that's what her mother said when trying to talk her out of going; that she had heard things; that a man named Boris would in all probability try to lure Eleanor to a seedy hotel where he would give her drugged cigarettes and then photograph her in compromising positions. Eleanor assured her mother that if she got as much as a whiff of the scented cigarettes of anyone called Boris she'd run a mile but that she had no intention of changing her plans. It wasn't that she was much of a ballet fan although she liked the cool, controlled formality of it, the emaciated bodies of the dancers, all muscle, no flesh. Reflecting her own somewhat passionless nature, perhaps, she preferred classical ballet to the sweaty contortions of modern dance. She understood that there wasn't much modern stuff in Soviet Russia, which was apparently why so many of the dancers there fled to the West. As far as Eleanor was concerned, she simply felt that, already in her thirties with time slipping by, she needed a change, new horizons, and acted on an impulse when she saw the holiday ad in a magazine.

She was determined to soak up the entire experience and so was even able to relish the cruise on the tacky Russian ship featuring bossy stewardesses with cruelly bleached hair and greasy vermilion lips. She ate everything that was put in front of her, unlike most of her fellow travellers who complained all the time, about the food, the service, the bar prices. They stopped in Copenhagen for a few hours and she dutifully wandered around with Dorothy, her cabin-mate, a large middle-aged woman in flowing purple, who insisted on spending most of the day sampling Danish pastries.

'This may be the last real food we get,' Dorothy muttered ominously, crunching almonds.

Come Helsinki, Eleanor was determined to give Dorothy the slip, and indeed lost her immediately in the bustle of the fish market on the quayside, thereafter spending a pleasant few hours by herself, wandering the streets of golden buildings until she bumped into her cabin-mate again, about to enter a department store.

'This may be our last chance to stock up with essentials,' Dorothy barked, dragging her in.

Just behind Dorothy's shoulder stood a tall woman, as tall as Eleanor herself, slim and elegant. She introduced herself as Gilda and when Eleanor, asking if she was on the tour and being told yes indeed, expressed surprise at not having seen her before, replied that she had been sea-sick for the first few days and only now felt up to mingling.

'Not the sea,' Dorothy shook her head, 'the food. That caviar last night was very suspect if you ask me.'

She was examining tights and wanted to buy four packets of the very cheapest.

'Gifts for the maids,' she announced. 'They prefer them to tips.'

Dorothy was a balletomane, a regular visitor to Leningrad and liked to think that, as she put it, she 'knew the ropes'. She claimed to be having a torrid love affair with a member of the Kirov ballet company who however was foolishly sticking to his marriage.

'One of these days I'll pop him in my suitcase and bring him home with me,' she promised.

Eleanor and Gilda exchanged looks across the glass counter, across the broad purple back of Dorothy.

The two women spent all their time together after that, sitting late into that last pale night on deck, sipping Pernod, staring out across the expanse of the Baltic broken only by the occasional wink of lights from a fishing boat. Later under the thinnest crescent of a waning moon they were joined by an actuary named Ronald, and Eleanor told him her father had been an actuary too.

'Had been?' asked Gilda. 'Is he already dead then?' As if she knew him. Which of course was impossible.

'No. Retired,' Eleanor answered, somewhat puzzled.

Twenty-four hours later, walking the streets of the city in a night that never grew dark, one of the magical white nights of St Petersburg, crossing the little bridges over the canals, over the river Fontanka, Eleanor had a vivid and disturbing sensation of familiarity. She knew that she had never been to this city before, but felt she had experienced this moment already, leaning over a parapet with Gilda, gazing at flowing silver water somewhere, sometime. Her head was spinning, the traffic noises faded, a large bird flew up past them silently, its wings fanning their faces. She raised her eyes, following its flight into the wide white expanse of sky until it disappeared, as if sucked in. Gilda reached across and brushed the hair away from Eleanor's cheek, from where it had caught on the dampness of her mouth.

'How lovely it is,' she sighed. 'Don't you wish it could stay like this for ever?'

'Yes,' said Eleanor. 'Oh yes.'

Back at the hotel, the tour guide approached her with a serious face.

'I'm so sorry,' she said.

There had been a call from the embassy. Eleanor's father had died suddenly. If possible, Eleanor's mother would like her to return at once. It was difficult, said the guide, but under the circumstances arrangements could be made.

Eleanor felt more irritation than grief. Her parents had never been particularly loveable; they had constantly given the impression of wanting more from her than she was able to give, and it was typical of them that one would choose to pass on at the moment likely to cause her the most disruption and difficulty. In view of her mother's opposition to the trip, Eleanor even imagined the grim satisfaction it would have given her to summon her daughter home, in the only way that allowed no refusal. She was tempted to ring and say it was impossible to arrange, you know how these Soviets are, particularly since she had started to enjoy herself, if that was the word, remembering with a shiver Gilda's light touch.

To Eleanor's amazement, her mother sobbed down the phone. Such an unprecedented show of emotion! Had she really loved her husband, despite those separate bedrooms, or was she just sorry for herself? What could Eleanor do other than promise to fly back at once? She didn't see Gilda again, although Dorothy embraced her with loud wails as if they were best buddies and Ronald accompanied her to the airport and carried her bags and waited with her through all the dreary formalities. The fact that his Russian was quite good was a help.

The funeral was quiet and mostly attended by dark-suited men who had worked with Eleanor's father over the years, men who shook her by the hand and muttered things like 'deepest condolences' and 'sadly missed' and drank the one whiskey or brandy etiquette demanded before swooping off in their black cars. Afterwards, Eleanor's mother couldn't bring herself to stay in the house until 'his' things had been removed from view, Eleanor being commissioned to perform the task, while her mother took off to stay with Auntie Vi for a few days in a house by the coast. Auntie Vi was the only person Eleanor's mother had kept up with from the old days, a boarding school friend and no one's real auntie.

So Eleanor stayed alone in the house, pokier than ever and dreary with its beige and brown decor. There was even a musty smell as if it had been empty and closed for some time. Eleanor tried to be brisk. She folded armfuls of grey and navy suits into cases, white and pale blue shirts, sober ties. The sensible lace-ups she put in black plastic bags to be retained, the socks and underwear and other items of an intimate nature she put in another plastic bag to be thrown out. Her mother's instructions had not been totally clear. Did she want it all out of the house or simply out of sight, in the loft or under the stairs, or did she want it sold to a dealer or donated to a charity? For the time being Eleanor, fearing not to do the right thing decided to store it all where it could easily be reached, under the stairs.

She opened the little odd-shaped door and was immediately transported back thirty years to her childhood. Probably by the evocative scent – of hard wax polishes mostly – still stored there. She flicked a switch and the light came on. It was the same as ever. There had been no reason to change it, for surely only the most wearisomely house-proud redecorated under the stairs. The hieroglyphics she'd scrawled on the wall were still there. She fitted herself in, with much more difficulty now that she was so tall, pulled the door shut and switched off the light again. This had been her retreat when the silence of the house had been too much for her, here she had come and... here she had come and...

There were two little girls squashed together in the pungent darkness, giggling with their hands over their mouths to muffle the sound, two little girls – how could she have forgotten? Here she'd come to meet her friend, in their den, to spend hours together while her mother rested upstairs with a damp cloth over her migraine-tormented head. It was black dark at first but then the thin line of light marking the odd-shaped door gradually illuminated the bulkier shapes, the two little girls giggling their secrets, squashed together, bare arms and bare legs touching, touching in the dark each other's secret places...

Eleanor flicked on the switch suddenly, a sick panic rising in her. The light bulb, knocked by her arm, swung violently in the small space, casting distorted shadows. She directed it to the niche between the third and fourth stair, too low for an adult to see. She crawled out to fetch something from her handbag, a little mirror which she brought back and held under the rough wood. There it was back to front but still clearly visible, a crudely drawn heart and the words inside, '*Eleanor and Gilda forever*'.

Before she could even begin to think what it all meant, there was a rap on the front door. She went to see. A looming shape was outlined against the light passing through the stained glass lozenges. Eleanor shivered. She didn't want to open the door, for some reason. But that would have been giving in to irrational fears and she had always thought of herself as even excessively sensible. In the event, it wasn't after all what she had dreaded. It was only Ronald, back from the trip, calling to find how she was bearing up.

'I tried to phone,' he said. 'They told me it had been disconnected.'

That was Eleanor's mother, terrified she wouldn't be able to manage on half a pension, not wanting to pay for a luxury she, with no one to call, didn't need.

The holiday hadn't been the same without her, Ronald claimed. Dorothy had made loud difficulties about the accommodation, the ticket allocation for the Kirov, the inadequacies of the sight-seeing trip to Peter the Great's Summer Palace (the famous fountain had been shut down awaiting repairs, a decent cup of coffee wasn't to be had...). She had introduced everyone to her lover but Ronald received the distinct impression the young man was more interested in him than in Dorothy.

'And Gilda?' Eleanor finally managed to ask.

'Which one was she?'

Eleanor let it pass. She thought she might be going mad.

She thought she might be going mad and that was why she let Ronald lead her upstairs to her mother's bed and make love to her all afternoon.

'Unfinished business,' he whispered in her ear. She couldn't think what he was referring to because they hadn't even touched before. And then, as he caressed her breasts and pressed himself against her belly and pushed her head down until she took him in her mouth, she heard a distinct giggle. But when she opened her eyes there was no one there, only Ronald, telling her she was a great girl.

Later, as they drank her mother's tea, he mentioned the reason he had called: there was to be a reunion the following week of everyone on the trip.

'I didn't think you should be left out,' he smiled.

Her father threw open the door and dragged her out, naked and all as she was, he dragged her out and slapped her arm. It was the only time he'd ever hit her.

'*You dirty dirty dirty little girl!*' *he shouted.*

She was screaming with sobs.

'*Shut up,*' *he screeched back,* '*your mother's trying to rest.*'

He pinched her arm and the marks remained as bruises for weeks afterwards.

'*You dirty bitch! So this is what you do by yourself in the dark.*'

He slapped her again and behind him she saw Gilda creep out from under the stairs, naked too, creep out and away. She screamed and bit her father's arm and he crashed his hand against the side of her head and she passed out.

When she came to, she was in her own little bed in her own room, wearing a nightdress, her mother sitting beside her. A strange man standing.

'*You were having a nightmare and fell out of bed, dear. We were quite worried. But doctor says you'll be all right.*'

The nightdress had long sleeves. They covered the bruises on her arms. But maybe it really had been a nightmare, because her father and mother never referred to the incident again, her father never raised his voice or hit her or even touched her again. Only under the stairs was crammed with things that never used to be there, the vacuum cleaner, a boot rack, spare rolls of linoleum. There was no room for her, no room for Gilda if she should ever try to return.

The reunion was taking place in a restaurant along the river. People Eleanor hardly remembered came up and embraced her. Dorothy gazed at her earnestly and told her she knew exactly how she felt. Of tall elegant Gilda there was no sign and for some reason Eleanor didn't want to ask. Ronald behaved in a proprietorial way, touching her a lot, on the arm, on the thigh, brushing her breasts. Eleanor couldn't help thinking it was largely for show, to inform the others, many of them hanging off each other, that he too had enjoyed a holiday romance, cruelly cut short, as Dorothy kept saying. When asked about her own affair, Dorothy shrugged significantly, 'toujours cette execrable épouse', in French presumably because she didn't know any

Russian except 'da', as Ronald giggled into Eleanor's ear. 'Da, da, da.'

She excused herself as if to go to the ladies. Instead she walked out into the gardens of the restaurant. It was nearly dusk. A white night, darkness hovering a blink away. The gardens smelt headily of roses. There was an ornamental bridge over the river and Eleanor went down there to gaze at the silver water rushing under it.

'It's deeper than you'd think,' Gilda said.

Eleanor didn't reply.

'You knew I'd come, didn't you,' Gilda asked, after a pause. 'I couldn't stay away.'

Eleanor turned to face her. 'Where is away?'

'Ah... Everywhere... and nowhere. Not very satisfactory, really. I thought I could get on by myself, without you. But of course, it wasn't possible. *Eleanor and Gilda forever.'*

Eleanor nearly swooned. She gripped the cold metal of the bridge to steady herself.

'Why have you come back now?'

'I want to live. I'm tired of being a shadow. You on the other hand would quite like it, wouldn't you?'

'What do you mean?'

'The way you live or partly live. Nibbling reluctantly at existence. It's all too much for you. We'd be better off swapping places.'

Eleanor looked into the other's eyes, fathomless hollows. She saw silence. Her head was spinning, the traffic noises faded, a large bird flew up past them, its wings fanning their faces. She raised her eyes, following its flight into the wide white expanse of sky until it disappeared, as if sucked in. Gilda reached across and brushed the hair away from Eleanor's cheek, from where it had caught on the dampness of her mouth.

'How lovely it is,' she sighed. 'Don't you wish it could stay like this forever?'

'Yes,' said Eleanor. 'Yes, yes, yes.'

It was easy. She simply climbed over the ornamental metalwork of the bridge and threw herself off into the silver water. As she sank down she saw the other lean over and look at her, as in a mirror.

Her imaginary friend, her mother said, joking at first, Eleanor's pretend friend, even going along with it, giving Eleanor a biscuit for herself and another one for Gilda. Then got concerned when it became obsessive. When Eleanor wanted her friend to have a share in everything. When Gilda became more and more demanding, stamping her foot to get her own way. Having screaming tantrums. Not like Eleanor, not like Eleanor at all. It isn't healthy, her mother finally said, clutching her throbbing head. You should have real friends like everyone else. (Well, not everyone. There was poor Mildred Smart as a terrible example of friendlessness.) Eleanor had to meet Gilda in secret after that. Under the stairs. Where her father had found her.

Now Eleanor could see that someone had joined Gilda on the bridge. It was Ronald come looking for her, the two of them gazing down into the fast flowing water. Eleanor felt it carry her away from them. She tried to raise heavy arms but they had turned to embrace each other and didn't see.

'Call me Gilda,' she heard. 'I prefer it.'

Then Ronald and Gilda turned and walked away towards the lights of the restaurant as the darkness crept up over the gardens, tarnishing the silver of the river and flowing cold through Eleanor, filling her eyes and ears and mouth as she was forgotten forever.

THE EPIPHANIC MOMENT

The audience clapped dutifully. Patrick, casting a languid eye over the assembly, observed the usual abundance of pudding-faced middle-aged women, a couple of flashier young ones, a sprinkling of men with beards. He smiled at them all.

'Thank you,' he said. 'Thank you so much. Now my next poem...'

Praise God, he thought – the God he didn't believe in – for the arts festivals that spread like a rash over the country from spring onwards. To make a living as a poet was impossible, and the fees he received from these readings were most welcome. Of course he had to eke it out with teaching, a generally distasteful occupation among wannabe poets who had hardly read a line of anyone else's work and hadn't even heard of Robert Lowell or Robert Frost or even Robert Service.

'Thank you,' he said, making eye-contact with the woman in the front row who, throughout the reading, had been calling attention to her fat legs by crossing and re-crossing them and then attempting to tug down the short tight skirt she was wearing to save her modesty.

No luck there, love, he thought. I can see your knickers.

She was over middle age, more like old. But no doubt imagined she had fooled everyone with her dyed bouffant hair, her thick make-up, her dangerously corseted hour-glass figure. Patrick was reminded of Swift's Corinna who takes herself apart at night when all the beaux have left: '*pulls out the rags contriv'd to prop/ her flabby dugs and down they drop*', and then the glass eye, the false teeth, the wig, and so on.

He grinned at the thought and the woman smiled back. No, those nicotine-stained teeth were all her own.

Patrick finished with the poem about his father. It always went down well, even if it was from his first collection, the one which, many years earlier, had established him as the latest 'one to watch'. He was now trying to flog his sixth, *Shades*, an elegant little volume featuring an abstract design on the cover in paler and darker greys. He'd had misgivings at the time. Grey, indeed. But his editor had persuaded him.

'So minimalist,' Kirsten had said. 'Like your work.'

A compliment, he supposed. But he still thought the cover a mistake. You needed something to jump out at you from the shelf, not fade discreetly into the background.

He finished the poem and the audience clapped a little more enthusiastically than before. It would be familiar to some of them, having been widely anthologised – not that he'd ever received a penny for that – and one year had even featured on a Leaving Cert paper as the unseen. Kirsten had laughed.

'I'd love to see what those spotty kids wrote about it,' she said.

Sometimes he thought Kirsten disliked both him and his work. Maybe because he had been careful never to make a pass at her. Women were strange that way. Even though she was sure to rebut him, perhaps she still wanted him to try it on.

'Now, if there are any questions,' he said, 'I'd be delighted to try and answer them.'

There followed the usual tedious litany. Where do you get your ideas from? How long does it take you to write a poem? When did you start writing? What made you want to become a poet?

'Ah,' he said. 'You see, I never wanted to become a poet.' He paused. 'It's more like a vocation, or even a disease or an addiction. Something that you get hooked on and then you can't shake off, however much you may want to. Let me tell you something that happened to me recently.' He paused again for effect. 'One day, while I was wrestling with the Muse, my phone rang and some man asked "Is that Pat Brennan the driving instructor?" And, d'you know, for a moment I thought of saying "Yes". I mean, how much simpler and happier life would be, if I just pottered around with people in cars, telling them what to do.'

The audience laughed. It was an anecdote he had told many times before, one that he had in fact stolen from another writer. To divert himself, Patrick varied the caller's queries. Sometimes a driving instructor, sometimes a painter and decorator, sometimes a plumber. When he was drunk, something a bit more outré, a taxidermist, an undertaker.

'Who's your favourite writer?' asked the fat-legged woman in the front row.

'Well now,' he looked thoughtful, 'I could say Shakespeare, I could say Milton, I could say Seamus Heaney. But if I am to be brutally honest, I have to say... myself.' A pause and then he winked.

They laughed because they thought he was joking.

'No,' he went on. 'I love the American confessional school, Lowell, Berryman, Roethke...'

He observed the customary blank expressions on the faces of the audience. The fat-legged woman was taking notes.

'Sylvia Plath.'

He threw her in, not because he particularly liked her stuff but as a sop to the audience. They had at least heard of her.

'And Irish poets?' someone said.

'Apart from Heaney? Well, Paul Muldoon, Eamonn Grennan, Michael Hartnett, John Montague...'

'All men! What about the women?' called out some dyke standing at the back, one of that army, Patrick noted, who deliberately dress in a confrontationally non-feminine way while insisting on promoting feminism. This one was sporting a man's baggy check shirt, equally baggy jeans, hair pulled back in a pony-tail, no make-up. She was possibly quite pretty and not overweight at all but the way she presented herself made her look fat and plain.

I mentioned Plath didn't I, you silly bitch.

'Well,' he said, 'to give the ladies their due' (ladies, she'd hate that!) 'Eavan Boland, Paula Meehan, of course. I adore their work. And,' pausing, 'Andrea Foy.'

Now the audience looked really puzzled.

'She's a new young poet. Actually, she was in one of my writing classes, something of a protégée of mine, in fact.' He smiled self-deprecatingly. 'I think you'll be hearing a lot more of Andrea Foy in the years to come. One to watch.'

That scrap of flattery should get the nubile Andrea to spread open those long well-epilated legs of hers for him again, as long as he made damned sure she heard about it. Andrea, he thought hungrily: long curling hair, skinny body, like a young boy's. Shame she was so earnest.

'Do you teach a lot of classes?'

'I have several. It's very rewarding, and, as in the case of Andrea, sometimes you discover a real gift. But, if I can make a confession here, I think I learn as much from my students as they do from me.'

'Can poetry writing be taught?'

'Someone once said that the chief value of writing classes was that they got indigent writers off the street.' He laughed. 'But of course I wouldn't be doing it unless I thought I could in some way draw out dormant talent. How did Gray put it? "*Many a flower born to bloom unseen/ and waste its sweetness on the desert air.*" My job is to stop that waste. However, all I can really do is present my classes with exercises in form, encourage their efforts, and then it's up to them.'

Now an elderly man in the third row put up his hand. The high colour on what had to be a habitually angry face, made him a paradigm, Patrick judged, for the choleric type, if you happened to be categorising people according to the Four Temperaments. Maybe there was a poem in that thought.

'I came along tonight with the wife,' the man said, indicating with a sharp jerk of his thumb a mousey little pink-faced grey-haired woman on his left. 'She's a divil for the poetry. But me, to be honest with you, I haven't read a poem since school.' He stated this with pride, as if poetry wasn't something for real men to bother with.

'I hope you enjoyed what you heard tonight.'

'No well, I'm wondering, friend, can you explain something that been puzzling me. All this modern stuff, your stuff, it doesn't seem to rhyme. And if it doesn't rhyme, in my book that's not a poem.'

There's always one, Patrick thought. And 'stuff' indeed! He smiled sweetly at the man.

'That means, *friend*, you're telling me Shakespeare wasn't a poet.'

The man looked at him, the belligerent set of his mouth loosening slightly.

'A lot of Shakespeare doesn't rhyme, you know.'

Patrick launched into the opening speech from *Twelfth Night*: '*If music be the food of love, play on...*' He knew, many had told him, he had a beautiful speaking voice. 'So,' he concluded, 'if that's not poetry, I'd like to know what it is.' But not to mortify the man too much – he had paid in after all, and Patrick wanted him to buy the book – he added, 'However, I understand your confusion, shared, I might add, by many,' and launched into the usual spiel justifying free verse.

'My work is all about what James Joyce termed the epiphanic moment,' he concluded, thinking these people wouldn't recognise an epiphanic moment if it reared up and bit them in the arse. 'A revelation, a showing forth. In lay terms a "wow" moment. That's what I want you as listeners and readers to experience. Rhyme, metre, yes, by all means, if that's what turns you. But the most important is the moment of recognition that, after the poem, the world, even in some small way, will never be quite the same ever again.' He smiled. 'That's my modest intention.'

The reading was over but not the poet's ordeal. He was now expected to sign his books and mingle with these people. They were in an upstairs function room in the hotel where Patrick was staying, so eventually he'd be able to escape down to the bar. Not yet, however.

'There's wine and nibbles,' announced the dumpy woman – Carmel something – who was secretary of the local art appreciation society. 'I'm sure Patrick will be delighted to answer any further questions you might have. He'll also be signing copies of his latest book... er...' She looked at him queryingly.

'*Shades*,' he said.

'Ah yes, of course. That's right. *Shades*. Such an evocative title.'

So evocative you forgot it.

Carmel took his arm and led him to a table where a grey pile of books sat hopefully, alongside a few copies of his earlier works, in case people were sufficiently enthusiastic about his oeuvre to want the complete collection.

'Red or white wine?' she asked.

'Just sparkling water, thanks.' He dreaded to think what sort of plonk these people would serve.

'I'm not sure if we have sparkling. We have fizzy orange.'

'Oh no, thank you. Just plain tap water will be fine.'

She bustled off.

The first to his table was Fat-legs.

'I love your work,' she said.

'Thank you so much.'

'I do some writing myself, you know.'

'Really.'

'Yes, I've published a book.'

'Great.'

'Erica Butterfield.' She held out a hand to be shaken, which he dutifully took, finding himself squeezed tightly by podgy beringed fingers. Then she rummaged in a large silvery handbag. 'Here,' she said, proffering a clearly self-published booklet, a dozen or so pages bound together. The cover featured a crudely executed painting of a lumpy female nude over the title *Cold Sweats and Hot Flushes*.

Patrick thumbed through it, aware of the queue of people waiting behind the dratted woman.

She picked up a copy of *Shades*.

'Fair exchange is no robbery,' she said. 'You sign yours and I'll sign mine.'

It seemed she had no intention of paying. Patrick was furious but not to make a scene, he icily scribbled his name on the title page of his book and gave it to her.

'Oh,' she said, studying it. 'You didn't dedicate it 'To Erica'.'

'No, I didn't.' He smiled wolfishly, 'That, my dear, would cost you eleven euro and ninety nine cent.' He pointed to the price on the back of the volume.

She grabbed the book and flounced off.

Most others in line behaved as a good audience should, buying *Shades* and sometimes one of the other volumes as well. Even the little wife of the choleric gentleman bought a copy, asking for it to be inscribed 'For Mary'.

'I so enjoyed the reading. You have such a lovely speaking voice,' she said, twitching her nose in a perfect imitation of a mouse and Patrick bowed his head slightly in acknowledgement.

'Thank you, Mary,' he said.

In the end, despite the oaf who fingered the book with one hand while holding a greasy sausage roll in the other, commenting 'We don't get much for our money, do we,' and finally not even buying it, Patrick couldn't complain. He had done well and the pile of *Shades* had gone right down.

Carmel, to whom he had gallantly presented a complimentary copy, accompanied him down to the hotel bar.

'I'm sure you need a drink after all that,' she said.

'A daiquiri would be most welcome,' he said.

She goggled at him. 'A what?'

'A daiquiri. It was Hemingway's drink, you know.'

'Ah well. I'm not sure if they'll have it. But we can always ask.'

'Otherwise, Bacardi and lime juice over ice will do fine,' Patrick said, sighing slightly.

They took a table at the side that could accommodate a few others if they wished to join them and Carmel went off to get the drinks. While Patrick was waiting, two women came over and asked could they sit with him. He nodded and smiled a welcome, noting they were both good-looking in a peroxide blonde, fortyish kind of a way. Mumsy, as Michael Caine put it in *Alfie*.

'Were you at the reading?' he asked,

'We missed it,' the smaller one said. 'But of course we know who you are.'

'My fame has preceded me, has it?'

The smaller one giggled and looked at the other, who asked, 'You don't remember me, do you?'

'Oh dear. Should I?'

'We met at Listowel, a couple of years ago.'

'Ah!'

'I attended your workshop.'

'Well...'

He hated that. People always expecting you to know who they were when, after all, you met so many in the course of your busy life. Even worse, they expected you to remember their stupid scribblings and he imagined that would be the woman's next sentence: 'I showed you my little poem, *Snowdrops*', or something similar. So it was opportune of Carmel to arrive just then with the drinks. Simultaneously, a large red-bearded man together with the feminist dyke plonked themselves down beside them. The man had a foaming pint of stout in his hand, as did she. Of course she did. What else would she have?

'Liam Long,' the man said, sticking out a hairy red hand.

'Liam's one of our local bards,' Carmel said.

The man chuckled. 'Not in your class, of course, Patrick. I don't write deep stuff. Songs mostly.'

'He's very good,' Carmel went on. 'One of his songs has been covered (is that the word, Liam?) by Jimmy Crowley no less.'

'Oh,' said Patrick. 'Very good.'

'We must have a bit of a session later.' Carmel patted the bard's hairy paw.

'Yeah well,' Liam replied. 'We'll see. If Moira will sing for us, too.'

He indicated the dyke.

'Moira Cullen,' the feminist introduced herself.

'Do you write too?' Patrick asked.

'No,' she said. 'I'm a reader.'

'Thank God for that. It's more readers we need, not more writers.' He laughed.

'Moira's also an excellent English teacher,' said Carmel.

Despite this rather unpromising start, Patrick found himself becoming more jovial as the night went on and the Bacardis slipped down. He offered to buy a round once but no one would let him.

'You're our guest.'

Adding to his pleasure was the sight of Erica Butterfield, sitting at the bar, glowering across at him. Carmel remarked on this once.

'I wonder why Erica hasn't joined us. She usually wants to hob-nob with fellow scribes.'

She waved at Fat-legs, who looked away.

'She gave me her *book*,' Patrick said with scornful emphasis, and was about to follow this with a cutting remark. But stopped himself in time. These people were neighbours, even friends of the woman. Possibly thought her stuff terrific. And they were feeding drink into him.

Instead, he turned away, towards the woman on his left, friend of the one he was supposed to have met before. She was already very drunk and giggled a lot. A pretty little thing, nonetheless. He noted the wedding ring but was reassured to discover hubby was at home, minding the kiddies.

'Do you have children, Patrick?' she asked.

'Alas, no. I'm not married... well, not any more.' He thought briefly of Elaine, his ex. She'd wanted kids and he hadn't. She had them now, with some Polish guy. Her new man. Good luck to them.

'Oh dear...'

Did he imagine it, did the woman snuggle up a bit closer? Behind her a mirror extended along the wall and he observed himself in it. He had to admit he looked well for a man on the cusp of middle age. Hair a bit thinner and grey at the temples, but barely. High cheek bones, slightly flushed from the heat of the room, but not unattractively. He smiled at himself. Good teeth, too.

The woman, Annette or something, was rabbiting on.

'I went to mass today,' she said.

Not that surprising. It was Sunday and this was Ireland.

'Oh, yes?'

'First time in five years.'

'Five years! You must have an awful lot on your conscience by now.'

She giggled at that. Then went on, 'It was terribly boring, Patrick. Made me remember why I'd stopped going in the first place.' Then she clapped pink varnished fingertips to her mouth. 'Oh dear! I hope I haven't offended you. Are you a Catholic?'

'No. Not at all. I'm an atheist.'

'Wow! Are you really? How interesting.' Her baby blue eyes bulged. 'Oh dear. All the religions they have these days. I can't get my head around them. Once everyone was Catholic and you knew where you were. Now there's... Mormons and Muslims and Hindus... er...'

'Buddhists and Jews and Rastafarians and Zoroastrians,' said Patrick helpfully. 'Not to mention Protestants.'

'Yes, that's what I mean. So complicated. But the way I look at it, Patrick, it doesn't matter one bit so long as you believe in God.'

Now it was Patrick's eyes which bulged.

'But I don't.'

'You don't!'

'That's what an atheist is, pet. Someone who doesn't believe in God.'

'Goodness! So what do you think' – he could see she was trying to get her silly little brain around the novel notion' – what happens to us when we die?'

'Nothing. We rot in the ground.'

'Goodness!' She slurped her drink. 'That's awful. But then who made us, if not God? I mean, someone must have.'

'Following that reasoning to a logical conclusion, pet, you also have to ask who made God?'

She looked troubled.

Patrick watched his reflection patiently explain it to her. 'God, my dear,' he said, 'is made up to comfort children who are afraid of the dark. I am one of those who have grown up and need no such comfort.'

'So if you don't believe in God, you can sin all you like and nothing bad will happen to you.'

Patrick laughed. 'Something like that.'

'Wow!' She gave him a tipsy, sexy look. 'You must be fun to hang around with.'

He leaned towards her and blew hot breath in her ear. 'I like to think so.'

She pulled back. 'Naughty,' she said. Her face creased with the effort of thinking. 'What I believe,' she went on, 'is that we come round again and again. Like, after I die, I'll come back as someone else.'

'Reincarnation,' said Patrick. He noted that his reflected smile was indulgent rather than patronising. Undoubtedly an attractive smile.

'Yes,' she replied, uncertainly.

'And what evidence do you have for this, pet?'

'Well,' she reached for the new drink someone had brought her. 'I often find myself talking to someone I've never met before and thinking that I know them.'

'Ah, you mean déjà vu all over again,' quipped Patrick, watching himself clink glasses with the woman. 'So do you get that feeling with me?'

She considered. 'No,' she said. 'Definitely not.'

'Unlike your friend.' He glanced at the other woman, in conversation with Carmel. 'But of course, she claims actually to have met me before in this present life.'

'Yes...'

A guitar twanged behind him and Patrick turned. Liam Long was preparing to entertain them.

'Oh dear,' Patrick whispered to the woman, who giggled and snuggled a bit more.

After a couple of songs which Liam was able to raise above the cringe-making lyrics only by the robustness of his voice, Patrick decided to make his move.

'We can't hear ourselves talk any more,' he murmured. 'How about getting out of this place?'

'And go where?'

'Why don't you come up to my room? We can share a bottle of champagne.'

'Champagne, ooh.'

'Isn't that an offer you can't refuse?'

'Well... it sounds nice, but...'

'I'll slip out first and order the booze and you follow. Pretend you're going to the ladies or something.'

He gave her his room number. Then, making his apologies during a lull in the singing, stood up to go out.

'Great, man,' he said to Liam. 'Rhymes and all! Well done.'

'Are you going already? You have to stay and hear Moira sing. She's a voice like an angel.'

'Oh, I'll be back. Wouldn't want to miss Moira.'

He went to the bar and found they had two types of champagne. He ordered the less expensive one. The barman said he'd get a lounge boy to bring a bottle up to his room in a bucket of ice, along with two glasses. With somewhat unsteady steps – how many Bacardis had he drunk? Ah, but on an empty stomach: he never ate before a reading – Patrick clambered up the thick patterned carpet to the first floor and his room.

He looked at the bed's candyfloss-pink satin spread. He pulled it down and then pulled it up again. Don't make things too obvious, he said to himself and caught his grinning face in the long wardrobe mirror.

'For fuck's sake, stop admiring yourself, Patrick.' He jumped at the sound of Elaine's voice. She wasn't there, of course, but the sudden intrusion even of the memory of her made him uncomfortable. 'You're such a fucking self-centred bastard,' she went on. 'You...'

'Go away, Elaine,' he said. 'Buzz off. I'm expecting company.'

'That's a surprise. Can't sleep by yourself, can you. Little boy still afraid of the dark.'

'No, no...'

There was a knock on the door. But it was only the lounge boy, a pasty, gangling youth. He put the bucket with the champagne on the dressing table, removing two glasses from it. Patrick fumbled for a coin to give him a tip, but all he could find was a note. Too much of course, and he was about to say 'Catch you later,' but at the last minute felt it wouldn't do. The lounge boy took the fiver with the disagreeable air of one who expected at least as much.

Patrick wondered if he should open the bottle at once. He could do with a drink.

No, he thought, the woman, whatever her name was, would probably get a kick out of hearing the cork go pop. So he sat and waited. And waited. Where the hell was she? Surely he wouldn't have to go and look for her. Not him, Patrick Brennan.

To pass the time, and having nothing better to hand except his own poems – and he'd had enough of them for one night – he took the copy of *Cold Sweats and Hot Flushes* out of his jacket pocket, shuddering again at its lurid cover, and started to read:

I flick my tongue
Athwart your lips
I lick your chin, your neck
The taste of you is sweet
But acrid too

Down I lick
Down the centre of your chest
Bypassing the twin peaks of your nipples
Rising in a slight swell
Like berries on whipped cream...

There was a rap on the door. Saved by the bell.

He picked up the bottle to hold in one hand as he welcomed her in. Opened the door.

'Oh!' he said. 'I thought... Where's er... er... Annette?'

'Anita?' It was the friend. 'She's not feeling very well. I told her to go to bed.' She looked at the bottle. 'Ah, champagne. What a surprise!'

'Why don't you come in and share it with me?'

'Thank you.'

She walked in and sat on the bed. This was easy.

'Sorry, I can't remember your name.'

'That's all right. It isn't important.' She sat looking up at him, a queer half-smile on her lips.

'Dear lady,' he started, sitting beside her.

She took the bottle from his grasp and studied the label.

'Second-best champagne. Ah, well, I don't suppose Anita would know the difference.' She started to open the bottle. The cork popped but not loudly and only a tiny dribble came out. 'Now what does that remind me of? Let me think.' Her tone was unpleasant. She stood up abruptly and Patrick shivered. He suddenly had an unmistakeable sense of déjà vu.

'Yes,' she said, observing realisation dawn. 'We have been here before, Patrick. Not here literally, of course. In similar, one might say identical circumstances two years ago at Writers' Week. Do you remember my poems, the cycle lamenting the destruction of the environment? You said they showed remarkable promise. You said that in the bar and then suggested we continue the discussion in your room, where it was quieter, over a bottle of champagne. We drank the champagne but somehow failed to discuss my work. In fact, I seem to remember you telling me, while rather ineffectively lying on top of me, and twisting my breast in an attempt at erotic play, that sex was the truest poetry of all. And then, after a bit more drunken groping, you packed me off back to my own room and never spoke to me again.'

'I...' For once Patrick was lost for words.

'You know what they started saying downstairs, after you left. How disappointed they all were with the reading. That you'd only ever written one good book, one good poem in your life. That you're past your sell-by date. Best before 1987.' She threw back her head and laughed. 'Rehashing stale ideas in unimaginative ways... Epiphanic moments, my eye... I'll give you an epiphanic moment.'

She turned the bottle upside down and emptied the fizzing contents over his head.

'Hey,' she remarked, studying him, 'Patrick Brennan, you're going bald.'

Then, chucking the bottle on the bed, she turned on her heel, and went out, slamming the door behind her.

For a long time he sat slumped, staring at his reflection in the long mirror, at the champagne dribbling down his face, spreading over the candyfloss counterpane, puddling expensively on the floor.

Stupid, he said to himself. What does she know anyway? What do any of them know?

He picked up the naked woman, opened the book, and with a plunging sense of terror and despair, read on.

OUT OF THE BLUE

The woman was still talking. Mouth opening and shutting, lips twisting. There was a contortion of sound, too. High squeaks and low grunts. A phrase or two out of the babble – *you know yerself, missus... two weeks... the seaside... the kiddies...* And beyond all, the blue, that dizzying, vomit-inducing, screaming blue.

'You all right, missus?'

Her hands fluttered blind. She grasped at air. She found her dark glasses and then found her eyes, to mask them.

The woman was gazing at her, silenced at last, slack mouth hanging open, the bright blue fleece muted now, browned through tinted plastic.

'Sorry,' Grace said. 'I'm not myself.'

'So anyway,' back to business, 'as I said, we'll be wanting the caravan next Thursday week. You'll be sure to be out by then?'

'Yes.' Please just go.

'You know the way it is. It was never meant to be permanent.'

The woman seemed apologetic now, Grace looking so white.

'No. I'll be sure to be gone by then.'

It wasn't as if the place was comfortable. It was cold and damp with condensation that dripped off the walls, even after she'd lit the oil stove that stank and sucked up the oxygen. But Grace had got used to it. She liked its fragility, the way it swayed in the wind. She liked the staccato of rain on the thin roof. Nature just half an inch away. Sometimes when it was really stormy she lay on the bunk and fancied that the little bubble she was in broke free of its moorings and got tossed up into the sky, over the drab streets of the outer suburb, up to the mountains or out across the nearby bay, the crashing breakers.

The woman had gone. Her and her blue fleece. That shade. Petrol blue? Electric blue? Grace had reacted before but never so strongly. She looked out the open door of the caravan. The woman was tottering off into the night down the hill towards the bungalow on stilettos that must be sinking with every step into the wet soil, leaving a weaving pattern of tiny holes. Grace imagined following behind her and dropping a seed into each one so that in the summer a path of flowers would mark the way the woman had taken. She had loved gardening before she got sick. But in any case now she wouldn't be here to see flowers bloom. Twelve days to find a new place to live. The woman glanced back and Grace raised a hand in acknowledgement. The woman didn't respond.

Grace vomited on the grass then sighed back into the caravan. Never such a strong reaction. Was she getting worse, then? The doctor said she must expect strange symptoms.

'Expect the unexpected, Miss Brock,' he'd said, chuckling. 'We're in uncharted territory here.'

She turned on the radio. A live broadcast from the New York Met was about to start. There it would be afternoon. She imagined New Yorkers hurrying through the March sleet to the opera house. She wondered what it would be like to be in New York. People said it seemed familiar because of TV shows. You felt you already knew it. But she didn't have a TV.

Tristan and Isolde. One of the greatest love stories of all time. She lay back on the bunk and let the lush melodies brush over her while the wind whipped up a storm outside and the bubble she was in trembled and shook.

'How did she take it? The troll.'

Preston watched his wife as she removed her fleece. God, she had gone to flesh round the middle. Stick insect legs and then those rolls of fat round her belly and back. He could see the outline of her bra through the tight jumper, cutting into the flab, losing the battle to pull up those dangling tits. She was letting herself go. The large mole near her mouth had dark bristles growing out of it, matching the roots of her bleached hair. An image of Junie rose before him, Junie, seventeen if she was telling the truth, more like fifteen, her swimmer's body taut, her big white teeth in that wide mouth made for cocksucking. He fidgeted.

His wife was talking.

'She gives me the creeps,' she was saying.

'Well, did she say she'd go?'

'I s'pose. Not sure how much she took in. She looked queer. Queerer than usual.'

Preston thought of their tenant. Even less delectable than his wife, with a squat body and extra large hands and feet. He'd fallen about laughing one night, when Jason was reading The Three Billy Goats Gruff to Celine and asked him about a word. He'd shown the picture to Fee.

'Who does that remind you of?'

'Wha'?' The kids had asked. 'Who?'

'Shh,' Fee had said, laughing despite herself, 'they'll only pass it on.'

Ever after to him the woman in the caravan was the troll.

'Anyway, she'll have to go or lump it.'

It had been his brainwave. Get a plot in a caravan park down Tramore way. For the kids, he'd told Fee. You can take them down there all summer if you want. Relax. Enjoy yourself. Leaving him in town with Junie. Or else taking Junie down there when the family was at home. A summer of screwing. He was growing hard at the thought.

'I feel bad about it,' Fee was saying. 'We should have given her more notice. She looked like she was having a fit.'

'We have to take the plot right now or Keith'll give it to someone else. She'll be grand. Find some bridge to live under.'

Fee laughed.

'Come here,' he said.

'Wha'? Wha'?'

Grace had vomited twice more. And during the Liebestod, at that. One of the most powerful moments in opera. Could it just be the effect of the electric blue fleece? There had to be more, surely.

'Photophobia,' the doctor had said. 'A very special form of it in which a certain shade of blue is the trigger. And of course, it's related to the rest of your illness.'

About which he remained silent except to say it had something to do with the immune system.

He doesn't know, Grace had thought. Uncharted territory. Anyway, she felt a bit better now. Too late to enjoy the opera, though.

Love stronger than death. Not something she had ever experienced, but she could imagine it. And as Violet L'Estrange, author of romantic novels, she had on occasion conveyed this to her readers. Since she'd got ill though, she hadn't been able to write. A few letters from fans had been forwarded on to her, asking when her next book would be coming out. Her publishers, however, weren't pushing it. Violet L'Estrange was old fashioned. A chaste kiss or two, but then, because her stories ended with the wedding day, what happened after was outside the scope of the book.

But that, Grace thought, was what appealed to her readers, mostly single women of a certain age or housewives beaten down by rearing families on little money. The woman in the electric blue fleece for instance. She probably read that sort of story, if she read anything. Grace sensed such people didn't want descriptions of sweaty gropings, or even the idealised sexual congress some writers went in for. 'Tristram awakened the woman in Antoinette' was as far as Grace would go. Leave the rest to the imagination.

The caravan jerked as a mighty gust hit it sideways on. Grace gasped as a cup fell from her tiny draining board and smashed to the floor. She never listened to the news so was unaware that near hurricane force winds had been predicted that night, that the seas would rise at high tide and that all along the coast sandbags had been placed in readiness, householders creating makeshift barriers against the floods. Another great thud hit the caravan. An electric blue flash engulfed her.

Preston, impaling his wife on the living-room floor for the second time that night, wasn't aware of the weather report either. He only ever watched the sport and only when Fee gave him a window between her soaps.

'Fucking hell, Fiona,' he screeched, grabbing the flesh of his wife's belly.

Every knobble on her backbone would be bruised the next day, she thought bitterly as he slammed her against the thin carpet.

Then 'Fuck!' as the wetness seeped into her. He thought she was getting excited for once and thumped down harder.

'Preston!' pushing him off her.

'What the fuck!'

Across the blue carpet with its design of stylised orange flowers a darker stain was spreading. Preston and Fee looked at it bewildered, then at the glass door leading out to the patio. A good foot of water was pressing up outside. And planted there in the water, staring at them with big goggly black eyes, was the troll.

'Bloody hell!' Preston pulled on his jeans. She must have seen everything. Me bollix.

Fee started screaming.

'It's an ill wind,' said Grace's brother Brian, reviewing the situation several weeks later.

'I wouldn't have wished it on them,' said Grace. 'But they weren't very nice to me.'

The night of the storm she had waded down to the bungalow, glad of her wellingtons as the waters rose up her ankles. She had tapped on the window, not sure at first what it was she was peering at. There was blue, she knew that, luckily toned down by her dark glasses. And two half-naked bodies writhing on the floor in a pool of water. The man had jumped up, followed by the woman. If Grace was astonished, she was too polite to show it. In any case, she had other things on her mind.

'The lights went out,' she'd shouted at them but they didn't seem to understand. 'The electrics are gone.'

They'd gone in the blue flash. At first she thought the colour had finally blinded her until vague shapes started emerging out of the blackness. But it had been a nasty few minutes.

Now the woman had gone off somewhere and the man was on a mobile phone, yelling at someone. Of course she realised they didn't want to open the door and let in more water, but still, there she was standing in the deluge, the water now lapping at the top of her boots. The man gestured at her to go away, or that's what she understood. He was a crude, rude person who always looked her up and down with a sneer on his ratty face and she preferred to deal with the woman. Back she trudged, away from the flood up to the caravan. Then stopped aghast. It was on fire. Ablaze in the rain. With all her stuff inside. But she didn't have much.

Soon she became aware of the woman at her side, clutching a child in her arms. Then the man holding hands with another one, slightly bigger. They were all gaping at the fire.

'So much for frigging Tramore,' the woman said.

'Fuck,' said the man. 'Fuck, fuck, fuck.'

The fireman investigating said the wiring was a disaster waiting to happen.

'Good thing,' he informed Grace, 'you was awake. If you was asleep you'da have been burned to a crisp.'

The oil stove hadn't helped. It had exploded as had the calor gas cylinder.

'You was living in a time bomb, missus,' said the fireman.

The man and woman's insurance company paid her a nice little sum. Brian said they could have got more if they'd gone to court but Grace said no. It was enough. Because of her illness, she had been re-housed in a cosy one bedroom apartment further from the sea but nearer the mountains. The walls had been blue but were being repainted, on Grace's instructions, a nice shade of mauve. Very restful to the eyes. Meanwhile, she had decided, in the wake of the trauma, and in the light of the little windfall, to take a cruise round France, Italy and Greece.

'Good idea,' said her doctor. 'Could work wonders. Sun, sea and dot dot dot,' he winked.

Grace sat on a lounger writing in a thick A4 pad. Occasionally she looked up for inspiration but mostly her pen raced across the page. *Iseult sat on the deck reading her book*, she wrote. *Little waves tripped by. Rare clouds danced across a pale blue sky.* Grace struck out *pale blue* and wrote *cerulean*. She thought for a moment then continued: *The tall man she had spotted earlier passed her again with a sideways glance. She pretended not to notice. She pretended she was engrossed in her book.* Grace stretched out, wriggling bare toes with pleasure. Through her dark glasses she watched the tall young man leaning with his back against the ship's railings, ogling the girls walking by. He was very good-looking in the arrogant way of Italians, dark-haired, swarthy skinned. No, olive-skinned. *The tall olive-skinned man...* Grace wrote. *'It must be a good story'*, the man *said*, *'to intrigue you so much.' Iseult looked up into eyes like burning coals...* Grace reread what she had written and inserted *in husky accents* after *the man said*. She sucked the end of her pen, and stared after the tall man as he swaggered off along the deck after a leggy brunette in a skimpy bikini. Then she changed *said* to *breathed*, *accents* to *tone* and added *flavoured with the spicy accents of the Mediterranean.* The new book, she thought with satisfaction, was going to be a cracker.

The girl pushed Preston's hand off her breast.

'I can't do it here,' she said. 'This place stinks. Makes me want to puke.'

She got up off the couch. There was a stain around the fabric of it marking how high the water had risen the night of the flood. Junie had oohed at the sight. 'Must have been sooo scary,' she'd said running the tip of a pink tongue along her teeth.

'Anyway, got to go,' she said now, briskly.

'Go? You've only arrived.'

'Yeah well...'

'We got the place to ourselves. For as long as we want.' That was a fucking fact.

'Yeah, but it's minging. Why can't we go to a hotel like we done before?'

Cos I can't afford it, you stupid cunt. Not now.

'Next time,' he said.

'Yeah, next time,' she mimicked, not pleasantly. 'Like, it's always next time. Anyway, have to dash.' She looked down at him with those baby blue eyes. 'Sorry Prez. Meeting some friends.'

'Who?'

'You don't know them.'

'A fella?'

She laughed and pecked his cheek but resisted when he tried to pull her down beside him again. He could have forced her, but what was the use.

'I only love you. Doncha know that?' She waggled her tight bum in its hipster jeans. Three inches of her flat belly bare above them. The ring in her navel he'd paid for that her da had hit the roof about.

'Junie...'

'See ya around, Prez.'

Her heels tapped away from him across the floor. And then she was gone.

Fee was gone too, to her bitch of a sister of all people.

'I just can't hack it any more,' she'd said, turning away. The kids had looked at him with solemn eyes, then skipped out after their ma. He'd been gobsmacked. He still was.

Preston stared at the bungalow, empty and stinking. At the glass door where that fucking troll had stood bringing her bad luck. At the floor, stripped now of the ruined blue carpet, the concrete underneath grey and blank.

STING-A-LING-A-LING

I'm afraid, Mr Blake, there's nothing more we can do for you,' the doctor was saying in a lugubrious voice. 'We've run out of options.'

'How long have I got?' Blake asked.

'Well, bluntly put, only a very short time. A few weeks at most.'

The doctor was pompous, short, fat and bald with a red complexion and a purple nose. Blake looked at him and started to splutter. Then he looked across at me. He winked.

'How long do any of us have?' he asked. And started to laugh. And I laughed too, it was so infectious. 'What about McSorley here?' (pointing at me.) 'Thirty, forty more years if he's lucky? A mere blink of time's eye.'

The doctor leaned forward, locking his fingers together and closing them over his knuckles.

'As for you, doc,' Blake went on, considering that nose, those bloodshot eyes, 'you might get another five years out of it. Or you might pop off tomorrow.'

'I'm glad,' the doctor replied, tight-lipped, which made us giggle all the more, 'you're able to be so philosophical about it. However, there's the issue of pain relief. Someone from the palliative care team will be in to see you in due course to discuss how this can be organised.'

Blake suddenly stopped smiling. 'You mean you want me to stay here... Here!' he gestured at the vomit green hospital walls. 'To wait for Death to come and nab me?'

'It would be preferable. The final stages of the disease can be distressing. Bodily functions out of control and so on and so forth. The main thing is that you be comfortable.'

'I understand,' Blake said, 'the sort of comfort you have in mind. Morphined into a zombie so I won't even hear the pitter-patter of Death's feet when he comes calling.'

'It's your choice of course,' the doctor said. 'We could perhaps arrange for the hospice to take you. Or you could go home, if...' he looked at me doubtfully, 'there's someone capable of looking after you.'

'No better fellow,' Blake said, swinging his arm around my shoulders and burying his fingers in my flesh. 'McSorley's the man for the job.'

Before we left the hospital, we had to wait to see the palliative care doctor. Sitting on hard grey plastic chairs in a room with a view out over the building site for the new extension. A digger was chewing lumps out of the remaining old structure like a hungry raptor. Blake had me tell him some jokes to pass the time, so I started with the one about the pope and the chewing gum. Even though I kept my voice down, we got dirty looks from the old wans waiting beside us. So then I raised my voice and told a couple of blue jokes to shock them even more. Blake liked that and laughed like a drain even though the jokes weren't very funny.

I could tell Blake wasn't impressed with the palliative care doctor. He was this tall skinny guy who leaned right into you and spoke loudly as though you had a hearing difficulty. He asked us to call him Frank. Or maybe he told us he was going to be frank. I was so busy thinking how loud he was I didn't pay much attention to what he said. He shook us both energetically by the hand.

'The main thing is your comfort,' he said looking from Blake to me and back again. Maybe he didn't know which of us was the dying man. 'We want you to be comfortable.'

'For me,' Blake said, 'that's not the main thing. I've never particularly wanted to be comfortable. I just want to have fun... you know, like the girls.'

Frank looked confused. Blake broke into song and after a few beats I joined in.

'*Girls just want to have fu-un. That's all they ever want...*'

'Right.' Frank looked solemn. Having fun was clearly the last thing on his mind. Singing about it even more inconceivable.

'I want to eat, drink and be merry...'

'Alcohol,' said Frank, shaking his head, 'with the medication you're on...'

'What? It might kill me?' Blake chortled.

'It might adversely react.'

'So what if I stopped the medication?'

Frank looked horrified.

'See, doc,' Blake said. 'If I gotta go, then I gotta go, as the incontinent nun said to the bishop. But, I don't want to go quiet. I want to go shouting and singing. Screw a few chicks, maybe, just for old time's sake. What do you say, McSorley?'

'Absolutely,' I said.

'McSorley will be the best nurse a man can have, Frank.' Blake leaned up to the doctor who now actually backed away. 'He'll bring me the right medication when I want it. A plate of fish and chips, swimming in vinegar and ketchup. A six pack. A girl with a nice fat ass. Won't you, old chum.'

'I most certainly will.' Though I had my doubts about the girl. With his lesions and flaking skin, his tremors and his falling hair, Blake wasn't the most attractive prospect on the planet.

'See, Frank. That's the sort of comfort I want.'

Blake had a hard night. I gave him strong painkillers but he vomited them up. His vomit was dark brown. So then I gave him the morphine injection and towards dawn he grew calmer. I sat watching him, listening to his rasping breath. I watched the sky brighten and heard the birds wake up in the ash tree outside the window.

When I opened my eyes again, the light was mid-morning hard. Blake was grinning across at me.

'Let's go out for the day,' he said. 'Let's do something outrageous.'

'What do you suggest?'

Blake looked thoughtful.

'Go to a church and shout curses to God?' I suggested. 'Feed the animals in the zoo where it specifically says not to? Wheel you round and round the sign that says DON'T WALK ON THE GRASS.'

'All quite good ideas,' he said. 'But I got a better one. Pass me the telephone directory.'

'Make abusive anonymous phone calls?' I asked. 'Ring up and ask for Diddy, first name Seymour?'

Blake checked a couple of names and addresses, made a note and said to me, 'Get me up. We're going out.'

It was a suburban front door of stained wood, with a heavy brass knocker in the shape of a lion's head.

'Should be a skull,' Blake muttered. 'And that,' banging on the door, 'should sound more like the knell of doom.'

A stout woman answered. She was wearing a wrap-around pink overall sprigged with purple flowers.

'Yes, can I help you?' She looked doubtfully from me to Blake in his wheelchair and back again. 'Are you collecting?'

'Is Mr Death in?' asked Blake.

Something pinched at her face. 'Mr De'Ath,' she corrected the pronunciation. 'No, he's out.'

'Are you Mrs Death?' Blake persisted.

'Mr De'Ath is a widower. I'm his housekeeper. What do you want?'

'Mrs Death is dead,' Blake giggled. 'What d'you make of that, McSorley? If only Death himself were dead.'

The woman's face expressed the belief that we were raving lunatics. She made to shut the door.

'Can't we come in and wait for him. Wait for Death,' said Blake. 'I'm sick and tired of waiting for him to find me.'

'No, you certainly can't come in. In any case, I think there's some mistake. I don't think Mr De'Ath is the person you're looking for.'

'Ah, go on,' said Blake. 'We'd sit quiet, wouldn't we, McSorley. As quiet as the grave.'

The woman tried to shut the door, but Blake had extended his foot across the threshold. She started to burble in a bit of a panic. 'Go away or I'll call the police. Go away.'

I reckoned the joke had gone on long enough and pulled the wheelchair back. The instant Blake's foot followed the rest of him, the woman slammed the door.

'Now why did you do that?' Blake asked. 'I wanted to meet him.'

'Maybe it really was a mistake,' I said. 'Isn't there someone else on your list?'

'One other. Will we go there? It's quite a distance.'

'It's a nice day,' I said.

Blake looked around. 'You're right. It is. And I hadn't even noticed.'

And as we went along the leafy suburban street, past manicured lawns and flowerbeds brilliant with late summer blooms, he started to sing in a quavery voice:

'The bells of hell go ting-a-ling-a-ling
For you but not for me,
O death, where is thy sting-a-ling-a-ling?
O grave, thy victory?
The bells of hell go ting-a-ling-a-ling
For you but not for me.'

We came eventually to a run-down neighbourhood where weeds grew up through cracked paving stones and snot-nosed children played football in the road. Blake indicated a house as dilapidated as the rest, with untrimmed fuchsia creating a red fire on either side of the broken wooden gate.

'Here,' he said.

The door was black – 'a good sign' said Blake – its paint blistered and peeling back to pale bare wood. I rang the bell which sounded out a jingly tune: *'You aint nuthin but a hound dog.'*

'Hmm,' said Blake. 'Not so promising.'

A faded old man opened the door almost at once, as if he had been waiting behind it. He was wearing a baggy cardigan and dirty corduroy trousers. Fuzzy slippers.

'Mr Death?' asked Blake.

'Sure thing. What can I do you for?'

Blake looked doubtful.

'I don't think this is the right place,' he said.

'Ah, you're here now. You might as well come in.' Death beckoned us into the hall, a brown tunnel of a place with a rickety stand from which hung a greasy cap and a shabby tweed overcoat.

I was tired after all that walking and pushing. Blake looked all in as well.

'Come in for a cuppa,' said Death. 'You look like you could do with it. And I'd enjoy the bit of company. Don't get many visitors, you know.'

I manoeuvred the wheelchair up over the doorstep and down the hall. Death shuffling ahead of us.

The kitchen was brighter, light revealing the poverty and dirt of the place. A red-topped formica table was heaped with crockery and knives and spoons, opened packets of tea and sugar and biscuits. It was sticky to the touch. A white press had grubby fingermarks round the door. A single unshaded bulb hung from a twisted flex. Cracked linoleum in a brown pattern covered the floor as best it could.

I sat on a wobbly wooden chair. Blake stared up at a framed photograph on the wall while Death filled the kettle.

'You're a real Elvis fan, then,' he said.

The picture, surrounded by fairy lights that flicked on and off sporadically like a nervous twitch, was of the singer in his white satin hey-day. It even looked to be signed.

'Yes indeedy,' said Death, his false teeth slipping into a grin. 'I seen him many times. Was even over in Graceland once. You like him?'

'I do,' said Blake, 'particularly the early stuff.'

'Wait a mo.' Death shuffled out. Blake and I looked at each other.

'I didn't know you like Elvis,' I said.

'Absolutely,' Blake replied and sang in a soft growl, '*I don't have a wooden heart, I have a wooden head.*'

After a while, Death re-entered. Now he was wearing a white satin cloak with 'THE KING' embroidered in gold across the back of it.

'Wow,' said Blake. 'I'm impressed.'

'Got this over there,' said Death. 'Souvenir.'

The tea was very weak as though the bag had been used several times before. Blake took a few sips. I drank up out of politeness. A packet of unnaturally pink wafers was opened but sat untouched on the table. Jimmy, as he had asked us to call him, looked at us expectantly. 'Heartbreak Hotel' blared tinnily out of a battered cassette player.

'Sorry, Jimmy, but it was your name brought us here,' Blake confessed. 'I thought it would be funny to go looking for Death, instead of waiting for him at home.'

Jimmy nodded like one of those dogs in the back of some people's cars.

'It was a bit mean of us, I suppose. A stupid joke.'

'Not at all, not at all. I'm glad of the company. As I said, not too many visitors and I don't get out as much as I did.'

We stayed a bit but the colour had drained out of Blake and I could tell he was shattered.

'I'd better bring you home,' I said.

'See you again,' said Jimmy.

That night Blake took a turn for the worse. He vomited the nothing he had eaten or drunk in a great brown whoosh. Then lay back on the bed. I wanted to call an ambulance but he said no. Told me to let him try and sleep.

I left him for a while and watched TV. It was one of those English detective series set in a stately home with painstaking attention to period detail, fabulous fashions and an excruciating plot. I turned to the news but it was all about melting Arctic ice and Iranian nuclear capabilities and floods in Bangladesh and yet another civil war in the

Middle East. Alternatives included a reality show asking if fat teens could hunt. Or a cookery programme with a famous chef who shouted at everyone and threw a wobbly over the asparagus tips. Or sport. I went back to the mincing detective and, while he paused to ruminate, tiptoed out to look at Blake.

He was lying across the bed naked. I knew what he looked like, from washing and changing him. But I could never get used to the sight of those skinny arms and wasted thighs, the bulbous belly.

I felt his feet. They were cold as ice. As I pulled the duvet over him he opened his eyes.

'Hi McSorley,' he whispered. Then he looked beyond me and smiled. 'Hi there, Jimmy.'

It was a couple of months or so later that I found myself back in Jimmy Death's neighbourhood. I'd been planning to call before but hadn't got around to it. There was a fresh coat of white paint on the door. The young woman who opened it was brisk. She wore yellow rubber gloves and was holding a spray cleaner.

'The old man?' she said. 'Went to a home I think. Or maybe he passed on. Or moved to somewhere else. The corpo cleared the place out. My God, you should have seen the state of it.'

I glimpsed beyond her the bareness of everything.

'I'd like to know,' I said.

She shrugged. 'Can't help you. Sorry.'

I left and walked back remembering the way I'd pushed Blake that last day in his wheelchair, his woolly hat covering his patchy baldness while his head twisted from side to side not to miss anything that was going on. Remembering his jokes and mockery. His songs. I shuffled through the dead brown leaves, looking up at the baring branches of the trees, tossing in the wind as if trying to throw off any remaining foliage.

'And what do I do now?' I whispered into the air. 'What now for the thirty or forty years left to me... if I'm lucky?' Then I thought of Blake and what he'd have to say about that. And I started to laugh. And then to sing:

'*The bells of hell go ting-a-ling-a-ling*
For you but not for me
O death, where is thy sting-a-ling-a-ling?
O grave, thy victory?'

The Dating Game

So there I was, staring at a white wine spritzer, watching how the tiny bubbles raced up through the pale liquid and burst. Short glorious lives. I almost envied them.

'I thought from your picture,' Cecil was saying, 'your boobs would be bigger. I was specifically looking for big boobs. And long legs.'

There was a lot I could have replied. Specifically that if I had big boobs and long legs I wouldn't have been sitting here with Cecil in the first place.

'And a bit of glamour,' he added.

That hurt. I'd put on blusher and lipstick in his honour, and even got Mairead to give me a nice trim and blow-dry.

'Still,' Cecil sighed, 'I suppose...'

What, I wondered. Beggars can't be choosers? No. Someone like Cecil would never think of himself as a beggar.

He was a short man. When I first met him in the pub I couldn't help noticing that the top of his head came level with my eyes, and I'm no giant, believe me. Also that he was wearing shoes with heels: Cuban heels, is that what they're called? He'd combed his hair over a bald patch and showed the beginnings of a paunch and if I were less polite I could have pointed out that he too bore little resemblance to the youthful picture he posted on the dating website. Then I realised he was still talking. That squeaky voice! It reminded me of chalk dragged on a blackboard.

'So anyway, Janice,' he was saying,' my place or yours?'

I tore my eyes away from the bubbles to look at him.

'I've a bottle of Chianti back at the apartment and a CD of Perry Como's greatest hits. They're selling them in Tesco's now: *Catch a Falling Star, Papa loves Mambo* AND *Hot Diggity* all for €4.99! And not just Perry: you can get Nat, Deano, Sammy, all the old favourites. So anyway, why don't we adjourn? They charge a small fortune for drinks in this dump.'

'I don't think so...' I told him, assertive for once.

'Listen, lovely.' A cloying odour hit me as he leaned forward. Those Lynx ads have a lot to answer for. 'We both know why we're here. So no point prancing around, right. Let's vamoose.'

He stood up. So did I.

'You've made a mistake,' I said, looking down on to his comb-over. 'I've made a mistake. I'm sorry.' And I started to leave.

He caught at my sleeve. 'Not so fast,' he said. 'I bought you a drink.'

So what? Was I supposed to go to bed with him for the price of a spritzer?

'Please let me go.' My voice shook. I hated that. I wanted to sound resolute.

'Well, piss off then,' he yelled, flopping down into his seat. Several people turned to stare across at us.

Once safely at the door, I glanced back. He was slumped forward, slurping up what remained of my drink.

This Cecil was just the latest in a line of disastrous encounters. I don't know why I bother. I suppose I'm an optimist and keep hoping the next will be The One. Mairead encourages me. She seems to know an endless number of people who've found true love through the Internet.

'Time's not on your side, chicken,' she'll add, snipping a stray hair at the nape of my neck. 'I had three by the time I was your age.' Which is thirty-one.

'Three husbands?' I ask.

'Three kids, yer wally.'

Mairead is in her fifties, long separated, face coarsened by life and cigarettes, but still ready to party. Sooty mascara round her eyes, heavy pancake over the folds in her skin, candyfloss pink lipstick, short blonde hair. And, if she's to be believed, a long line of admirers.

Up to now there haven't been many men in my life. I teach infants at National School and the only ones I meet there are the daddies. At college I was secretly madly in love with Pete but he never looked twice at me. Once, in desperation at a party, I'd let Pete's friend Damien push his tongue down my throat. Then Damien, who wasn't much to look at, a loser the other girls called him, had gone around boasting I was his girlfriend, after which I'd spent my time avoiding both him and Pete and his pitying looks.

There have been a few other brief... well, you couldn't even call them flings, let alone relationships. Gerald, for instance, that I met at a music appreciation night class, who lived with his mother and grumbled endlessly about his job in an accountant's office where everyone apparently had it in for him. He expected me to remember the names of all these spiteful colleagues.

'I told you about Victor already, Janice,' he'd snap. 'Don't you ever listen when I talk to you?'

And then there was Paul, an Irish-language speaker whom at first I found rather sweet but who sweated and mumbled and trembled in a creepy way. I'd met him at a ceili in the Irish club and we went to the cinema a few times, where his clammy hand would hunt out mine in the dark, and I'd wait with dread for the inevitable moment when he'd press his lips to my ear and whisper 'mavourneen'. The end came abruptly. In the middle of The Walls of Limerick he'd pulled me closer than Irish dancing required so I could feel against my stomach exactly how much he fancied me. I finished the dance somehow, excused myself to go to the ladies, dashed out the door, and never returned. Which was a pity, because I enjoyed the jigs and the reels.

It was after Paul that Mairead suggested Internet dating.

'That's the modern way,' she said, rubbing in some conditioner.

So I've been trying it but to date without much success. The clientele have all been slightly off, at least the ones who want to meet me.

More than slightly off, to tell the truth. Just before Cecil, there was Brendan whom, at the first meeting, I really liked.

A man in his forties, neatly dressed, with a sincere face. He explained how his wife had left him, taking the kiddies, which nearly broke his heart. I found this encouraging: a man not afraid to express his emotions, devoted to his family. But when we met for the second date – a cheap and cheerful dinner in Ciao Pizza – he came dressed in a suit, which sounds fine except that, as well as the tailored jacket, he wore a sensible pleated skirt, Marks and Spencer footgloves with little heels, and, to finish off the ensemble, a perky hat perched on a curly brown wig. He explained he wasn't sure if he wasn't really Brenda and had hoped I could help him sort himself out.

Mairead chuckled at the news, remarking as she brandished the drier that he must have small feet if he could wear women's shoes off the peg. I said I hadn't noticed, so then she added, 'Take it from one who knows, chicken. Check the feet first and steer clear of a man with small ones. He's lacking in at least one important respect,' her laugh turning into a smoker's hacking cough.

But now I think maybe I've met him at long last. The One. Anthony. He's thirty-nine, and divorced, with a fourteen-year-old daughter. We've been out a few times and really hit it off, so I've invited him round to dinner. I live in the house I inherited from my parents, a semi-detached in a convenient suburb, and I like to keep it nice. Because I'd be uneasy alone with a man, even a gentleman like Anthony, Mairead is coming along too, bringing a friend.

Actually when I meet the friend, I'm a bit taken aback. He has a shaved head and a nose ring and is at least twenty years younger than Mairead. His name is Eddy. Mairead looks amazing with bare fake-tanned legs in a leather mini-skirt shorter, and heels higher, than anything I'd ever dare to wear. Her neckline plunges below safety levels and I can see Anthony studying her thoughtfully. But we all get on well enough, helped by the wine, as well as the whiskey Anthony's brought, although he follows me out to the kitchen at one point, puts his arm round me and tells me I have a lovely place and that he thought we were going to be alone.

Mairead comes out later, while I'm straining the potatoes, and informs me that in her opinion Anthony is older than thirty-nine.

'More like forty-nine, chicken. But he has lovely big feet. Almost as big as Eddy's.' Her breasts wobble with laughter.

Later, after the wine and whiskey levels have gone right down, she presses him on the point. He gives me a little smile and says, 'Actually yes, I'm forty-seven. Can you forgive me, Janice? Can you still like me?'

'Oh,' I say. 'Yes,' I say.

Now I don't generally drink much, but I'm nervous and someone keeps filling my glass – though it's white wine I'm on, not whiskey. So I turn to Eddy and start asking him about himself. He's a bit cagey at first, but Mairead says, 'We're among friends here, Eddy, love. You can tell them.' It turns out he's just come out of the 'Joy', as he calls it, for stealing cars 'and that'. And then, blow me down, doesn't Anthony admit that he was inside too for a short spell, for embezzlement.

'I think it's only fair, Janice,' he says to me, 'because I want to be totally honest with you, to put my cards on the table. I've turned over a new leaf since those dark days.'

They exchange a couple of prison stories and I say it must have been terrible. But Anthony explains, not really: he wasn't in with the rough crowd but with a better class of inmate, white collar criminals. Then he says 'no offence' to Eddy, who replies, 'forgeddaboudit.'

My head is spinning with all this new information and I tune in and out of some long story Anthony is telling about how his wife got the house and everything, so that, after he lost his job because of the embezzling, he's now ended up living in a one-room flat in the north inner city on social welfare.

'Life's a bitch, love,' says Mairead.

I stumble off to the kitchen to make coffee. Mairead comes out to help me.

'He's a nice man,' she says. 'You could do worse.'

'Yes, but what about his age, the prison stuff?'

'You're as old as you feel, love. Just look at me. And a man's entitled to make one mistake. Take Eddy. He's going straight since he met me... Well, straight-ish,' and she laughs.

It's true I find Anthony attractive in a rugged kind of way. And anyway beggars can't be choosers. I set the tray with an embroidered linen cloth and dainty cups and saucers, together with a plate of chocolate digestives.

'By God,' Anthony says. 'Is that real coffee?'

'I never use instant,' I reply.

'She's a treasure, isn't she?' Mairead says.

Anthony looks around the table, around the room. 'A diamond in a gold setting,' he says. 'Tell you what, Janice, why don't you marry me?'

I gasp. Mairead and Eddy smile and nod. I notice Eddy is missing a front tooth.

'That's right,' Anthony says. 'Marry me, and then after a bit I'll poison you, inherit your savings and get the house.'

I read an article the other day. It said that there's far too much pressure on women to enter into relationships and that they're often better off by themselves. Meanwhile, someone called Richard found my details on the website before I took them down and has asked me to go on a date with him. I haven't replied yet. I don't think I will.

But then again, maybe he's The One...

MAMMY WAKE UP

'Wake up, Mammy,' I say. 'Mammy, wake up.'

I catch hold of her blue skirt with the lace on it and pull.

'Wake up, Mammy.'

I pull at her top with the pretty blue and white flowers. Mammy looks nice in her best clothes. She has put on lipstick. Her nails are painted pink. Mine are too. She put some on for me yesterday but it's starting to come off where I bite it.

'Mammy.'

She's sitting at the kitchen table, resting her head on it. She must be very tired. It's night time and I only woke up because the baby started crying. The baby's crying now. Screaming. But Mammy doesn't wake up.

Maybe she can't hear. That must be why. Maybe she can't hear properly any more, like Granddad, who has a box behind his ear.

Her eyes are a bit open. I can see them. I put my face right up to her.

'Mammy!'

Perhaps she needs her glasses. I look for them but they aren't on the table or in her bag. I go up to the bedroom to look for them. They are beside the bed. Daddy isn't in the bed. He mustn't be home yet. I pick up the glasses and then have a good idea. I go to my room and get my crayons and some paper. I go down the stairs.

Mammy is still lying across the kitchen table. I get the paper and write in big red letters: MAMMY WAKE UP. Then I try and put her glasses on her. They are a bit wonky but I hold the note in front of her and pull at her top.

She makes a noise, like she has a pain but doesn't wake up. The baby is still screaming. I find a bottle and put some milk in it. Then I put it in the microwave like Mammy does, just for a little while. Baby Jean doesn't like it too hot.

I take the bottle out and go upstairs again. Baby Jean is standing up in her cot and screaming. Her face is red and wet from crying. When she sees the bottle she quiets down. I get her to lie down in her cot and take the bottle. I think she has dirtied herself, because I can smell it.

I sit on the floor and look at the stripes on the mat, pink and red and gold. I think it would be nice if it was a magic carpet and I could sit on it and fly out of the window. I could take baby Jean too if she wanted to go. And Mammy. We could go to a magic land, like in the story my teacher reads us, where the sun always shines and sweets grow on trees.

Sometimes when Mammy is shouting at Daddy or when she is walking about downstairs by herself crying or when she screams at me and hits me then hugs me tight and tells me sorry sorry or when she sits staring into space for hours, I go and sit on the mat and wish really hard to fly out the window.

Mostly I wish it when Mammy cuts herself and starts to bleed.

I hear a noise in the kitchen and go downstairs again. Maybe Mammy has woken up.

She has fallen off the chair and is lying on the floor. She is making funny noises and spit is coming out of her mouth. I push at her but she doesn't move. Maybe she will be more comfortable lying on the floor. I touch her hands. They are cold. I get the red and black throw from the couch in the room with the TV and spread it over her and tuck it round her so she won't be cold any more.

Baby Jean is crying again.

I look for Mammy's mobile in her handbag. It says 3:47. That means the middle of the night. I know how to ring Daddy's number and hope he won't be cross if I wake him up. I ring and ring but he doesn't answer.

Baby Jean is screaming.

I go upstairs and pick up the bottle which has fallen on the floor. I lift baby Jean out of the cot and hold her. She smells bad and I put her down on the mat. The nappies are in a bag on the floor and I get one out. I have never changed baby Jean before but I have seen Mammy and Daddy do it. I give her the bottle and she quiets down. I unpop her babygro and take her little legs out of it. I pull off the nappy. It is very dirty and sticky and I want to be sick. But I get a baby wipe and take off all the yellow poo from round her bottom and legs. Her bottom looks red and sore but I don't know if we have any cream. She is clean now anyway and I try to get the new nappy on to her. It is quite easy after the first try when it was the wrong way round.

She is happy with a clean bottom and her bottle but I pick her up. It's nice to feel how soft and warm she is. I put my face into her neck. She smells good again. I kiss her head.

We go down to the kitchen. Mammy is still on the floor making those noises.

'Here, Mammy, here's baby Jean,' I say. But Mammy doesn't wake up.

I wish she would.

I go into the hall with baby Jean and open the front door. The street lights are on but there are no lights in any windows. Everyone must be asleep. I go next door to Maureen's and knock but no one answers. Maybe they have gone on their holidays. I go back into the house. Mammy has stopped making noises now.

I see a piece of paper on the table under where she was lying. It has words on it. It says I AM SORRY I LOVE YOU ALL I AM NO GOOD YOU ARE BETTER WITHOUT ME I LOVE YOU ROBERT CIARA AND JEAN I AM SO SO SORRY FOR EVERYTHING

Ciara is me. Robert is my daddy. I take the note and throw it in the rubbish.

I take baby Jean and go into the room with the TV. I put baby Jean on the couch. I get the remote and turn on the DVD. It is Peppa Pig, Jean's favourite. We snuggle up to watch. Baby Jean starts to laugh. We watch Peppa Pig for a bit, jumping in muddy puddles and eating ice cream on the beach with her brother George. His ice cream melts and he starts to cry. Tears spurt out of his eyes. Mammy Pig lets him have some of Daddy Pig's ice cream and he is happy again.

Jean wants ice cream too, so I get some from the fridge in the kitchen. I ask Mammy if she wants some but she just makes little snoring noises. I take a spoon and go back to baby Jean. We eat it in turns, me popping a spoonful into baby Jean's little mouth then taking one myself. It tastes of strawberries. Jean has had enough and turns her face away. I put the pot on the floor for later.

We watch Peppa Pig make sandcastles with her brother George.

It is morning time. The light is coming through the curtains. I am not in my bed in my bedroom. I am on the couch with baby Jean asleep beside me. The ice cream has melted in the pot and Mammy will be cross. Then I remember she is asleep in the kitchen. I go in to see if she has woken up but she is still lying on the floor.

'Wake up, Mammy,' I say and pull at her blue skirt. 'Mammy, wake up.'

The clock says 8:05. I fetch baby Jean and we go next door to see if Maureen is awake.

She opens the door. She is in a dressing-gown and I am still in my pyjamas.

'What is it, Ciara?' she says.

'Mammy won't wake up.'

'Holy God,' she says. 'Brendan!' she calls. Brendan is her husband.

He comes down the stairs in pyjama bottoms and vest. He is a fat man. They come with me back into the house just the way they are.

'Holy God,' says Maureen again, when she sees Mammy on the floor.

'Where's your daddy?' asks Brendan.

'I don't know.'

Maureen sits baby Jean in her high chair and gets us some Weetabix and milk.

A bit later the ambulance arrives to take Mammy to the hospital.

'What did she take?' one ambulance man asks.

'I don't know,' Maureen says. 'No sign of any bottles.'

'Have a look around, would you, and call emergency. It's important we know what she's taken.' He writes down a number on a piece of paper and gives it to her.

'I will. How is she?'

'Can't say for sure,' he glances at me and lowers his voice but I can still hear. 'She's pretty far gone. Shame we didn't get to her earlier.'

He smiles at me and pats my head.

'Can you mind the chisellers?' he asks Maureen. Chisellers means Jean and me. It's what Granddad calls us.

'Of course,' says Maureen.

They put Mammy on a bed with wheels and take her away. Maureen looks around.

'Do you know where Mammy's pills are, Ciara?' she asks.

I show her the drawer beside mammy's bed but it is empty. She looks in the rubbish bin in the kitchen. She finds the note. She smooths it out and reads it.

'Holy God,' she says. Then she looks at me. 'Did you throw this away, Ciara?'

I start to cry. 'I didn't want Mammy to get into trouble,' I say.

I tell her how I came down in the night and found Mammy at the table and how she wouldn't wake up. I show her the note I wrote and she looks at it for a while. I tell her how I knocked at her door in the night but no one answered. Maureen blesses herself. Then I tell her how I tried to phone Daddy but he didn't answer. How I covered up Mammy because she was cold.

'You're a great girl,' she says, shaking her head and wiping her eye.

I give her Mammy's phone and show her how to ring Daddy. She talks to him.

'Where the hell are you, Robert?' Maureen says into the phone. 'Jacinta's taken an overdose again. It looks serious this time.'

Jacinta is my Mammy. I cry some more.

'Don't worry about the babies,' Maureen says. 'I'll mind them. You get to the hospital.'

'Daddy!' I say, but he has gone.

'It's OK, chicken,' says Maureen 'You did what you could. You tried to help your Mammy. And weren't you great, looking after baby Jean, and all.'

I tell Maureen about the ice cream and how Mammy will be cross I let it melt.

'Don't you worry about that,' she said. 'We can always buy some more.'

She hugs me to her big soft chest but she is shaking. I look up into her face. It has gone all red and then I see that she is crying too.

I look out the kitchen window and for a minute I think I see me and baby Jean and Mammy, beautiful in her best clothes and lipstick and pink nails, flying away on the magic carpet. Mammy is looking happy. We are going up high, away to the country where the sun shines all the time and sweets grow on the trees. Then I blink and I see that there is nothing there but sky. Nothing at all.

It's Hard To Die In Springtime

For her it was bluebottles. For David Attenborough, apparently, it was worms.

One day she had heard the famous naturalist on the radio, explaining why he was an agnostic. He couldn't believe in a kind and loving God, he said, after seeing the suffering of innocent children in Africa, afflicted by a worm that burrowed into their eyes and made them blind.

Over the years, Josie's own doubts had grown. She regarded God's creation mostly with wonder, but also with some puzzlement. It wasn't all good, after all. Why bluebottles, for instance.

'They serve in the putrefaction process,' her clever granddaughter Maeve had told her. 'You may not like them, but they perform a useful job nonetheless.'

'Not when they lay their eggs on my nice roast chicken.'

If Maeve thought the chicken should have been safely locked away in the fridge and not left out on the counter, she was too polite to say.

'Well, anyway Gran, I don't think bluebottles disprove the existence of God. Not by themselves.'

But now Josie had to contend not simply with doubts and David Attenborough but also with the young men and women in the same ward as herself.

'It's a form of leukaemia,' the consultant told her after all the tests. 'A progressive form. Unfortunately, you've had it undiagnosed for years and now it's at quite an advanced stage.'

What did that mean? But she couldn't bring herself to ask how long.

'On the plus side, Josephine,' he said, 'some wonderful new treatments have been developed. We'll give them a try, will we?'

He smiled at her encouragingly. She smiled back, wondering if she should inform him that no one had called her Josephine since the disapproving nuns at school. And what would he say if she started calling him Barry? On the other hand, all this talk of Josephine made her think that perhaps they were referring to someone else. Not her.

'Now then, Josephine,' the nurse, different nurses would say when she came for her weekly blood test, all smiling that professionally kind, unengaged smile. 'Let's see how we are today,' thrusting the needle into a vein if they could find one that hadn't collapsed.

'You're too nice,' her daughter Carmel said, when Josie came home, weak with fatigue. 'You should make a fuss. It's not right that a sick person should be left waiting around all day on a hard chair. I've a good mind to come in with you next time and give them a piece of my mind.'

'They're doing their best,' Josie replied, wishing Carmel would let her stretch out on the couch for a snooze and not be bothering her with her outrage. 'They're overworked. There must have been fifty people alongside me, all waiting. I can't expect special treatment.'

'It's the system that's at fault, then,' said Carmel. 'You should write a letter to your TD, the one who always makes out he can fix things.'

Josie sighed and closed her eyes. But Carmel wasn't finished.

'That's the trouble with you, Mam. You always try to please. You've tried to please people all your life and look where it's got you.'

No one mentioned Thomas, Josie's late husband. A cantankerous demanding man who'd died of a heart attack some eight years previously, leaving his wife a legacy of peace and quiet, at least when Carmel wasn't visiting. Josie never said, but she was almost as intimidated by her daughter as she had been by her husband.

But now the disease had progressed to the stage where she needed to be hospitalised frequently. That was when she met the young women and men who had an aggressive form of the illness and that was when she started to wonder again about the goodness of a God who could grab lives so randomly before they had even properly started.

'It's not fair, 'she said to Maeve.

Her granddaughter sat back looking at her. Maeve with her short hair dyed – what was it this week, pink? purple? blue? In her little vest, puffed tutu of a skirt, black tights and heavy boots. Her multiple piercings.

'My God, what do you look like!' Carmel would explode.

Josie and Carmel's big oaf of a husband Leo would catch each other's eye. Josie thought Leo secretly agreed that Maeve looked rather fine. She certainly cheered up the ward when she came in.

'Who said it was supposed to be fair?' Maeve now asked her grandmother.

'That's true, but...'

'It's like saying 'why me?' when what people should be asking is 'why not me?''

This was getting too deep for Josie.

'Anyway,' she said. 'It's very sad.'

Several days after this conversation a new patient was wheeled into the bed beside Josie. She was a slip of a thing, who slept a lot. Come visiting time, Josie noticed how Maeve kept peering across at her.

'Don't stare,' she whispered.

'I'm sure I know her,' Maeve whispered back. 'Isn't she that singer?'

'What singer?'

'I'm sure she is. The one who does all the Jacques Brel stuff.'

Josie looked bewildered.

'She was on the Late Late Show once. Talked about growing up in one of those homes.'

Josie remembered vaguely. A voice like an angel's.

'No,' she said. 'That one was quite chubby.'

'Grandma! She's sick, she's lost weight. Like you.'

Josie didn't have it to lose and was starting to scare herself, she looked so skeletal.

'I'm sure it's her.'

The nurses didn't know. They called the girl Margaret. Maeve was disappointed.

'The singer was Peggy something.'

'But Peggy's short for Margaret,' Josie told her, glad to be the one giving information for once.

'Really! That's great! I mean... It isn't great. It's terrible.' Poor Maeve looked desolate and Josie patted her hand.

The next morning the girl in the next bed was a little more awake.

'My granddaughter thinks she recognises you,' Josie said.

'Ah. Well maybe.'

'She says you're a singer.'

'Yes.'

'That must be lovely.'

'Mm.'

'That's a silly thing to say. Sorry.'

'No, you're right. It's lovely to sing. It's lovely to have people listen and enjoy. Only... I'm not sure if I'll ever sing again.'

Josie was about to say 'of course you will', then she remembered the bluebottles and the worms and the tainted blood pumping through both their veins. 'Let's hope you do,' she said. 'At least, so I can hear you.'

Peggy laughed at that, a tinkling sound. 'I'll give a recital some night,' she said. 'Strictly for the moribund.'

'What, dear?'

'The bedridden.'

A smiling young man came and visited the girl most days. He would wheel her out for a cigarette.

'I know I shouldn't,' she said to Josie. 'But what the hell! When they open me up after I'm gone, it'll give them more to talk about.'

'That's very morbid talk.'

'No, I'm leaving my body to science.'

Josie was shocked until Peggy explained it to her.

'It's the last useful thing you can do. No one will want my organs for transplants but at least they can be used to educate new doctors. And it gets round all the religious quackery associated with funerals. I couldn't stand that. Some priest who doesn't know me spouting on about the after life, and being at peace and all that shit.'

'You don't believe in God.'

'I believe in life, not afterwards.' Her eyes flashed.

She didn't have family, she told Josie.

'So there'd be no one to carry my coffin anyway.' Just Ben, the smiling young man. 'He's good to me.'

One time, when Maeve was taking Josie for a little constitutional along the corridor they met the pair coming back.

'Did you see his face?' Maeve asked.

Behind Peggy's back, pushing the chair, Ben looked ravaged by grief.

Later Peggy said to Josie, 'I think we'd better have that concert tonight. I'm in the mood for it. But apologies if my voice isn't quite what it should be. With all the ciggies.'

She got one of the nurses to help her stand up using a zimmer frame.

'Any requests,' she asked the other patients. 'Assuming I know the words.'

She sang *On Raglan Road*, *She Walked through the Fair*, *Dublin in the rare Oul' Times*. Her voice was nearly as clear as Josie remembered it, but with an occasional heart-breaking crack. The six-bed room was soon crammed with patients from other wards. The nurses clucked a bit, but not too much.

'I'm going to finish now,' she said, 'with a Jacques Brel song. He was a Belgian singer, a poet. He died of cancer.'

The song, she said, was called *Le Moribond*, the man about to die. She glanced at Josie and winked.

'I'll translate, so you've an idea what it's about. He says to his friends 'Goodbye. I'm going to die. It's hard to die in Springtime. But I'm leaving with the flowers, peace in my heart. I want you all to dance, to laugh like mad, when they put me in the ground.'

Peggy launched into the song, her voice cracking, her knuckles white with the effort of holding the frame to stay upright. Tears starting streaming down her face into the second verse and to the end, and down the faces of some of her listeners as well. It isn't fair, Josie said to herself, no matter what.

That night Peggy suffered a terrible nosebleed. They had to bind a thick cloth around her face to catch the blood that wouldn't stop. The following morning, Barry the consultant, arrived with his entourage and a grim expression. They pulled the curtains round Peggy's bed. Josie heard them muttering.

'They're moving me to intensive care,' Peggy told Josie later.

'I hope it wasn't the singing brought it on.'

'Speeded up the inevitable,' she tried to smile behind that ghastly bandage. 'Tell your lovely granddaughter from me to laugh, to dance, as long as she can. And you too, Josie.'

'Dance!' exclaimed Josie.

Peggy winked.

Then the porters came and Josie never saw her again.

A week later, when she was being discharged – 'For the time being, Josephine,' Barry said with a merry smile, 'I know you can't stay away from us for long' – Maeve broke the news that Peggy had died.

'No one told me,' Josie said, indignant.

'It was in the papers. But the nurses probably didn't want to upset you.'

Josie went not home but to Carmel's house in Drumcondra, with carers coming in while Carmel and Leo were at work. Maeve filled in when her studies permitted.

'Let's go for a walk,' she suggested one bright March day.

'I can't, dear.'

'In the wheelchair.'

'Oh, I don't know...'

'It's lovely out. Do you good.'

So Maeve took her, well-wrapped up, to the Botanical Gardens. The daffodils were at their best, dancing in the breeze. Fat buds of blossom were starting to burst open.

'It's hard to die in Springtime,' said Josie.

'What? Grandma, you're not dying quite yet.'

'My dear,' said Josie. 'It's the words of a song.'

They sat under pine trees by the ornamental lake, gazing across at a tree that was already a mass of pink blossom, while overly tame squirrels came right up to them hoping for titbits.

'Maeve,' said Josie after a while, 'I've decided to leave my body to science.'

A pause, then 'Mother will hit the roof.'

'She will. But I'm going to do what she's always telling me to do and please myself. It's all set up.'

'OK, so. Great!'

'Will you tell her?'

'No, grandma!'

'Will you be there when I tell her, then, and back me up.'

'Of course.' Maeve chuckled. 'Wow, gran! You're full of surprises.'

They laughed together.

The wind shifted. A few stray petals fell from the tree and floated down onto the rippling water. Birds chirruped, ducks and moorhens dabbled.

'Hold my hand, dear,' said Josie. And they stayed like that for a long while in silence, listening and looking.

LED INTO TEMPTATION

I blame God.

'Lead us not into temptation,' we keep asking him. But he never listens. I must have said that prayer almost every day of my life since I learned to speak, but it makes no difference. I'm being led into temptation all the time.

Like that business when I was ten, the business with Mavis Price's ribbons. It wasn't my fault. I was led into temptation. Miss Atkins put her sitting in front of me in class, so all I was looking at all day were her ribbons, wide rose pink ones tied round her two fat plaits. I'd never seen anything as pretty as those ribbons and I wanted some too. My mam said, 'Regina, what would you be doing with ribbons, with your hair the way it is?' True enough, though it was mam who chopped my hair that short in the first place because of the nits. But, as I pointed out to her, it'll grow. 'I'd like ribbons,' I said, 'for when it grows. Meantime I'll keep them safe in my treasure box.' But she said she couldn't be spending hard-earned money on ribbons. Lone parent's allowance hard earned? Don't make me laugh. I didn't say it, though, because she'd give me a clatter for being smart. So I just thought it.

I could tell Mavis Price's plaits annoyed her, the way they kept banging on her back whenever she went skipping in the school yard. Mavis Price was round like a bun, with white hair and pink eyes. 'It's an affliction,' my mam said. I thought Mavis looked a bit like the white mice my cousin Kieran feeds to his pet python. Only bigger.

So anyway, there I was day after day staring at those ribbons. Led into temptation, you see. The ribbons would be different colours: green or red or pale blue, but I liked the pink ones best. The day it happened, she was wearing pink ribbons. I must have known she would because that was the day I brought my mam's big scissors into school.

I thought I was doing her a favour. I truly did. I thought the way those fat plaits kept banging on her back must annoy her. And when I said it to her after school and waved the scissors under her pink eyes, I thought she agreed with me.

Seemingly when her mam and da saw what had happened they started screaming and so she started screaming too and said I'd attacked her. Her da came round to our flat and shouted at my mam, who wanted nothing to do with it. Mavis's da demanded the plaits back, so I took him down the school yard and showed him where I left them. He just looked at me and picked up the two fat plaits, which, with nothing to hold them in place, had started unravelling at both ends. He stared at them for a bit and then took them, I don't know why. Did he think he could glue them on again? Anyway, he never asked about the ribbons, so I put them in my treasure box for when my hair grew long enough to wear them.

It never did. Anyway, I prefer it short now.

My new teacher in the new school was much nicer than Miss Atkins, the bitch. It was her fault I had to go to a new school. Seemingly she told my mam that I was a bad influence if you please, and the business with Mavis Price's plaits was the last straw that broke the camel's back. Actually I never believed that thing about the straw. It couldn't just have been one single straw. More like a bunch. And how could you put straw on a camel's back anyway? With that hump in the way it would all fall off.

My new teacher's name was Sarah Moke. It was the sort of school where you knew teachers' first names, even though you were still supposed to call them Miss. Sarah Moke wasn't married, but I bet she had lots of men after her because she was beautiful, with a pale face and dark eyes and long bony fingers. She played the piano in prayers. My favourite hymn was *There is a Green Hill Far Away*, but we only sang that at Easter. I liked to think of that far away green hill. The next line says 'without a city wall', which I thought was stupid until Sarah Moke explained that it meant 'outside a city wall' and not that there was no city wall at all. Mostly we sang *Onward Christian Soldiers*, because that was the school hymn. I never understood about the soldiers. I always thought Jesus was against fighting and stuff.

Nothing bad would have happened if Mrs McCafferty wasn't a gardener. I was being led into temptation all over again. You see, one day we were reading some poetry with Sarah Moke, all about flowers, and nature and things, and I asked her, Miss, what's your favourite flower?

'Well, Regina,' she said after a moment's thought – she looked nice when she was thinking, tilting her head a bit and gazing into the distance – 'I'm afraid I'm going to be very obvious here and say roses. I love roses,' she said.

So anyway, if Mrs McCafferty, who lives in the house on the corner near our flats, hadn't had a garden full of roses, I'd never have thought of it. But that very day, on my way home from school, I noticed them all of a sudden, all those bushes covered with great blooming heads in shades of pink, yellow and red. The big pink ones were nicest and smelt the best when I stuffed my face in them. Next thing, up pops Mrs McCafferty's head from the bushes where she was pulling weeds or something. 'Lovely flowers,' I said, but she just gave me a nasty look. Anyway, a few days later, I took my mother's big scissors and, after it got dark, I crept along to Mrs McCafferty's garden while mam was agog watching *Desperate Housewives* and drinking a glass of wine like they have in the advert. I suppose mam liked to think she was a bit of a desperate housewife herself, like that Susan one, with just an annoying teenage daughter. But Mam's built like a tank – you could put all four desperate housewives inside her and still have space over.

I'd taken a black plastic bag from the kitchen and put the roses in that. Then I got up really early and set off for school, so I could be in the classroom before anyone else.

It didn't have quite the effect I'd expected. I'd heaped them up on Sarah Moke's desk and since there were loads of them, around the place as well. It was like in that poem where the poet strews, if that's the right word, rose petals under the feet of the beloved so she doesn't have to walk on the hard cold ground. So anyway I strewed rose petals around the desk. When the other girls came in they started giggling. But Sarah Moke looked very stern. 'Who is responsible for this?' she asked. The other girls all pointed at me, the bitches.

She took me outside and asked me whatever had I been thinking. I said it was because she loved roses and she said, 'Not butchered ones.' But she said it quite nicely. I think she knew I meant to please her, because she added, 'Regina, flowers look so lovely when they're growing. When we pick them, they die quicker.' That was certainly true of Mrs McCafferty's roses which I couldn't help noticing had gone quite wilted and bruised looking after a night spent in the black plastic bag. Sarah Moke asked me why I'd just cut off the heads without the stalks, because with the stalks on they could have been put into water and lasted longer. So I showed her where the thorns had torn stripes in my hands and arms. 'They fought back,' I told her. 'Roses are spiteful flowers.' Then Sarah Moke gave me a funny look and made me clear up what she called the mess, while the other girls recited their tables. Afterwards she kept me in at break and made me recite my tables all by myself. I didn't mind because I like tables, I like the way you just chant them without having to think too much, and anyway I knew the other girls were waiting in the yard to gang up on me. Already someone had written 'REGINA CROW LOVES SARAH MOKE' and 'REGINA CROWS A LEZZIE' all over my copy books.

It was true in a way that I loved her, though not like a lezzie. I didn't want sex with her or anything. But I kept one of the roses, a pink one, and pressed the petals between the pages of my bible and then when they were dry and thinner than paper, I put them in my treasure box where they still kept their faint scent.

That wasn't the end of it, however. You couldn't help noticing when you passed Mrs McCafferty's garden how it looked like one of those Egyptian plagues had passed over, eating the ripe rose heads. The bare thorny stalks stood ugly and vicious, like people are really, no matter how beautiful they seem to be. I don't mean Sarah Moke. She was nice to me for the rest of the term, even though it was probably her who suggested to my mam that I might be happier in another school, because of the other girls and that. But the stalk thing is generally my experience of the world up to now.

Mrs McCafferty of course went ballistic. I don't know who told her. Probably that bitch Lilian Green. Or Lilian put two and two together, the rose heads in the classroom, the decapitated rose bushes in Mrs McCafferty's garden and Lilian told her mam who told Mrs McCafferty. That's probably how it was. Anyway, Mrs McCafferty came storming round to ours and told my mam how losing her roses was even worse than when Mr McCafferty died. I remember him, a weasly little man who was always trying to sniff back the drops of water that hung off the tip of his nose. I wasn't surprised that she missed her roses more than him. I'd miss anything more than him. Then she added, 'At least Mr McCafferty had a long-term illness and I had time to inwardly prepare. This was a shocking sudden death.' My mam nodded and said she understood and not to worry, she'd beat the living daylights out of me as soon as Mrs McCafferty had gone. And then Mrs McCafferty said, 'I'm not looking for violence, Mrs Crow. If that's your answer to problems, then no wonder your daughter is the way she is.' My mam gave her one of her looks that would curdle milk but Mrs McCafferty didn't notice and went on, 'In the normal course,' she said, 'this would be a case for the police or at least I'd be looking for some sort of monetary recompense for the loss of so many valuable flowers, but in view of the circumstances...' (she looked around the kitchen like she could smell something bad, which she couldn't because mam had sprayed some stuff called Summer Blossoms round the place just before she came in) 'On this occasion,' she concluded, 'we'll say no more about it.'

Never mind what Mrs McCafferty said, my mam did beat the living daylights out of me after, if that's what they were. I saw stars, anyway, and had twilight-coloured bruises for days.

Actually, I think what Mrs McCafferty had said to her riled her so much she was even more heavy-handed than usual.

The next time I was led into temptation was last year when I was thirteen. There was this boy on our road that I kind of liked the look of. He was about fifteen I guess, tall and skinny with a big load of a fringe that flopped over one eye. He walked past our flats every day but not because of me. I don't think he knew at first that I existed. He had this dog that he walked, a big hairy black thing. The first thing I ever said to this boy was, 'That's a nice dog,' and tried to pet him, but the boy jerked the chain round the dog's neck and walked off without saying anything. I suppose he was a bit shy. Later I found out his name. It was Keith Foy. The dog was called Edward.

I must say I didn't like the way the dog had a chain around his neck. It seemed very cruel to me, the way it got tighter when you pulled it. Tighter and tighter. I thought I'd like the dog to have a proper collar and then, being led into temptation, I remembered my aunt Phillippa.

Actually, aunt Phillippa is really my great-aunt. She is my mother's father's sister and about ninety-nine years old. Her only companion is her dog Clytie, a snapping, yapping fat little ball of brown hair, with teeth like needles that she likes to sink into my ankles when I try and kick her. My mam tells me off. She says aunt Phillippa is probably loaded and we should be nice to her and her dog. I say I only kick her because she yaps and tries to get under my feet.

Anyway, Clytie has all sorts of doggie accessories – a little plaid jacket for when it gets cold, a cushion to sleep on and so on. And a lovely collar with diamonds on it. Well, of course they aren't real diamonds, just glass probably. But I can't help think how nice that collar would look on Edward, instead of the chain.

The next weekend I called on aunt Phillippa and asked her if I could take Clytie for a walk. 'What!' she said, making me repeat myself, and then looked at me in astonishment. 'I didn't think you liked her,' she said. 'I love dogs,' I said. 'I want to be friends with Clytie as well and she doesn't get walked much.' That was true. Aunt Phillippa was as ball-shaped as her dog and never ever took any exercise. She looked a bit doubtful but finally let me off. We went down the road a bit, me dragging Clytie. Then Clytie started to snap at my hand when I tried to get at her collar. I had brought my mother's big scissors with me in case I had to cut the thing off, but in the end that wasn't necessary. I suddenly remembered I had some chocolate biscuits in my pocket. I'd swiped them when aunt Phillippa wasn't watching. Clytie is very greedy and loves chocolate. So while she was guzzling, I slipped off the collar. The trouble was, I hadn't thought it all through and when Clytie suddenly found she was free, she went haring off down the road. Never mind, I thought. Dogs are good at finding their way home again. It could even turn out to be good luck. When she got back without her collar, I could say she ran off and someone must have stolen it.

So anyway, I lurked around waiting for Keith Foy. I knew he'd be along sooner or later and luckily it was sooner because it was cold standing in the street. Also, people were giving me funny looks, so I kept pretending I was waiting for someone (well, I was) and looking at my watch. I didn't actually have a watch, but they didn't know that.

Finally Keith Foy turned the corner with his dog. I thought he looked like he was going to cross the road when he saw me, but there was too much traffic, so he had to keep coming. 'This is for Edward,' I said, holding out the collar. Keith Foy stopped in his tracks. 'What?' he said. This was the first time I heard his voice. It was kind of shrill. 'A collar for Edward,' I repeated, 'instead of that chain.' Keith Foy took the collar and looked at it. 'It's too small,' he said. I could see he was right but I said, 'Take it anyway. I don't want it.' He didn't say anything. He was examining a tag that hung off the collar. 'It says Clive or something,' he said. Shit, I should have looked at the thing properly instead of just stuffing it in my pocket. 'I thought Clive would be a nicer name for your dog than Edward,' I said. 'How do you know my dog is called Edward?' he asked rather nastily, I thought, 'And there's a telephone number too,' he said,

twisting the tag in the light. 'And the name isn't Clive, it's...'
By now his voice was annoying me, like when you don't put
oil on a squeaky gate. 'If you don't want it,' I said, 'I'll have it
back.' 'Where did you get it?' he asked. 'Did you steal it?' 'No,'
I said. How rude of him! 'I didn't. I found it.' 'I expect someone
is looking for it,' he said. 'You should phone that number.' And
off he went with Edward on a chain. Keith Foy never walked
past our flat with the dog again but I didn't care. I didn't like
him any more.

There was hell to pay about Clytie. I told Aunt Phillippa that
the collar must have been too loose, because the dog's head
had just slipped through it and she'd run off. Aunt Phillippa
started having hysterics. 'She'll come home,' I said. 'Dogs have
an instinct.'

'She's not a bloody homing pigeon,' shouted Aunt Phillippa,
'you stupid, stupid girl.'

The upshot was that I had to go around the whole
neighbourhood sticking up posters with pictures of Clytie and
aunt Phillippa's phone number. After a couple of days, someone
found her in their garden, near where she ran off. She came back
all bedraggled and trembling and quite thin-looking but soon
enough was back to her old snappy, yappy ways, my mam said.
I don't know. Apparently aunt Phillippa said she never wanted
to see me ever again.

You'd think that would stop me being led into temptation, but
no. Not a bit. See, our curate at the church died this year aged
eighty-three and was replaced by a young man, the Reverend
Arthur Blower. When I say young, what I mean is younger. I
suppose he is in his thirties, but good-looking in a blond Jude
Law kind of way. The Reverend Arthur Blower is married to
Mrs Frances Blower, who doesn't look like a film star at all.

Now I was coming up to my confirmation and attending
classes at the church. My mam laughed at me over religion and
said that if it was the Roman church I'd probably become a
nun. 'Or maybe you'll be a lady vicar,' she added and laughed
some more and Ray, her new boyfriend, laughed too. I don't

like Ray. He has a tattoo on his chest that says 'DEBBIE'. My mam's name is Linda. Anyway, the Reverend Arthur Blower was taking the confirmation class and giving a group of us the low-down on the Christian religion, five of us, four girls and one boy, Roland Dobson, who was short with red and yellow spots. With Roland the only alternative, all us girls had a crush on Arthur but no one wanted to do anything about it except me. I was racking my brains to get Arthur alone, and at last came up with a brainwave. One evening after the class I told him I had doubts. He got terribly earnest and concerned and asked if I thought I'd like to talk it over with him and I said I would.

So Arthur and me had a cosy meeting the next night, just the two of us, in a room off the church hall.

'What is the nature of your doubts?' he asked, clasping his hands in front of him on the table and looking like a dream-boat. 'God,' I said. 'I don't really know if there's a God. What's the proof? I mean we ask him to lead us not into temptation,' I said, looking into Arthur Blower's blue eyes, 'but I'm being led there all the time. All the time.' He coughed. 'We have to have faith,' he said. 'Pray for faith and it will come to you.' Which seemed a bit of a cop-out to me. 'Then,' I said, 'there's all that business about Jesus rising from the dead and all. I can't get my head around it,' I said. 'That's because it's a miracle. If you have faith you'll stop worrying about it.' 'I have doubts about the after-life,' I went on. 'I mean where are we all going to go? How will we all fit in? How will there be room for us all in heaven? And why would God want us all there? And will everyone be there just like they are here?' I was thinking of Aunt Phillippa and Keith Foy and Mrs McCafferty, and how I didn't particularly want to bump into them in heaven. 'And how about,' I went on, 'the virgin birth? That sounds like something a girl would think up to cover up the fact she'd been screwing around.' The Reverend Arthur Blower looked at me. Actually, to tell the truth, I hadn't realised until then how many doubts I really had. 'And can we be sure there is no hell?' I went on. He said something quietly. 'What?' I asked. 'No,' he said. 'No, we can't be sure.' Perhaps he thought he was already in hell, there with me in the room bothering him. Suddenly I felt awfully sorry for him, looking downcast and probably full of doubts himself and worrying about hell. I couldn't resist any more and leaned right across the table and kissed him full on the lips. Now here's the funny part. For a second, just a second, I swear his soft rose-pink lips pushed back against mine. Then he drew back. 'Regina!' he said in a shocked voice.

Of course I said I was sorry, and left after thanking him for the extra session. But I couldn't get the feel of his lips out of my head, so soft and plump. When I thought about it, I got tingling feelings inside.

Then I expected him to avoid me after, like Keith Foy, only Keith Foy didn't know I couldn't have cared less by then. Not with his unoiled gate of a voice. But the Reverend Arthur Blower, who has a deep velvety voice, was especially nice to me all the time and kept asking me if I was all right. I told him I was and he'd give me a little smile, which forced me to look at those lips of his and remember. Then I'd look at the lips of Mrs Frances Blower – two thin lines of orange lipstick – and I'd feel sorry for the Reverend for having to kiss those all the time. I have full lips too. Boys have told me I kiss great but how would they know, most of them.

One day the Reverend Arthur Blower gave me a leaflet which he said might help me with my doubts. It didn't but I put it in my treasure box with everything else. It was called 'Who moved the Stone?'

Anyway, I suppose I got a bit fixated on him after that and started getting funny thoughts, like if it wasn't for Mrs Frances Blower then we could be together forever. I often seemed to catch him looking at me in a searching kind of a way, which proved to me that he was as interested in me as I was in him. I still went to confirmation class, but stayed away from the other girls and never voiced doubts again even though I thought them.

Then one day I was in town waiting at the bus stop and I was led into temptation yet again. For who was standing in front of me in the queue only Mrs Frances Blower with her bags from Next and Marks and Spencer's and Clarke's. I said hello to her and she gave me a vague sort of a glance. Then more focussed. 'Hello,' she said. 'Don't I know you from St Mildred's?' 'Yes,' I said. It turned out she was a regular chatterbox and only waiting for an opening. 'My husband's the curate there,' she said. 'I know,' I said. 'I'm in his confirmation class.' 'What's your name?' she asked, looking sharp. I don't know why but I said I was Vivienne Snell, who was another girl in the class. She looked relieved, then asked if I knew Regina Crow. 'Of course,' I said, 'she's in the class too.' Mrs Frances Blower shook her head. 'Hmm,' she said. 'What?' I asked. 'What do you think of her?' asked Mrs F. 'She's all right, I suppose,' I said (Vivienne Snell hates me, after I wrote VIV SNELL SMELLS on the church wall. That was years ago when we were kids, but she still hates me, I can tell). 'A bit on the wild side, said Mrs F. 'But what can you expect. After all her mother... No wonder she's troubled...' Then she bit her lip and went silent. I said nothing, thinking about my mam and Ray, and wishing I had my mam's big scissors with me. 'I guess all you girls have a crush on Arthur,' Mrs Frances Blower said, laughing. Had he told her about the kiss? Surely not. She was probably the jealous type. 'Oh yes,' I said. 'We're all crazy about him. He looks just like Jude Law.' She laughed like a drain at that. In the distance I saw the bus was coming, stopped at the lights. People behind me were starting to push forwards. Suddenly I got this notion in my head, an accident, a terrible tragic accident, and the Reverend Arthur Blower would be a free man. 'Poor Arthur,' she was saying. 'What he has to put up with from all you girls.'

The lights changed and the bus moved forwards. Just a little shove would do it. I leaned towards Mrs Frances Blower's lilac-polyester covered back, thinking of the Reverend Arthur Blower's soft lips, I pushed as hard as I could with my two hands and...

'Vivienne, are you all right? Vivienne?' I opened my eyes. I was lying in the road with the bus inches from me, the sky hanging white above me. 'What happened?' I heard people asking. 'What happened to her?' 'She fainted,' said Mrs Frances Blower. 'Lucky you was there, Missus,' said a man. 'Only but for you, could have been a tragic accident.' 'We could have been reading about it in the evening papers,' said an old one. She wished.

'Oh well,' said Mrs Frances Blower. 'I just happened to be in the right place at the right time.' Her face with its thin orange lips looked down at me with concern. She looked really worried about me, actually. I'd like to see, I thought to myself, I'd like to see my mam looking at me like that just once in my life.

I told her I was OK. No need for an ambulance. Just hunger, probably. Or my period. Actually, I really did feel OK, just a bit dizzy.

'Come and sit next to me, Vivienne,' said Mrs Frances Blower, bustling me on to the bus.

But I went upstairs. You can see things better from up there.

SHRINE

Her friends plagued her with advice. It wasn't the end
of the world, they said, however much it seemed like
it. Life must go on. Think of the children, they said.
The grandchildren. She should pull herself together. Michael
wouldn't have wanted her to fall apart like this.

The clichés made her want to scream but she knew they
meant well. And they were right, of course, but knowing it
made no difference. There was this aching void inside her all
the time. Sometimes she just started howling, a primitive wail
that came from deep within. It could happen anywhere, often
at home alone but sometimes in public places too. In the café
where she had gone with Ruth, who believed fervently in the
healing power of cake. Lizzie had tried to control herself but the
sobs burst out of her anyway and Ruth had been mortified.

Everything had been so quick. No time to prepare. From the
diagnosis to Michael's death – his agonising final pain blanked
out at least by the mercies of the morphine drip – was just six
weeks. Before that a few aches and twinges you might well have
thought were just the usual symptoms of ageing. At fifty-seven
you expected the machine to start to wear down, as Michael
used to say. But the cancer was in his lungs and his bones and
the doctors shook their heads and told them it was very far
advanced, very aggressive.

They had given him chemo anyway, huge blasts of the stuff
that bloated him up and made him sick, made all his lovely
black hair fall out. Lizzie secretly vowed to herself that if, God
forbid, she were to be similarly diagnosed she would say no
thank you to the chemo and take her chances.

She sat by him for hours while they pumped it into him.
Holding his pale hand and stroking the dark little tufts of hair

on his fingers, wondering how this could possibly have happened to them. She would creep out when he fell asleep and sit in the hospital canteen drinking tea and staring into space, or, if the weather was good, go for a walk in a nearby park and look at the elderly couples shuffling along happily, holding each others arms.

That was supposed to be us, she thought.

The children were great but they didn't understand either. They grieved for their father but their lives had moved on. Sara had her two small children to distract her and was pregnant again. Joe and his girlfriend Helena were planning to get married the next spring. Timmy, at twenty the baby of the family, was the most affected but even he had got over it and thrown himself back into his studies, hoping to get an Erasmus scholarship to Sweden in the autumn.

Lizzie was glad for them all but as for herself, she couldn't see beyond the moment. She couldn't imagine a time when her life would retrieve its colour, when she would look forward again instead of back. It was only now that he was gone she realised how much of her life had been bound up with Michael's. They had done everything together, shared interests. Since they had got married very young – childhood sweethearts almost – she hadn't worked outside the home. Apart from a couple of girls from her schooldays – Ruth and Margaret – his friends had become. hers.

'I wish now,' she said to Ruth, 'I'd had more independent a life. It's like there's nothing left for me. Nothing to do.'

Ruth, a single woman the same age as Lizzie – mid-fifties – didn't get it.

'You're still young enough to start again.' She squashed into the eclair with her fork. 'You might even meet someone else. In time, of course.'

Ruth forked the chocolaty pastry into her mouth, licking the cream off her lips. Lizzie watched, thinking she didn't want to meet anyone else ever. She just wanted Michael back.

Ruth attended tea dances, where serious professional men occasionally invited her to dinner or a film or play. Maybe there was more to it: Lizzie had never asked. But none of these relationships seemed to last.

Margaret, their other old friend, was married like Lizzie with grown-up children. Brisk and practical, she ran her home like a military operation.

'I'll come over and help you sort through his stuff,' she told Lizzie. 'Vincent de Paul will be glad of it.'

Lizzie was shocked. 'I'm not throwing anything out.'

'You can't keep it. What for?'

Lizzie said nothing. Not how much it comforted her to see Michael's coat hanging in the hall. How she buried her face in it sometimes to try and get his scent. How she washed his shirts from time to time to freshen them up. Even ironed them and hung them in the press. Sobbed into them.

She had been invited to Sara's for Christmas but said she would prefer to stay home. So all the family came to her bearing various food items to save her the trouble, although she would have preferred to be busy. They were clearly taken aback to find that she had laid a place at the table for Michael.

'That's too weird,' said Timmy.

'That's granddad's place,' Sara told three-year-old Cian when he tried to climb up to sit there and the boy looked around with big eyes to see where granddad was hiding. Throughout the meal everyone glanced uneasily at the empty chair and Cian was shh'ed when he asked.

For her present they had clubbed together to pay for a weekend away in a luxury hotel near Westport. A weekend for two. She looked at them aghast.

'You could take Ruth,' they suggested hastily. 'Or Margaret.'

In the end, she went by herself.

The first night she sat having dinner in the hotel restaurant, surrounded by couples and families, wondering what the hell she was doing there. She drank two glasses of wine with the beef stroganoff and a brandy with the coffee and then went up to her room, stretching out on the chintz bedcover and gazing at the hunting scene on the wall. She felt that she was disappearing.

The next day it rained so she drove to the Museum of Country Life. A leaflet in the hotel had extolled its delights and, without any great expectations, she reckoned it would put down a few hours. Perhaps the rain would clear after and she could go for a tramp through the countryside.

The museum engaged her more than she had expected it would. It was both soothing and fascinating to see the way people had lived over the centuries, to look at the artefacts, the woven baskets, the shoes, bowls, necklaces, made with care and skill by unknown hands.

The display that caught her attention in particular was a strange contrivance that looked like a belt, but seemed far too rigid and heavy to fit around anyone's waist. A belt shrine, she read on the inscription, discovered in a Sligo bog in the 1940s by a man cutting turf. It was exquisite, hinged bronze inset with small silver panels beaten into elaborate Celtic designs and studded with coloured glass and enamel. Made to house the leather belt of an unknown saint.

As she looked at this sacred object, Lizzie was overwhelmed with a sudden sense of connectedness. She felt it radiate out of her, a chain of light linking her to John Towey now dead but aged eighteen when he had dug the relic up and left it on a sod of turf all the rest of the working day because he didn't know what it was; to the restorers who had cleaned off the muck of centuries, wondering to see its intricacies emerge under their soft brushes; to the craftsman who had fashioned it so lovingly so very long ago. And finally to the long forgotten saint who had once tied round his waist the strip of leather encased in the shrine. Such belts, she read further, were thought to have miraculous powers to cure illness.

What a pity, Lizzie thought, it's too late for us.

Leaving the museum at last she found the sun had indeed come out into a clear blue sky. She took deep breaths of sharp February air and walked into hills rusty with last year's shrubs, showing the first signs of new shoots. As she went her mind buzzed with thoughts of the belt shrine and the other artefacts on display. One thing had always puzzled her: that there weren't more around. Considering the millions of folk who had passed over the surface of the earth for hundreds of thousands of years, living, loving, making, you would think you'd forever be stumbling over their pots and their tools and their jewellery, the relics of their lives. So many hopes and dreams gone without trace.

Back in Westport she went exploring. In a little side street she found the sort of junk shop she and Michael had loved to visit, picking up all manner of what his mother dismissed as 'clutter' to furnish their first little house. So much of that had gone too, she thought sadly, in the clearout when they moved. She picked up a small and battered metal box. Running her fingers over it, she had a sudden idea and laughed aloud, causing the shop assistant to glance up at her.

'How much?' she asked.

It was for nothing.

Once home she searched out Timmy's box of enamel paints that he'd got as a boy to colour his model soldiers. Some were dried up but others were still fine. First she painted the box all over in shiny black and let it dry. Then she started decorating the box with a Celtic bird design copied from an old coin. It looked good, the long beak, the swirling tail. She had always been artistic that way. Michael had encouraged her but somehow she'd never had the time.

When it was completely dry she fetched Michael's leather belt, the one she had bought him when they were on honeymoon in Barcelona. They had tried to dance a flamenco that night in their hotel room but soon collapsed on the bed laughing. She remembered the difficulty she'd had in unbuckling the belt and how Michael had said it was his chastity belt. He'd always called it that after. 'Where's my chastity belt, Lizzie?' he'd shout out.

'Don't mind him,' she'd tell the astonished children.

Now she rolled it up and placed it in the box, together with a note: *This belt was the property of Michael Gallagher, 1951-*

2008. He was no saint but I loved him. Then she signed her name: *Elizabeth Gallagher.*

She took the box and went out to the back garden. There she dug a hole under the cherry tree Michael had planted when they moved in nearly twenty years before. The tree would be flowering again soon, its buds now tight as a baby's fist. She buried the box quite deep and patted the soil firm over the top of it. Maybe one day someone would dig it up and read her message and feel the same connections she had felt in the museum.

Sara rang her that evening to find how the weekend had been.

'Grand, love,' she said. 'Thanks so much for making me go. It did me the world of good. Actually I'm thinking of going back there. They run painting courses and I'd love to take that up again. Take it more seriously. Your dad always said I had a gift.'

Later that evening she propped a postcard of the belt shrine up on the mantelpiece. The power to heal, they said. To heal heart sickness too maybe, she thought. Or at least to comfort and soothe. She looked at the photograph of Michael beside it, fit and smiling and full of love, and she smiled back.

THE FILM WORLD

Melissa McDermott was in a film. It was progressing
slowly but she tried not to mind, being fully aware
that much of the footage would anyway finally find
its way on to the cutting room floor. That was how it worked
in films, much more material was shot than was ever used.
She had looked into it and that's how it was. She would have
preferred perhaps more actual contact with the director but she
understood that his way was stealth. That the player, herself,
was never to be quite sure of the position of the camera. So she
constantly ensured that she was presenting a pleasing view from
ever angle.

Melissa McDermott knew she was in a film because
everywhere she went she was accompanied by music. She only
had to walk into a supermarket or cafe for the orchestra to
strike up. Just to pass a shop in the street.

She wasn't sure what part she was playing, or even what sort
of film it was, but she felt in her heart that she had a starring
role. In any case, all would become clear in due course. She
mustn't be impatient.

It was lucky chance that had changed her first name from the
mundane Maureen to the much more appropriate cognomen she
now used. Someone had once asked her what she called herself
and astonishment at the directness of the query had thrown her
into confusion.

'M.. Miss er McDermott,' she had replied.

'Melissa,' the person – a man of course – had misheard.
'What a pretty name!' And he had smiled at her before passing
out of her life.

Now she wore the name proudly pinned to her chest at
the supermarket checkout where she sat every day awaiting

developments in the film she was in. 'Melissa McDermott' – it seemed so appropriate for a star. MM like Marilyn Monroe, who had also changed her name from something more homely.

Every morning she prepared for the day in the shabby little bed-sitting room she herself had so carefully embellished with pastel drapes, a small reproduction of Monet's 'Water Lilies' and a pale china shepherdess (she understood that on grounds of authenticity the director preferred to forego the efforts of an artistic designer) to fit the character she felt herself to be playing, a wistful, sensitive, solitary girl awaiting the moment when she would be sparked into self-fulfilment.

She would look at herself in the mirror, and observe a small face, a frail slightly hunched body, all framed by pink plastic. Immediately she would – self-consciously, even though there was no one to see her except possibly the director with his hidden camera – throw out her breasts until the slightest bumps became discernible under her blouse. For Melissa McDermott, though sharing initials, was not endowed like Marilyn Monroe. But then of course voluptuousness was not appropriate for the character she was playing. She wore minimal make-up and just hoped it was good enough for the camera. Most of her fellow check-out workers had heavy pancake that ended under the chin, giving the effect of a mask, blusher, glinting eye-shadow, mascara that made their lashes stand out spikily, gloss on pouting lips. But she understood that it was for contrast, like their permed and brashly highlighted hair, so unlike her own natural light brown bob.

She knew exactly what she was waiting for. What the director intended. At a certain moment, HE would appear, the male lead. Undoubtedly the director was taking his time and she couldn't help wishing secretly, that they could move to that part of the film which would surely have more action. It wasn't her place to tell a director his business, but she felt that if she were a spectator instead of a participant, she would have lost interest long before. She tried to stop herself gazing hopefully at any young male who came to her check-out with his basket of baked beans, small sliced pan and frozen meal for one. In the cafe where she went for her lunch, she would wait with sickening nerves in her stomach for some nice-looking man to ask politely if the other seat at her table was free, and if he did, stare at her cheese sandwich waiting for him to make some remark. And if he asked if she was using the sugar or salt, she would mumble something unintelligible and push it at him so violently that on more than one occasion it had crashed to the floor.

Melissa McDermott had an aunt who lived in the city where she worked and whom she visited most Sundays for her lunch. There, over boiled meat, she would be subjected to three hours of intimate details regarding the old woman's irritable bowel. Melissa never quite believed the film continued here, particularly since there was never any music to alleviate the tedium of the conversation but only the constant patter of the television, a match, a black and white cowboy film, a quiz in which ugly people won unlikely domestic appliances or holidays in the Caribbean.

Once a month she took the bus down the country to the family home on the edge of a small town. Her mother was always too harassed by the demands of the numerous little ones to bother too much with 'Maureen' as she still called her, after the first searching look in her face (the eyes inevitably dropping to see if there was any evidence of a swelling in the region of her belly). Melissa found she no long resented minding the younger girls, with their naive questionings about the city. She had acquired prestige as one who had gone away to better, stranger things. At Sunday Mass, she sang out almost loudly, the light of devotion in her eyes. Was there not perhaps a camera lens peering at her from behind a pillar, the shadowy director lurking in a side chapel.

On her return to the city from such a visit one dull Sunday night as she dozed in the window seat, someone banged down next to her. He lit a cigarette. The fumes roused her.

'No smoking,' she said.

The man shrugged and continued to puff away.

'Don't you see the notice?' Melissa asked, respect for the rules overriding her shyness. The man muttered something that might have been a curse. He smelt sour, like he had spilt drink, maybe even urine on his clothes.

'I'll tell the driver,' Melissa persisted. Once she had seen a picture of tar-coated lungs and it had filled her with dread.

'Driver's smoking too.'

That was true enough.

'One rule for them, another rule for us. It's always the way.' The man smiled. His teeth were discoloured. 'But seeing as how you asked me so nicely,' he went on, 'and cos I can't resist a pretty face...' he ground out his cigarette.

'Thank you,' Melissa said and turned her blush towards the mirroring window again. Pretty, he said. He actually said she was pretty.

His name was Eddie. Like herself he had family in the country, a job – of sorts – in the city. It seemed that he had been to visit his mam to squeeze some money out of her.

'Can't keep meself in smokes the price they are with what I get on the valeting.'

It took Melissa a while to realise that he was not a footman in a grand house but a cleaner of cars.

When they reached the city he asked her to come for a quick jar before closing time. She refused politely but he grabbed her hand in his rough one and pulled her across the road. She couldn't break free: he was carrying her bag as well as his own back-pack.

The pub was yellow with old smoke. A few men sat at the bar, some of whom greeted Eddie and looked her over. He found her a torn mock leather seat and went to get the drinks – the glass of cider she had requested and a pint of stout for himself. While he was standing at the bar waiting for the beer to settle, she studied him. Quite old, thirtyish, skinny with thinning hair, certainly not the matinee idol she had been expecting. However, the music was playing, the cameras were evidently rolling and she would have to go along with it.

He talked, not seeming to mind that her replies were mumbles. What he said she couldn't have repeated: lots of incomprehensible information about people she didn't know, people who often, it seemed, tried to put one over on Eddie, apparently without much success. He grinned, barely those discoloured teeth.

'See, I wasn't born yesterday,' he told her. And she had to agree with that.

The pub seemed to ignore normal closing time and Melissa suddenly realised she had missed the last bus out to the suburb where she lived. She would have to get a taxi but, never having done such a thing, was unsure how to go about it. In other films, people stepped into the street, clicking their fingers and shouting 'taxi!' but she didn't think, with several drinks taken at this stage, that she was up to it. Anyway, Eddie had her bag under his legs and she would have to wait until he went to the bar again before she could make a lunge for it.

In the meantime she needed to pay a visit to the Ladies. Flushed faces loomed at her through the smoke as she passed by. People laughed loudly. Not at her, surely. The lavatory was dirty with a wet floor. She could hardly bear to use it but had to. There was no water in the taps, so she couldn't even rinse her hands.

Later she couldn't remember how they had got to the dark alleyway where she found Eddie on top of her, hurting her, pressing her back against the hard ground, grabbing her tiny breasts, forcing himself between her legs, probing her most secret party with a hard warm wet stick. She struggled and sobbed while he hissed in her ear, 'You're a great girl. Oh dear God!... Oh fucking Christ!'

As the man sank his teeth – those brown teeth – into her neck, Melissa McDermott rolled back her head in protest at the pain. Her open eyes saw a red light, the back window of the club where she suddenly remembered they had gone after the bar. He had held her tight in a dance that was no dance but an opportunity to rub himself against her. He had pressed wet lips against her and forced a snaking tongue into her mouth. She had taste his sourness and ran outside to vomit. He had come after her, clasping her breasts from behind as the cider she had been drinking all evening poured out of her in a jerky stream.

Now pounding, throbbing dance music filled the alleyway as the man on top of her reached his climax. Again, as his mouth searched for hers, she twisted away and suddenly glimpsed a figure outlined against the street lights of the main road beyond, looking straight at her.

The director lowered his camera, turned on his heel and strode off into the city. It was, as they say in the film world, a wrap.

Wetting The Baby's Head

S
o far so good, Helen Flanagan was thinking, sipping her Britvic orange. Of course, the fact that Desmond had refused to come, that she didn't have to look at his tight face, those pursed lips, all helped her survive the experience. And the baby helped, too. They were all united in oohing and aahing over little Setanta, forgetting differences for a while.

Setanta – Helen smiled to herself in satisfaction. That had been a good victory. She glanced across at red-faced Bernadette Cummins and remembered how the woman – arms crossed over that huge bosom – had asked beefily what class of a name was that, what were they thinking of, saddling the poor little mite with a girl's name. And Helen had been unable to keep a sneer of superciliousness out of her voice when she replied that it was from ancient Irish, Cuchulain's name before he killed the hound.

'I don't know,' Bernadette had retorted, 'if they wanted an Irish name why they didn't call him Darren. That's a nice name, Darren.'

'But hardly Irish,' Helen had commented.

The woman had turned to her then, a gleam of triumph in her eyes, and Helen even now wasn't certain whether she had been serious.

'Course it is,' she had said. 'What about Darren islands!'

'Can I get you a drink, Mrs Flanagan?' the godfather was asking her. Paul his name was, a nice polite young man, though more a friend of Dolores than of Henry.

'Oh... thank you, that's very kind.' She was conscious of chirping, as Desmond called it. It always irritated him. 'Just an orange, then... a Britvic orange.'

'Nothing stronger? To give you strength.'

For an instant she wondered with alarm how he knew. But of course he didn't. She could tell from his face. He was just joking.

'Well... I'll take a drop of vodka in it, then. Just this once. Thanks very much.'

They said vodka didn't smell on your breath but she never knew whether this was true. She smiled amiably at Paul's girlfriend, Cerise or something, Celia. The girl was very young and quite pretty, but had too much shimmering make-up on eye-lids, cheek-bones and lips. Her nails were silver.

'Isn't the baby gorgeous,' the girl said. 'I love babies.'

Helen smiled. 'Mmm.'

They drifted over to peer at it again.

'Look at him... aaah...' Celia or Cerise was saying. 'Isn't he a dote!'

The dote had twisted its features into contortions and was turning red. Evidently it was building up to a howl. It's eyes opened a crack and looked straight at Helen with a vindictive expression.

'Oh dear!' she said. It looked just like Desmond.

Paul returned with the drinks and Helen took hers gratefully.

'Cheers,' they all said.

'So Mr Flanagan couldn't come?' Paul asked.

'No, he didn't feel too well.'

'What a shame!' the girl said. It was Celine, Helen suddenly remembered. Like that singer.

She drifted off after a few more polite exchanges. She wanted a word with Henry but by the time she reached him, forgot what she had intended to say.

'All right?' he asked her.

'I'm grand.'

'We'll be having the dinner in about twenty minutes. If you can hang on till then.'

He turned away. Whatever had he meant?

She went up to the bar and ordered another drink. She tapped two fingers on the counter and looked meaningfully at the barman.

'One Britvic orange,' he said briskly and took her fiver.

She nearly jumped out of her skin when Jack Cummins put his arm around her. She could smell the whiskey on his breath, his face was that close to hers.

'Footloose and fancy free, heh,' he chuckled, actually squeezing her as she tried to wriggle away.

'Desmond had some important work to do for tomorrow.' She tried to sound dignified. 'He was raging he couldn't come.'

'I'll bet.' Then he muttered something that sounded suspiciously like 'fecking old grouch'. Maybe that's what it was.

'What're you drinking?' he went on.

'Orange.'

'Orange! You're codding me! The christening of your first grandchild and you're drinking orange!'

'Well... if you insist, I'll take a drop of vodka in it. For once.'

'Double vodka and orange, Dermo!' Jack called. 'And a pint and a Paddy and Red and a snowball for herself.'

'A double! Oh goodness...'

'Put colour in your cheeks,' Jack said jovially, smacking her lower back. 'Which cheeks, says you?.. No offence.'

It was unbelievable. What had Henry been thinking of, uniting himself with such a family! The man shuffled off and the next instant she heard him roaring with laughter. Not at her, she trusted.

Helen was suddenly sick of socialising, her face aching in a smiling rictus. She stayed sitting at the bar gazing at her two orange drinks. She glanced up and saw her reflection looking back at her. Her hat was a bit crooked. She straightened it. Now all was well. She sipped from one orange drink, then the other. They tasted the same. Maybe vodka, as well as having no smell had no taste. Then she remembered tapping with two fingers on the bar when she'd ordered. No change from a fiver.

'There's nothing more comforting,' she said to the man sitting next to her, a stranger, 'than an understanding barman.'

She wasn't sure if he'd heard her. He said nothing.

'You aren't in the party, are you,' she persisted.

'No,' he replied, slouching further over his drink.

'It's my grandson's christening. Setanta.'

'Get away,' said the man.

In the mirror she saw her dear Henry reflected. The apple of her eye. The apple – what a strange expression. Whatever could it mean? She debated asking the man next to her but he didn't look encouraging. Anyway, it was almost certain that he wouldn't know. People never did when she put such questions to them, just gazed at her queerly. The orange pippin of my eye, she thought. The golden delicious. With her – Dolores, beside him. Still looked pregnant in that dress, her belly still bulging. Helen recalled that after Henry was born, her own belly had just snapped back into place. She had told Dolores as much but as usual the woman hadn't even pretended interest. She had just looked as sour as ever. Now the couple seemed to be exchanging words. Arms were being flung in the air, fingers pointed. It all looked very far away. Through the looking-glass, she thought. Like Alice. As a child she'd always wanted to be Alice, to go through the mirror into another world. She'd still like to try it. She caught the barman's eye and tapped one finger on the counter.

'Britvic orange?' he asked impassively. She nodded.

'Vitamin C,' she said to the man next to her. 'It keeps all sorts away, you know... Colds, cancer...'

She was chirping again. Of course it didn't matter. Desmond wasn't around to complain. He would later, of course, but she'd be insulated by then. No doubt he was at that very moment sitting in front of the unlit fire, his face composed into a frown, his lips pursed, rehearsing what he'd say, getting, as time passed, more and more sulky. She giggled, thinking of how the baby resembled him. The baby, who even now was screaming. Or was it? Maybe there was another baby. There seemed to be a lot of screaming.

She gave the barman a fiver and waved away the change.

No, she didn't want to go through the looking-glass. She didn't want the Queen of Hearts to chop off her head. She would like to become an explorer like one of those intrepid Victorian ladies. There had been a series of programmes about them on the radio. Isabella Bird, for example, who didn't set off on her first expedition until she was fifty and then continued into her seventies. Helen was only fifty-five, fit enough. She shut her eyes. It was almost as if she could feel the damp leaves of the rain forest splat against her face, hear the screech of parakeets...

Someone tapped her arm.

'We have to go outside.'

It was the godmother, Maureen, whom Helen had always liked. The sort of sensible, educated person who would have suited Henry as a wife. Someone from his own class.

'Is it for photos?' she asked, grabbing her full glass at the same moment.

Maureen appeared tense. Her grip on Helen's arm was almost painful.

Outside the cold air hit her like a sock in the stomach. She could tell from the faces that something terrible had happened. Cerise was sobbing. Paul looked agonised. Dolores was clutching the baby and still screaming. Beefy Bernadette was screaming. Jack looked black with rage. And her son? He was sitting on the curb, his head in his hands.

'What is it?' Helen turned her face to Maureen.

'Dolores says the baby isn't Henry's,' she said tragically. 'It's Paul's.'

Helen started to laugh. People turned to look at her. That only made her laugh more. Even Henry turned at last. He came over to her.

'Shut up, mother,' he said. 'Don't make a worse show of us.'

She thought for a moment he was going to hit her but instead he fell into her arms and started crying like when he was a little boy.

'There, there,' she said, patting the head that was already beginning to lose its hair. 'Of course it's yours, Henry. Isn't it the living spit of your father.'

Later she made an excuse to go back into the bar. No one had banned her. She hadn't shouted bad language, she hadn't engaged in fisticuffs. Her hat had gone crooked again, as she ascertained in the mirror. But otherwise she appeared the respectable, middle-aged, middle-class woman that she was. She caught the barman's eye and tapped two fingers on the counter.

'You can overdo the orange juice, you know,' he said gently.

'It's good for me,' she replied as steadily as she could. 'I need it.'

She watched him tip the orange into the glass and add the two measures of clear vodka. Dear little water, that's what the word meant in Russian, someone had once told her. Dear little water.

'The food's in there if you want to eat,' he told her, taking the twenty. 'It's a shame to let it go to waste.'

But she shook her head and sipped her drink. She would like to go to the Rocky Mountains, like Isabella Bird. To ride a mule up the Grand Canyon, deeper and deeper, away from civilisation. Away from people. In the mirror she spotted the loud-mouthed priest, Father Bill, as he liked to be called, sidling off into the private room where the food was. Please God he wouldn't see her and insist on looking after her. Take her under his wing, as he'd said once already, much earlier when he'd learnt that Desmond wasn't with her. Under his wing, indeed, as if he were some large ungainly black bird and she some helpless little chick. She took off her hat to be less noticeable. How stupid it looked, all moulded felt and tulle! She was done with hats from now on unless they were pith helmets. Pith – piss with a lisp! She started to laugh again. It was all so ridiculous. She rocked with suppressed mirth but it wouldn't be held in. Out it spluttered at last in chortles, chuckles, guffaws. A wonderful exuberant fountain of merry laughter. A waterfall, a cataract, a Niagara, gushing, spouting, overflowing, sweeping her away into an ocean of joy.

THE ICING ON THE CAKE

May sighed. It was over. Now at long last she could rest. A deeper sigh as the words brushed over her. As she smelt the sweet oil and felt it drip on to her forehead.

He was a young priest. Although to her they nearly all looked young now, even in their fifties. They say your life passes fast, blink and it's over. But she felt the weight of her eighty years dragging her down. It would be so good to let it all go.

Voices. Not the priest's. A muttering in the background. They all kept telling her she was deaf, but she wasn't. Just selective in what she heard, a skill she had mastered over the years. Now she tuned in. A sharp high voice, a lower drone, like a drill. Sylvia and Frances, who else, the two snakes.

'She had the nerve to tell me she had her eye on the Boulle press. No way I said, Mam definitely wants me to have it. Well, you know that, Frances. I told you before.'

'The cheek of it.'

'And in case she had any ideas, I told her, Frances has her name on the mahogany sideboard. Well, you do, don't you, Frances.'

'I certainly don't intend she should get it. Or the contents.'

'That's right. So then I spelt out exactly what we had decided, who'd get what and so on, and then... you're going to laugh at this, Frances... she got all red in the face and started on about how she didn't want the ottoman, where would she put an ottoman, and so forth.'

'I hope you told her exactly where she could put it, Sylvia.'

'I wish I had, Frances. And then she brought up the silver service.'

'Not again.'

'No way. I said. That was mam and dad's wedding present and by rights goes to the first-born, which is you, Frances. But she went on about how Anthony should have it being the sole male heir.'

'She said that? She didn't!'

'Honest to God. Her very words. The sole male heir.'

'And what did Anthony say?'

'He just stood there as usual like a big lump and let her do all the talking.'

'I'd say she's got her eye on the house, Sylvia.'

'Of course she has. Her and her sole male heir. It'll be share and share alike on that one. Not that they need a share. It's not as if they have any children themselves. When I think of what it's going to cost us to put Jason and Brittany through secondary... Well, you know yourself, Frances...'

Suddenly May opened her eyes, startling the young priest. This wouldn't do. This wouldn't do at all. How could she possibly have imagined that it was over. That she could rest in peace.

'I think she's rallying,' the priest called to the women. They rushed to her side.

'Mam!' Sylvia bent her face down towards her. It was an orange face that abruptly turned grey-white at the neck where Sylvia had omitted to rub on more pancake. Her eyelashes were spiky, her lips greasy red. So close May could see the grey roots of her buttercup blonde hair.

Frances stood behind her sister, gaunt and white. No attempt made to soften her hard lines. Sharp nose, thin lips cracked open, pale eyes bulging behind strong-lensed glasses. Grey hair pulled back into a ferocious bun.

May tried to remember them as babies. She tried to hear their children's voices. Her lips moved, calling them back.

'God be praised!' said Sylvia. 'She's still with us.'

Behind her, Frances turned away.

It was a miracle, Sylvia kept saying, waving some amulet around. May wished she would shut up and leave her in peace. She had things to think about.

May was lying on the ottoman – what was wrong with it and why did none of them want it? Sylvia was there and Anthony and Beverly, his little shrew of a wife. Frances was at work, thank God. One less, at least.

She closed her eyes in a vain attempt to shut them out. Sylvia, who had never had much imagination assumed she was asleep.

'I mean, it can't go on like this.'

'What?' The shrew.

'She can't look after herself properly. Meals on wheels are all right and the health board send around a woman each day to get her up and put her to bed. I do what I can, but it can't go on.'

'What do you suggest? Do her in?'

'Bev!' That was Anthony's wary growl.

'She's asleep. Anyhow, she's stone deaf.'

'We can't rule out a nursing home,' Sylvia said.

There was silence. She knew what they were all thinking. The money. The money haemorrhaging. Maybe the house being sold.

'Let's hope it doesn't come to that,' Sylvia said at last. 'Though I have to say, I think it would be better for Mam to go quickly and peacefully.'

Anthony and his wife murmured agreement.

Finally, they shuffled out without placing a pillow over her face, probably to do an inventory of the linen press. Once she was sure that they were gone, May took her mobile out from under the cushion and dialled a certain number.

There was a photograph of the whole family on the mantelpiece, taken shortly before Vincent died. May couldn't remember exactly but thought it was probably Jason's confirmation. A miserable event where Sylvia had gone around telling the guests how much money Jason had received at the last count, like it was a charity fund-raiser. 'Thirty five more and he'll hit the five hundred.'

It was the only fairly recent picture of herself, but Mr Ali said it would do fine, unless she wanted another one taken.

'Not like I am now,' she'd said. 'At least show me standing on my own two feet.'

No bother, Mr Ali said. They'd be able to scan the whole lot in to the computer and then wipe out the other figures. She liked the sound of that.

Whatever she asked him, he did without question, which she also liked. It was by chance that he wasn't an Irishman, nor even a European, nor even a Christian, but so much the better. If he thought what she was doing was bizarre, he never said anything. Although why should he, it was in his interest to go along with it all. And she was no doddery old woman. The contract was properly drawn up, witnessed and so on. Copper-fastened, as they say.

Mr Ali reminded her a little of the priest who had conducted the last rites – she hoped she wasn't being blasphemous in so thinking – a good-looking man in his forties, energetic, showing large white teeth when he smiled, which in Mr Ali's case was often. May tried not to think of Vincent, but staring at his solid, blocky image in the photograph caused him to rise up in front of her, laughing his sneery little laugh, finding fault with everything she said, finding fault with her silence. The old priest had told her to offer it up. The doctor had prescribed pills for her depression. Finally, Vincent had dropped dead on the golf course but too late to make a difference to her or the children. Now, when Mr Ali touched her arm, as he sometimes did, she couldn't help thinking of what else might have been.

At least Vincent was powerless now. How furious he would have been. She chuckled as she handed Mr Ali the photograph.

'Go on,' she said. 'Wipe them all out.'

Frances marched in while May was dozing on the ottoman.

'What's going on!' Frances shouted. 'What's all this about?' She waved the newspaper in May's face.

'There are going to be a few changes,' May said, more steadily that she felt. She had been afraid of her eldest daughter for as long as she could remember.

'This is a joke, right! A stupid, senseless and expensive joke.'

'Well, I suppose it is quite funny...'

'You crazy old woman. I'll get Dr Doyle to certify you... Lock you away where you belong.'

Akumbe came running in. Frances looked twice but then must have assumed she was the woman from the health board.

'It's all right, she said. 'I'm her daughter.'

'Not all right,' said Akumbe firmly. 'This old lady not to be disturbed.'

Frances argued for a bit but Akumbe was having none of it. She politely got rid of her. What a treasure.

'What's she got her knickers in a twist about?' Akumbe asked, bringing in two cups of tea.

'Oh...' May waved at the newspaper, open on the floor.

Akumbe looked at it. At the picture. 'This you, May. This your picture.' She smiled broadly – she too had white teeth, and started to read aloud: '*Yes, it's me. I have taken this advertisement to inform the members of my family that I am sick of all your fighting and bickering and plotting. I am not dead yet and it is not seemly to distribute the goods before I am gone. In fact, do not count your chickens before they are hatched. I have a big surprise for you all.*' Akumbe looked at her. 'Big surprise? Me?'

'Oh you're only part of it, Akumbe. Now pass the biscuits. Oh, and phone a locksmith. I need to change the locks.'

Vincent had never liked black people or Jews. Not that he knew any, but that hadn't stopped him. In fact he had never liked anyone who wasn't Irish. And you could limit that further to exclude anyone of the female sex.

'That's what's good about the club,' he used to say, meaning the golf club, 'No wogs and no women.'

So it gave May a special pleasure to fill the house with Akumbe and her five children. Akumbe was a Nigerian woman of generous build. Mr Ali had told May that she was a particularly deserving case, having fled from an abusive husband who had beaten her, Mr Ali said, shaking his head within an inch of her life. How she had ended up in Ireland was still vague to May, but what was certain was that Akumbe was an excellent carer, a jolly companion and a great singer of hymns, even if they were Protestant ones. Her children were delightful: the eldest girl, Miriam, was able to mind May in the evenings, when Akumbe went out to her job, and the younger ones played beside the ottoman and listened to her stories. They told her stories too, children's stories from Africa, and displayed their dances for her.

Sylvia had arrived in the middle of one of these sessions with Sylvia's husband Liam, the only one of the whole lot that May had any time for, a slow-speaking Ulsterman with a droll wit.

'Where's the furniture?' Sylvia asked. 'Where's the Boulle, where's the sideboard?'

'I never liked them,' May told her, 'and Mr Ali said that they were good pieces and would fetch a good price at auction.'

'You sold them!' Sylvia went white under her orange pancake.

'There's more space now, don't you agree. More room for the children to play.'

They called in doctors and lawyers of course, but May, with Mr Ali standing behind her, his hand on her shoulder, explained reasonably to the family why she had done what she had done.

'The agreement lets me live here for the rest of my life but the house now belongs to the trust. The Refugee Support Trust, 'May told them.

'The house...' Frances looked ready to bite her to death. 'You've sold the house to a charity!'

'You've all got nice houses of your own, dear,' May said.

'And the money,' asked Sylvia. 'Where's the money?'

'I've willed it to the Trust. It needs it more than you. After all...'

But the clamour drowned her out.

She had to be mad. That man, that coloured man, must have used undue influence, the black woman must have used voodoo on her. In fact, May thought, watching them rant and rave, the men in white coats would have more cause to drag them away than herself.

'Father must be turning in his grave,' said Frances, as Akumbe pushed them out.

'I certainly hope so, dear,' said May. 'After all, that would be the icing on the cake.'

Ka-Pow!

Geoffrey was beginning to think his latest career move had been a mistake. He had been sitting in the old woman's living room for over an hour now, clutching a cold cup of tea and listening to Vicky's babble. It was like some endless form of torture and he found himself hankering for Dunne & Sons, the funeral parlour where he had worked for the past several months, its calm quiet, the waxen faces of the corpses who never answered back.

Uncle Ronald hadn't actually sacked him. He had simply told Geoffrey's mam that Geoffrey had an inappropriately facetious attitude for an undertaker and that he might be happier in another occupation.

'Have you got a facetious attitude, Geoffrey?' his mam had asked him, her hands clasped worriedly across her vast bosom.

'I dunno.' If at least he knew what it meant.

'Oh dear. I had hoped you'd do well there, son.'

His granddad, mam's and Ronald's dad, had set up the funeral parlour back in the sixties and, because Ronald only had daughters who weren't interested, his mam, ever optimistic, had encouraged Geoffrey to go into the family business, with a view, eventually, to inheriting it. Geoffrey had at least been willing to give it a try but it had started badly. Uncle Ronald, a small ball-shaped man with a bald head and a black pencil moustache, who for professional purposes cultivated a hushed voice and lugubrious demeanour, proved to be not one bit impressed with Geoffrey's suggestion for new advertising slogans.

'Something catchy,' Geoffrey said. 'To draw in the punters, like.'

'Thank you for your interest,' Uncle Ronald sighed in his funereal way, 'But you see, Geoffrey, in the first place we don't refer to the bereaved as punters and in the second case I hardly think 'Dunne In' or 'Dunne and Dusted' or 'What's Dunne is Dunne', would attract anyone. Never mind 'Dunne Roamin'.'

Geoffrey was disappointed. The last slogan in particular he had reckoned was really slick.

'You see,' he explained, 'this house I passed had a plaque outside with the name on – Dun Roamin' – and I figured out it meant the people in the house had stopped roaming to settle down only they spelt 'done' wrong, as a joke, like, and so cos your name is Dunne and cos dead people have stopped roaming...'

'Yes, Geoffrey, I get it. But, trust me when I tell you, it isn't appropriate.'

'I just thought it might cheer people up at a sad time. Mam says laughter is the best medicine.'

'Not in this instance, Geoffrey. At Dunne & Sons we have always prided ourselves on maintaining an atmosphere of quiet and solemn dignity.'

Geoffrey's next attempt at improvements had met with an even icier reaction.

'It can't be true,' his mother said, shocked, 'Tell me it's not true, Geoffrey.'

'What?'

'Ron told me you put funny make-up on the... the... dead people.'

That morning Uncle Ronald had called Geoffrey into his office, all carved mahogany and purple plush and white lilies.

'Can you imagine, Geoffrey,' he had said, leaning forward elbows on the desk, rhythmically tapping the fingertips of his plump raised hands together. 'Can you begin to imagine, the pain of the bereaved, coming in the parlour only to discover their dear departed grandmother plastered in rouge and mascara like a common tart.'

'I was trying to make her look better... So their last memory would be beautiful, like.'

'Well, be that as it may. I'm willing to give you the benefit of the doubt in this case and accept that your youthful enthusiasm got the better of you. But that hardly explains Mr Hapgood.'

'Ah well.'

Admittedly, Geoffrey had got carried away when it came to Mr Hapgood. His excuse was that he had been bored out of his mind with nothing to do once he had applied the required flesh-coloured make-up to the late gentleman's face, there being a shortage of stiffs to fiddle around with that day. It had started innocently enough with a lipsticked trickle of blood running from the mouth down the chin but had got out of hand when Geoffrey, in rising excitement, realised what amazing effects could be produced with white and blue face paint.

'Dracula!' expostulated Uncle Ronald. 'You turned Mr Hapgood into Dracula!'

Geoffrey didn't know what all the fuss was about. The make-up had wiped off pretty easily, all except the stuff making dark hollows of the eyes. Anyway, the mourners had later filed past without comment, hadn't they.

Since the decision, mutually reached, to cease work at the funeral parlour, this job with Vicky was his third endeavour. That is, if you counted the modelling. He'd only lasted two days at that. The artists complained he kept fidgeting. Well, wouldn't anyone, expected to hold the same position for hours without going for a piss. Anyhow, his mam had hit the roof when she found out the gory details.

'In your nude!' she'd shrieked. 'Even I, your own mother, haven't seen you naked since you were nine.'

The other job, in the corner shop, had lasted a few weeks, until they discovered discrepancies in the till at the end of the day and traced it back to him. They accepted he wasn't pilfering but simply making mistakes with the change. He had never been much good at sums.

'If at least it was occasionally to the benefit of the shop,' Mrs O had complained. 'But the shoppers always seem to notice when they're short and never say a word when they get given too much. Geoffrey, I'm sorry but you're a liability I can't afford. You're costing me a fortune.'

Mrs O, in his opinion, was making a big fuss about nothing. She was paying him peanuts anyway, so saved on proper wages. However, as she kept telling him, she had only given him the job in the first place to oblige his mother. 'That poor widow,' she would say, even though Geoffrey's mam wasn't one. Although they hadn't heard from him for years and years, Geoffrey's father, as far as anyone knew, was alive and presumably kicking someone else.

After Mrs O made it clear she wasn't prepared to give him any more chances, Geoffrey found himself at a loss as to what to do next. Or at least, he would have been happy enough to draw the dole but his mother wasn't having it.

'No son of mine will lay himself open to charges of sponging off the state,' she'd said, no doubt recalling Geoffrey's father who sponged off everyone.

Clutching at the last straw, she asked his sister June if there were any openings in the beauty salon where June worked.

'What! And have that little squirt do to the living what up to now he has merely perpetrated against the dead!' June laughed her racking smoker's cough. 'No mam, I don't think so.'

It was his mate, Deco, who had put him on to the present job.

'All you have to do is go around houses and put the frighteners on the owners so they'll buy a burglar alarm off you.'

Deco would give anyone the frighteners with his beefy build, shaved head, tattoos and pierced eyebrow.

'If you ever come home looking like that, Geoffrey,' his mother had warned him, 'I'll change the locks.'

After Deco got in a fight not of his own making – he was despite appearances a bit of a wimp – and ended up with an ugly scar down one cheek, the alarm company decided to put him to work in the office, rather than on the road, and as result there was a vacancy for a trainee sales rep. Unlike his friend, Geoffrey – neat-haired, skinny and with a customary blameless expression – would, Deco said without rancour, present an acceptable face for the company.

'I dunno,' said Geoffrey. 'They don't pay much.'

'Yeah but that's just the basic,' Deco explained. 'You get more if you sell the product. Commission, see.'

Geoffrey told his mother he was convinced that his persuasive manner would soon make his fortune and she smiled proudly, imagining his rapid rise within the company. However, before he was allowed out by himself, he had to accompany a more experienced member of staff 'in the field', as they put it, to see how to operate effectively.

And that was how he came to be sitting in the old woman's living room, uncomfortable in his scratchy black undertaker's suit and tie, his mind floating while Vicky ran through her spiel.

Vicky had been with the company three months and considered herself an old hand. She was a plain, fat girl with thick spectacles and braces over her teeth. To distract from her appearance perhaps or maybe she was like that anyway, she cultivated a bubbly personality. She had confessed to Geoffrey, rather breathlessly as they walked the streets and between banging on the doors that most often banged shut back in their faces, how she had picked him out of the new recruits to be her apprentice.

'When I read your career aspirations,' she said, 'I knew you were the boy for me.'

Actually, it had been Deco who told him what to put on the form. Geoffrey wouldn't have had a clue about goals and ambitions and where he saw himself within the company in years ahead and why burglar alarms were close to his heart.

'But now,' she went on, 'I want to get to know you better. What makes the real Geoffrey tick?'

'Dunno,' he said, grinning sideways.

'Well, like, do you have a girlfriend for instance?'

Although the question had been lightly tossed at him, Geoffrey recognised the pleading glint behind the spectacles.

'Yes,' he lied. 'I do actually.'

'Oh, that's great. Terrific. I bet she's lovely. What's her name?'

He looked away. There were flowers blooming in the garden they happened to be passing.

'Tulip,' he said. And then immediately regretted it.

'Goodness. Never heard that one before,' Vicky said.

'It's a nickname.'

'Ah.'

'Her real name's... Karen.' That was the name of one of his sister June's friends, someone he quite fancied, actually, even though at twenty-seven, she was a much older woman.

'Karen, that's nice, Geoffrey. So why do you call her Tulip?'

'Er... It's her favourite flower, like.'

'Really... Mine's... red roses, I suppose. Not very imaginative.' She giggled.

'Roses are nice.'

'Yes, they are. I'm glad you agree with me, Geoffrey. I feel, you know – I hope you don't mind me saying this – that we have so much in common.'

They talked a lot, or rather, Vicky did, that day out in the field. The old woman had been the first one to show the slightest interest in the product.

Vicky had explained to him in advance how it worked. You established a friendly tone, showed your photo ID ('Mine's ghastly' she laughed, flashing it at him. It looked exactly like her) and gained the person's trust by presenting yourself to them as trustworthy ('You'll have no problem with that, Geoffrey,' patting his arm). Then you asked if you might, without any obligation on their part, enter their house and see what sort of a package might suit their requirements. Getting them to invite you in was a big part of the strategy, apparently. Then, once inside you described how the product operated, while at the same time showing an interest in the person, and dropping hints about the grave dangers of an unprotected house, an approach that seemed to work particularly well with lone women.

'But we must never be cynical, Geoffrey. It is important for you yourself to believe in the product. To believe that this is the best possible product on the market.'

'Yeah,' said Geoffrey. He had merely skimmed the brochures he had been given before coming out.

'You do believe that?' Vicky asked earnestly. 'Because, you see, this belief of yours will convey itself to the customer.'

'Yeah, why not. Yeah. I believe in it.'

'Good. So do I. In fact, I have the product installed in my own little apartment. You can call in and see how it works some time if you like.'

'Yeah, maybe.'

'Oh, good. When would suit?'

But that was the moment the old woman opened the door with a friendly but questioning expression on her face.

'Yes, my dears,' she asked. 'What can I do for you?'

Vicky explained, showing her ID. The woman looked at it.

'Victoria!' she said. 'That's a nice name.'

Geoffrey didn't yet have ID, but that was okay, Vicky said, because he was with her and she vouched for him. Anyhow, the old woman didn't question him and agreed to let them in to tell her more about it.

She led them into the sitting room, where they sank into big armchairs. She had a fire going, even though it was spring and warm out, and the atmosphere was stuffy and airless.

'You must feel the cold,' Vicky said brightly. Then, before the woman had time to answer, exclaimed at the décor. 'It's lovely the way you've done the room. Isn't it lovely, Geoffrey?'

Geoffrey agreed that it was even though it didn't seem special to him. Just old people's style.

'I love the wallpaper,' Vicky went on.

Geoffrey looked at the sprigged flowers on the walls.

'Did your husband put that up?'

'No, dear. I had the decorators in.'

'It's very nice. And oh look Geoffrey, what lovely ornaments! "Souvenir of Majorca",' she read off a little vase. 'Did you go there with your husband?'

Geoffrey knew what Vicky was trying to do, establish if there was a man about the house.

'No dear, a friend brought it back for me. I've never been abroad.'

'Oh I know what you mean,' Vicky said. 'Why travel abroad and go through all that hassle when Ireland's so nice, with so much to see here. I couldn't agree more.'

'Well, I suppose I never got the opportunity, dear. I wouldn't have said no, if I'd ever got the opportunity.'

'I know what you mean,' Vicky said. 'Travel certainly broadens the mind, as they say. I was in Kusadasi last year and it was only gorgeous.' She giggled. 'Sun, sea and well... enough said about that little adventure.'

The old woman picked up a cloth bag and extracted some knitting from it, a heap of pink.

'I hope you don't mind if I get on with this while you're talking. Only it helps me concentrate.'

'Not at all,' Vicky said. 'What a lovely colour! What are you making?'

The old woman held it up. It looked pretty shapeless to Geoffrey.

'It's a jumper.'

'Lovely. Oh, I wish I could knit, don't you, Geoffrey.' And then Vicky laughed. 'What am I saying! That's not a manly enough occupation for you, is it. Does Tulip knit?'

'Er... I dunno.'

'Tulip's his girlfriend,' she told the old woman, who nodded politely while counting stitches and consulting a pattern. 'Short for Karen.'

'Very nice, dear,' said the old woman.

'I thought Tulip was a funny name. But then he explained it was her favourite flower. Do you like tulips... sorry, what's your name?'

'I'm Peg, dear,' the old woman replied. 'Tulips? I can take them or leave them.'

'Me too, Peg. Roses are my favourite.'

'Roses are nice.'

'Geoffrey told me he likes roses too. Better than tulips,' she giggled. 'Didn't you, Geoffrey?'

'Well...'

'Peg.' Vicky motored on. 'That's short for... What's it short for? I can't remember. Do you know, Geoffrey?'

'Margaret,' the old woman said. 'It's short for Margaret. But nobody calls me that.'

'Well, Peg's a nice name.' Vicky started to open her folder, 'Anyway, Peg, we can't sit here gossiping all day. I wonder,' she went on, 'if I could trouble you for a glass of water first. Only we've been walking around for hours and, I don't know about Geoffrey, but I'm gasping.'

'Of course, dear,' the old woman said. 'What about a nice cup of tea?'

'We don't want to put you to any trouble, after you've been kind enough to ask us in, do we Geoffrey?'

'No,' said Geoffrey, who didn't like tea.

'I was going to make some for myself anyway.'

'Well, in that case, tea would be lovely, wouldn't it Geoffrey?'

'Er...' said Geoffrey, about to ask if he could have coffee instead.

'Lovely,' said Vicky. 'Can I help you at all?'

'No, dear, the kettle's just boiled.'

But Vicky followed the old woman out, leaving Geoffrey sitting by himself.

They seemed to be gone a long time and overcome with heat and boredom, Geoffrey started dropping off. He was starting to think you had to work very hard in this job to make your commission. He yawned. Maybe he'd rethink his career options.

When the women came back it was Vicky who was carrying the tray, laden with mugs and a plate of chocolate digestives.

'Oh, Geoffrey,' Vicky said, 'You should see Peg's kitchen. It's dotey. And she's cooking the most delicious-smelling stew. Makes me feel quite hungry.'

She handed him a drink.

'And just look at these mugs. They're priceless. Have you ever seen anything like them?'

Geoffrey looked. His mug featured a cartoon pig dressed as a ballerina in a tutu and standing on its hind legs. The old woman's said KA-POW! in yellow comic strip letters, while Vicky's was emblazoned with a crazy looking person at a desk, hair standing on end, and the message *You don't have to be mad to work here, but it helps.*

'Tell me where you bought this, Peg,' said Vicky. 'I just have to get one for the office.'

The old woman couldn't remember. She'd had the mugs a long time, she told them.

At last Vicky got round to describing the product and the way it worked. It seemed very complicated to Geoffrey, all electronic beams and a box named DEREK.

'Direct Electronic Routing Control,' explained Vicky. 'It's an... an acronym – the initials stand for words – or they would if you spelt it Derec with a C instead of a K and had another word beginning with E in there. But we at the company thought DEREK sounded nice and friendly, to reflect the service that we give our clients.'

The old woman nodded in an agreeable manner. Geoffrey could tell Vicky was getting optimistic at last about a sale. But still, it was important, as she had impressed on him, to find out if the old woman was the sole owner of the property and therefore entitled to sign the consent form that Vicky would whip out when she decided enough softening up had been done.

'They have to sign on the spot, Geoffrey,' Vicky had told him. 'We don't ever come back, tell them (even though we do sometimes). This is a special offer and to avail of it they have to commit at once. Also, tell them we're only allowed sell three in any given area. Put them under pressure to decide and let them think this is the last one left. If they have time to think about it, they're likely to change their minds.'

Geoffrey considered it all a bit dishonest. It reminded him of the time his mam had been talked into signing up for a set of encyclopaedias she didn't want by a salesman who had caught her unawares and charmed her into spending much more than she could afford. Not only that, they'd had to buy a special

bookcase for the things and then no one ever looked at them
except Geoffrey, who casually flipping through one time, had
found a section on native tribes that featured women showing
off their bare boobs.

'Think of the peace of mind you'll have, Peg,' Vicky was
explaining, 'knowing that no one can move around the house
without setting the thing off and alerting the authorities.

The old woman looked concerned for the first time. 'I don't
know about that,' she said. 'What about Bobs?'

'Who's Bobs? Your husband?'

'No, Sidney's my husband. Bobs is the cat.'

'Oh, no fears about that. We can position the beams higher
than Bobs can jump.'

'Bobs jumps very high,' said the old woman. 'On to the
curtain rail sometimes.'

Vicky and Geoffrey looked at the curtain rail. It was about
twenty centimetres from the ceiling.

'Well, Peg, you can turn it off, via DEREK, from any room
Bobs happens to be in.'

'So what if an intruder starts wandering about the room
when it's turned off?'

'Okay, say it's in here. The beam will pick up the intruder
when he goes into the hall.'

'Yes, but Bobs goes into the hall, all the time.'

'Can't you keep the cat in one room with you?' Vicky
snapped. Geoffrey sensed she was losing her grip. She recovered
fast, however, and smiled sweetly again. 'I'm sure Bobs likes to
be with his mistress all the time.'

'Well, that's true.'

'I love cats. Don't you love cats, Geoffrey? Where is the little
pet?'

'Oh, around,' said the old woman. 'Hiding probably. He
doesn't care for visitors much.'

'Mm. Pity... So, anyway, Peg, your husband's called Sidney.
That's a nice name. Unusual.'

'Well...' said the old woman.

'Where is he? I mean I have to explain to you, Peg, that in the event of your wanting to avail of our product we would need the signatures... Oh!!'

Geoffrey and the old woman both jumped.

'Oh, Geoffrey, would you ever look at that picture.' Vicky gestured to a reproduction painting on the wall of a raggedy little boy with a tear in his eye. Geoffrey had been looking at it on and off in a vague sort of way, deciding he didn't care for it, but apparently Vicky had only just spotted it. 'Isn't that lovely! Have you ever seen anything as lovely as that! Peg, where did you get it. I'd love one like that in my little flat.'

'I've had it years,' the old woman said. 'Can't remember where it came from now.'

'Sidney probably bought it for you.'

'No...'

'Or you bought it for him. Or maybe one of your children bought it for you. Do you have children, Peg?'

'No... No kiddies...'

'You're better off. My sister, Caroline, has two and, Peg, they've taken over her entire life. The noise they make! The mess! You wouldn't believe it. She doesn't have a life of her own any more.'

'I would have liked some kiddies. They just never came along.' The old woman stared at the picture of the little boy.

'I know what you mean, Peg. Children are a blessing really, aren't they. Despite everything. And then of course they can look after you in your old age.'

The old woman bent over her knitting. Geoffrey wished Vicky would shut up and get on with it.

'Anyway' – it seemed she was at last about to – 'I was just saying that we would need the signatures of all the householders, not just yours, if you understand what I'm saying. Is... er... Sidney at home today?' Vicky cast her eyes around the room as if she might somehow have failed to notice him in the same way as she had overlooked the painting.

'Not really, no.'

'Oh!' Vicky's pudgy fingers clapped against her mouth. 'I hope I haven't stirred sad memories, Peg. I mean, is Sidney... still with us?'

'I'm the sole householder, Victoria.'

Vicky leaned forward and put her hand on the old woman's knee.

'I understand. Believe me, Peg. I haven't been through what you've been through, but I hope you'll believe me when I tell you how much I, and Geoffrey, of course, sympathise with you at this difficult time.'

The old woman looked at Vicky's hand on her knee. She said nothing.

'In view of your circumstances,' Vicky went on, 'I would urge you most strongly to consider our product for your own peace of mind. You very kindly admitted us to your house and luckily for you our intentions are honourable. But there may be occasions in the future where unscrupulous people inveigle their way into your home to take advantage of you. You are lucky that our offer today includes a free alarm activating pad that you can attach to your key-ring, so that if, Peg, you were to find yourself in the unhappy position I have just outlined, you could summon help at the discreet press of a button.' She rummaged in her handbag. 'See, here I have the aforementioned object attached to my own key-ring.' She drew it out like a magician producing a rabbit from a hat. 'This would usually cost you €90 but as I say, it comes free today if you sign up for our product. It is, as you can see, small but ultra-efficient. If I were to press this green button here the authorities would be alerted and would arrive post-haste, so to speak, to come to my assistance. Well, that is to say, if I were at home, which I'm not.'

Vicky had shown Geoffrey the gizmo earlier in the day. The green button you pressed as she had described to the old woman. Then there was the red button. She'd probably get on to that next.

'Say for instance, Geoffrey,' Vicky had explained to him, eyes goggling behind her glasses, 'you were to try and attack me or rape me or something.' She had giggled. 'I would then press this red button here and the authorities would be alerted and come immediately to save me, no matter where I might be. There's a built-in tracking device, see.'

She had pressed the red button and giggled some more. He stared at her.

'No, don't worry. I'm not landing you in it, promise. To avoid the possibility that the button be pressed in error, you twice have to press this white button first. That activates the pad.'

It had all seemed a bit complicated to Geoffrey. Would anyone remember all that in a moment of crisis? Now, as Vicky took a breath about to launch into further explanations, he stood up. He reckoned he'd just about had enough. Vicky and the old woman looked at him.

'Can I use your toilet?' he asked.

'Of course, dear, top of the stairs,' the old woman said.

Vicky gave him a look. He had broken her flow.

However, he could hear her resume after he left the room.

'It's your fault, Peg,' she was saying. 'Your tea. I might have to avail of the facilities myself later.'

Her voice faded to a mumble as he went up the stairs and into the bathroom. He did what he had to do but didn't flush immediately, being in no hurry to join them downstairs again. At the rate she was going, Vicky still had a good twenty minutes of explaining to do. The bathroom was dull and functional and after he had appraised himself in the mirror and squeezed out a blackhead on his nose, he went on to the landing. Deco had told him to take a look around and see if there was anything of value in the houses they visited.

'Even if they sign up for the product,' he said, 'there's a delay before it's installed.'

Deco's brother had done time for robbing and had connections. Apparently, if Geoffrey pointed them in the right direction, there'd be a little bonus coming his way with no risk at all to himself. Geoffrey doubted that the old woman had anything of value – he hadn't spotted anything so far – but you never knew. Carefully, quietly, he pushed open a bedroom door. A neat room, the old woman's probably, with nothing there to catch his eye except for a cat curled up on the floor. The thing didn't move at his approach and suddenly he realised there was something off about it. It wasn't moving at all. He tipped it with his toe. Nothing. Then he noticed it was lying on some sort of a wooden tray. Looking at it closer he saw this was a base with a name carved into it 'BOBS' and the dates 1999-2010. The bloody thing was dead, or rather dead and stuffed. At any rate, its days of climbing up curtain rails were over for good.

Geoffrey smiled to himself at the old woman's cunning. Using the cat as an excuse, she'd given herself a let-out clause. Poor old Vicky, he thought, expending all that hot air for nothing.

There seemed to his eye to be nothing more of interest in there – the jewellery box he opened looked to contain only cheap stuff – so he crossed the landing to the other room. The door was closed shut and he debated whether he should try entering it at all. Curiosity and the prospect of a bonus decided him and as quietly as possible he turned the knob and pushed open the door. Then stopped stock still on the threshold. A skinny old man was sitting up in bed, staring right at him.

Now Geoffrey, having spent time around corpses, knew a dead body when he saw one. He approached cautiously. The old boy was definitely a stiff, that waxen hue, those sunken eyes. Dead a few hours, rigor mortis having set in. Moreover, it looked as though he hadn't died peacefully in his sleep. A bowl of some sort of congealed mess sat on a tray on his lap and the old boy was clutching a spoon in his right hand. His tongue was hanging out of his mouth and it was blue. Geoffrey carefully backed out of the room again and only after he'd closed the door realised he hadn't even noticed if there was anything of value in the place. He decided not to go back in and check. Instead, he flushed the loo and descended the stairs.

Vicky was sitting in the living room by herself. She gave him a dirty look.

'You took your time,' she said.

'I'm a martyr to constipation,' he told her, lifting a phrase from his mam's repertoire.

'Too much information, Geoffrey.'

'Well, you asked. Listen, where's your wan? We need to…'

At that moment the old woman re-entered with a tray on which stood two steaming bowls.

'Peg's very kindly offered us some of her delicious home-made lamb stew, for us to eat while she reads over and signs the papers,' Vicky said. 'Isn't that very good of her, Geoffrey.'

'Mm,' said Geoffrey, thinking faster than he had ever thought before, 'only see I'm a vegetarian. Can't eat meat.'

In retrospect, he realised what he should have done. Seized Vicky by the hand and rushed out with her. However, to be fair, the evidence at that point was only circumstantial. The old boy had probably had a heart attack eating his dinner and either the old woman wasn't aware of it yet, or else was, as June liked to say about her overweight friend Monica who blamed her obesity on glands, in denial.

The old woman looked innocent, he had to admit, her eyes twinkling at them, her hands again busy with the knitting.

'Don't forget to sign the papers,' Vicky said, tucking in.

'I won't forget, dear,' said the old woman. 'I'm just casting off first.'

'This is lovely Geoffrey. You don't know what you're missing.'

Prophetic words that proved to be the last uttered by Vicky in this world. She suddenly started gasping and grabbing at her throat, eyes bulging at them behind her spectacles.

'Something gone down the wrong way, dear,' said the old woman calmly, needles clicking.

Before Geoffrey could blink twice, Vicky had slumped back into the armchair. He jumped up to examine her but she was already limp and lifeless.

'Why?' he asked, staring back in horror at the old woman. 'Why?'

'I thought she'd never shut up. And I could tell she was lying about liking cats. There was insincerity in her voice…' The old woman was rummaging in her knitting bag. 'Where the goodness is it? I'm certain it's in here somewhere. Ah…' She pulled out a little pistol and pointed it at Geoffrey. 'I know you went in there and found Sidney,' she went on. 'I heard the floorboards creak.'

'Why?' he asked again. Other words failed him.

'Sidney killed Bobs,' she said. 'Strangled him in a fit of rage simply because the cat did its business in his shoe. Said Bobs had the evil eye, of all things. Said the cat had never liked him. Said it watched him all the time. Have you ever heard the like!' She looked angrily at Geoffrey.

'Mad!' he said.

'You're telling me. Anyway, that was the first straw. Then, you know, Sidney was just like that Victoria one, wouldn't stop going on and on and on. Especially when he took sick. Forever calling me up those stairs on one pretext or another. Just so he could start going on and on and on again. I couldn't stand it. That was the last straw.'

She waved the gun, then took aim.

'You don't have to kill me,' Geoffrey said. 'I don't say much and I'm good at keeping secrets. I won't tell.'

'You won't,' the old woman said. 'Not when I'm finished with you. Only I wish you'd eaten the stew. This way is so noisy and messy.' She cocked the gun.

'No, listen,' Geoffrey said. While he talked, his fingers abstractedly played with the emergency alert pad Vicky had left on the table. 'I can help you. I can help you dispose of the bodies so no one will know. Otherwise, it's just a matter of time till they come and get you. They'll lock you up, missus, and throw away the key. And they won't let you take Bobs with you into prison. That's for sure.'

'How can you help me?'

Geoffrey explained about the funeral parlour. Then he told the old woman about Dunne Roamin' and she laughed.

'That's a good one,' she said. 'That slogan would certainly attract my attention. So anyway, what's your plan?'

'Well, I'd have to give it a bit of thought. I'd be able to get back into the place no prob. They know me there, see. The family business, like. So then maybe, first off I could embalm these bodies for you so they don't decompose so quick.' Admittedly, he was embellishing his capabilities. He'd never actually done any embalming himself, though he'd watched Uncle Ronald a couple of times. 'Then,' he continued, 'I could maybe smuggle them into coffins with other people.'

Geoffrey had recently seen an episode of a detective series on TV where the villain had done just that.

The old woman looked dubious.

'Sidney's skinny enough but that Victoria one is a big girl. She'd take up all the space herself.

Geoffrey had to admit that was a good point.

'How about this,' the old woman went on. 'Chop her up and put her in a bit at a time?'

'Mm,' Geoffrey said. 'That's possible, I suppose. But I've never chopped anyone up before.'

'How difficult can it be?'

Geoffrey noticed the old woman had relaxed her grip on the gun a bit and it was now pointing down. He wondered how long the authorities would take to arrive. It was only a couple of minutes since he had twice pressed the white and then the red button, after all remembering to get it right in an emergency situation. But he would have to distract the old woman a bit longer.

'Perhaps you could let me examine Sidney,' he suggested. 'Then I'd get a better notion of what was involved, like. How much embalming fluid we'd need, that sort of thing.'

'All right,' the old woman said, raising the gun again. 'But no funny business. You go first.'

It was, as he told his mam later, just as well he hadn't sat waiting for help to arrive.

'I'm that disgusted with the product,' he told her, 'They're selling it under false pretences. I can't in all honesty continue to promote it. I've handed in my notice.'

'Ah, Geoffrey!' his mam said sadly.

'No,' he told her. 'I have another career in mind. And this time I think it's the one for me.'

Walking up the stairs ahead of the old woman, he had been surprised at how calm he was. Well, she was old and he was young. Her reactions would be slower.

'Very sad about poor Bobs,' he said conversationally. 'I'm a cat lover myself. A genuine one.'

So when the old woman started to tell him the story all over again of how Bobs met his demise, she was off guard when Geoffrey, grasping the banister at the top of the stairs, pushed hard against her, causing her to tumble backwards all the way down. He then nimbly leapt after her and grabbed the gun, but in any case she was winded and unable to get up.

'I think my leg's broken, Geoffrey,' she said. 'Why did you do that? I wasn't really going to...' And she passed out.

It was only when the authorities finally arrived, half an hour after Geoffrey had phoned them on his mobile, that she started to come round.

'What's going on here then?' the burly guard had asked regarding Geoffrey with deep suspicion. After all, here was a youth, albeit respectably dressed, but with a gun and standing over what seemed to be a dear little old lady.

'After I explained,' Geoffrey told his mam, 'and they looked round the place themselves, the same guard clapped me on the back and told me I'd shown great presence of mind. He told me they could do with more young men like me in the force and if I wanted he'd put in a good word. So that's what I'm going to do, mam. I'm going to apply to become a guard.'

'Geoffrey!' His mam's face was radiant with pride, and something else. 'But tell me,' she went on, 'had the poor soul really broken her leg?'

'Don't think so. Just twisted it a bit.'

'And what about the alarm button you pressed?'

'Yeah, those fellers arrived an hour after the guards I called. When I argued with them, they told me I had to take my place in the queue like everyone else. It was a busy evening, they said. People pressing their alarm buttons all over the place. Then they said I shouldn't have pressed the button at all because I wasn't the keyholder and where was she anyway. So then I told them she was in the living room in an armchair in front of the fire. Poisoned to death.'

'Oh Geoffrey! And that could have been you, too. It doesn't bear thinking about.'

'Can you imagine that, mam! Killed because she talked too much! Well, the old girl was clearly off her rocker. I mean, doing in her old man, like that? I mean to say. Murdering him in cold blood, over a cat!'

Suddenly his mam came over all shifty. 'There's probably much more to it than we'll ever know, Geoffrey,' she said. 'Sometimes a woman gets driven to the brink and can't see any other way out. She's desperate and not thinking straight. So she raises the knife and... ka-pow! Lucky for her if she has access to a means of permanently disposing of the body. Lucky for her.'

Geoffrey looked at his mam and she looked back at him.

'It wasn't a knife, mam.'

'Yes, it was, son,' she said softly. 'Yes it was.'

MOUSE

That fat woman, huffing and puffing down the bus, was about to sit next to her. Sabrina recognised the hypnotic glint in the woman's eye. The predator singling out its victim. Slowly slowly she took her plastic bag, as she had to, off the vacant space beside her and put it on her lap. The woman plumped down heavily.

'Great to get a seat,' she says to no one in particular.

Sabrina stared out of the window.

'Not a bad evening, howsomever, thank God.'

Howsomever?

Sabrina tried and failed not to turn towards the woman and make a whimpering noise. The woman composed her cheery red face for conversation. Sabrina looked away again, at the long street with its dreary houses and mean shops. She exhaled on to the glass and miraculously the scene disappeared.

'What I always say is...' the woman started.

Sabrina sighed in resignation. If only she could exhale on the woman.

'Hiya Dolores. Howaya?'

The sudden croak behind her ear made Sabrina jump.

'Howaya, love. Howaya, Carmel.'

An old woman with a long thin face, brown as a kipper, had unwittingly come to the rescue. The fat woman swivelled round so Sabrina was squashed even more towards the window. She tried not to listen but couldn't help hearing.

'...He hasn't!' kipper-face exclaimed.

'He has. Running for the bus.'

'Ah well now you see. That's something I'd never do. That's only asking for trouble, if you ask me.'

'There's always the next one.'

'Eventually.'

'Mind you, I couldn't blame anyone for running, the service the way it is. An hour and a half I stood the other day, waiting on one of these yokes.'

'In the pouring rain, I suppose.'

'And just to think, I saw him Tuesday in Mooneys with a rake of pints in front of him. Mind you, he didn't look good then. I remember thinking it at the time, Carmel. Funny colour on him.'

'Always had a funny colour, didn't he, Dolores, though. Kind of maroo-on.'

'That what you call it? I'd say more purple.'

'Violet.'

'Heliotrope.'

'*Je veux manger*,' thought Sabrina. She was on her way home from her Thursday night French class. '*J'ai faim*. I have hunger.'

She thought of the chicken breasts – two of them – she had cooked before she went out, cooling in the oven, ready to be popped into the fridge. You shouldn't put hot things in the fridge, she read in a magazine. It creates bacteria.

'...She had to have it cut out, but that won't be the end of it if you ask me.'

'It always stays in the system, that class of a yoke.'

'You can't escape your fate, Dolores, not if you ask me.'

As the bus passes a church. Sabrina noticed that while the fat woman blessed herself, the two elderly nuns in the seat in front of them didn't. Maybe they were exempt. Maybe they didn't need a blessing. But while she was considering this, already it was too late. The bus had driven past the church and was now in front of a butcher's shop. Sabrina couldn't be seen to bless herself alongside lamb chops and braising steak.

A chicken sandwich with mayonnaise. Some cucumber and a slice of red pepper. Finely chopped onion. A touch of mustard or maybe mango chutney if she still had some. She was starving, having skipped dinner before going to the class. Perhaps that was why she now felt low. Nothing at all to do with the fact that the man she chatted to in the first two classes had failed to turn up for the third time and possibly, probably, wouldn't return now. The teacher got them all to choose French names and his was Antoine. Perhaps his real name was Anthony, Tony. She didn't know. Perhaps it wasn't. Her own French name was Thérèse. Not after the saint, the Little Flower, which is what people assumed, but after a murderess in a book she once read. To christen her Sabrina was her dad's idea, after a dumb blonde who appeared on a TV show back in the days, along with a squat, balding, bespectacled comedian, who looked just like Sabrina's dad. The dumb blonde, tall, with huge breasts, and a very visible cleavage in the sequinned swimsuit they made her wear, was literally dumb, only uttering a single sentence at the end of every half-hour show, to the merriment of the audience and the feigned astonishment of the balding man, amazed that she could string more than two words together. But this Sabrina hadn't lived up to her namesake. She was timid, plain and flat-chested, with mousey hair, a big nose, poor eyesight and thick spectacles to compensate. The only similarity being that she didn't talk much.

Her dad was long dead and Sabrina's mother, too, from whom she has inherited only absence and lack of colour.

'No oomph, the pair of you,' her dad had liked to say. He had always prided himself on his oomph.

Sabrina squeezed past the fat woman to get out.

'Cheer up, love,' the woman smiled. 'It might never happen.'

That's just the point, Sabrina thought. If only it, something, would.

But at least there was the comfort of the chicken mayonnaise sandwich to look forward to. And a hot chocolate drink. And some comedy programme on television.

It was a five-minute walk from the bus-stop to her flat in a converted convent, down dark streets lit only flickeringly by amber lamps caught in the branches of huge trees, roots cracking the concrete of the pavement around them as if about to break free.

Sabrina opened the security lock of the outer gate by punching in a code number that she always dreaded she would get wrong and, as she supposed, set off flashing lights and sirens. But she got it right as ever; the gate clicked open and she was able to walk across the courtyard to the steps that lead up to her block. Some evenings as now, she seemed to glimpse veiled heads peeping from the shadows, while long black skirts swished away from her round stone walls along with the autumn leaves. In some ways it was ironic that she had landed in this place. At school, the nuns were always suggesting to her – perhaps her plainness led to an assumption of piety – that she might have a vocation. The memory even now made her shiver, although her way of life was surely dull and austere enough for the most demanding of gods. But still she had her secret fantasies, her small indulgences as those now awaiting her.

She climbed the stairs to the first floor and glanced at the door opposite her own, where Eileen lived. Eileen dabbled in astrology but even so gave the impression of being much more down to earth than Sabrina herself, perhaps because she worked in waste disposal. (Sabrina herself was a clerical officer whose main occupations were photocopying and filing documents written in impenetrable bureaucratese). Just now Eileen's door was blank as a blind eye – no sound of flamenco music escaped from under it, no garlicky odour of paella. Anyway, Sabrina wasn't in the mood for chat. *Non, absolument pas.*

Her own apartment struck her as a little chilly. October already. She would have to turn the heating up though she liked to delay this move as long as possible, for reasons of economy. Sabrina carefully put her bag down on the sofa that doubled as her bed. Eileen always expressed amazement that Sabrina bothered to tidy it back each morning since she so seldom had visitors. For Sabrina's own part, she reckoned it would be the thin end of some inexorable wedge to leave it the way Eileen did, simply throwing a few coloured scraps of cloth over it during the day in loose concealment.

Supposing a man called! Whatever would he think, the bed in full view!

She took off her coat and scarf and hung them on a hook in the tiny area that served her as a hall. Then she went through to the kitchen area, taking a deep anticipatory breath along with a spatula. She opened the oven door.

And screamed.

Her two breasts sat as she had left them, nice and brown and crisp, and flecked with tarragon. But crouched on one, interrupted in the very process of devouring it, was a small grey mouse.

Unperturbed by her scream, the mouse continued to regard her with bright inquisitive eyes. She slammed the door shut and then opened it again. The mouse had retreated to the bottom of the oven, by the gas burner, the way, no doubt, he entered. Still he looked at her as if asking did she really mean him to leave before finishing his dinner. Not very charitable! Finally, she banged on the metal tray with the spatula, and the mouse scurried down behind the burner.

She couldn't touch either of the bits of meat and threw them out. Then she looked around for further clues. She noticed how the bread bin was speckled with little crumbs that were too black to have come even from a granary loaf. Mouse droppings! She observed how a corner of the waxed paper wrapping had been chewed away and the crust within nibbled off. My God, she thought, how long has this creature been feasting on my food. She might have caught a disease. Hadn't she read recently how a man died after (inexplicably) licking rat urine off a golf ball? The symptoms were described as resembling those of 'flu. Sabrina had been sniffing more than usual. The bread followed the chicken into the bin.

There was nothing now to eat except a bit of cucumber, an onion and a red pepper. She took milk from the fridge – presumably mouse proof – and made herself a hot chocolate drink which she swallowed without relish. The television comedy wasn't funny. That night she slept badly, imagining she could hear the little creature scurrying around. Creature? Creatures? There was probably a whole dynasty.

On her way home from work the next day, she visited a hardware store and bought three mousetraps.

'It's the cold drives them in,' the man said as he puts them in a bag. He looked vaguely familiar to her, a gingery individual with big freckled hands, the skin of his face scraped red raw from shaving or the weather, since an icy blast continuously blew in the open door. 'This doesn't work, you might like to try poison.' He smiled, showing sparse teeth.

Sabrina nodded, knowing from her reading, however, that the creatures suffer agony after ingesting the blue crystals. The traps were at least quick.

At home, she cut off a lump of the cheese she had purchased, mousetrap cheese her dad used to call it, hard and yellow and sour ('bit like yer mam, wha'!'). She divided the lump into three small cubes and carefully positioned one piece on each of the traps. She then placed them around the kitchen area – one in the oven, one next to the bread bin, one on the floor leading out to the room where she slept.

It was Friday and she had no work the next day so she sat up late, grimly watching a film, something about gangsters drilling other gangsters in their knees because they had double-crossed them, and then inexplicably going to Venice and having a gondola chase on the canals. She couldn't concentrate because she was constantly listening out for the snap of the trap. None came. Not until past three in the morning while she lay in bed, eyes wide open. It made her jump, sounding like a sharp hand-clap in the darkness. She couldn't bring herself to look and tossed and turned until dawn. Then in a grey light, she crossed over to her kitchen area and examined the traps. It was the one by the bread-bin that had been sprung: a little furry body curled around as if asleep, a single bead of black blood on the counter. Sabrina got a plastic bag and managed to lift the whole thing without touching the mouse at all. But before she disposed of the bag, she thought she caught a glimpse of a bright eye peeping out at her as if to say, No, not charitable at all!

Nevertheless, the mouse was certainly dead and already stiff. In her plastic lined bin it went beside the chicken and bread of the previous night. Then she mopped up the blood with some kitchen paper drenched in disinfectant and threw that away, too. She lifted out the rubbish and took it to the wheelie bins that serve the whole of the block. No way was Sabrina staying one more minute in the same room as a dead mouse.

She clambered back into her still cosy bed and slept heavily, with dreams that swam off like glittering little fishes when she tried on waking to recapture them.

Later in the day, she met Eileen on the landing (she had been listening out for her) and told her of her adventure.

'An old building like this,' Eileen said, 'must be crawling with all sorts of wild life.'

And even though Sabrina caught no more mice in the traps that she laid out each night, she felt uneasy, like when you get an uncontrollable itch when talking about fleas, sure that she could hear scratching sounds, tiny feet racing over hard surfaces. Above all, she remembered the rather sweet face of the creature in the oven when it looked over at her as if to say, But aren't we sisters under the skin? And isn't there enough here for both of us?

It was the following weekend and she was sharing a bottle of Rioja and some nacho cheese tortilla chips with Eileen in Eileen's Spanish-flavoured apartment – fans and castanets on the walls and a reproduction of Salvador Dali's melting clock. Eileen had been in love with a Catalan separatist before he turned out to be gay but she remained in love with the place he called home. She was reclining on the bed, a large woman in her late thirties, long greasy hair piled untidily on her head, with dangling silver ear-rings, black leggings and a baggy black tee-shirt emblazoned with the message *No Pasaran*. There were tortilla chip fragments all down it.

'You should borrow Koshka,' Eileen opined.

Koshka, it turned out, was a three-legged cat belonging to one of her work colleagues, a waste-disposal expert who had recently heartbreakingly discovered that he was allergic to his pet.

'You could mind him while Tomás looks out for a good home.'

Sabrina looked dubious.

'I'd take him – he's such a sweetie – only Pablito wouldn't have it.'

Pablito was Eileen's stout ginger cat, now sitting on Sabrina's lap and occasionally sinking his claws through her skirt into her thighs. Eileen was under the erroneous impression that Sabrina and Pablito liked each other.

'He always comes to you,' she said.

Sabrina suspected this was because Pablito knew that she hated him.

'What do you think?'

'Well...'

'It's a great idea, Sabrina. Koshka's an indoor cat and even though short a leg is extremely agile. I'm sure he's an excellent mouser.'

Seizing on Sabrina's hesitancy, Eileen made the necessary arrangements and Koshka arrived that very evening, brought over by Tomás, a small neat man with red eyes and a runny nose. He couldn't stop sneezing and Sabrina turned her head slightly to avoid the germs. But you couldn't catch allergies, could you?

'Maybe you'll take to each other,' he said. 'Maybe you'll want to keep him.'

'Maybe,' she replied, eyeing the malevolent white face behind the bars of the cage.

Tomás gave her detailed instructions about Koshka's likes, dislikes and needs, as well as a large supply of gourmet cat food.

'He just doesn't care for the cheaper varieties and don't give him scraps: they aren't good for him. (*Atishoo*! excuse me) Some lightly poached whiting goes down a treat and he is fond of his bickies but make sure he has plenty of fresh water to go with them or he may get dehydrated... He's got a bit of rot between his toes, so here's the cream you have to put on after cleaning the black stuff away with warm water and cotton-wool buds... You have cotton-wool buds, I suppose?' he asked in a sudden panic. Sabrina assured him that she had. They could be so useful in so many ways.

Tomás departed in a miasma of moist exhalations, with a final distant wave to his three-legged friend. Sabrina and the now-at-large white cat considered each other in silence. Then the cat turned his back and walked over to the sofa, springing on to the place where Sabrina liked to sit. He established himself there, looking at her as if daring her to try and move him.

During the day, when she was at work, the cat was confined to the flat. It was therefore a mystery to her to return on the second evening to find that he had caught not a mouse but a frog. As far as she knew there had never been any frogs in her apartment before. It lay under the radiator, twitching slightly and therefore still alive. She took the spatula from the drawer, aware of the cat's eyes glittering at her, and lifted the frog off the floor. The poor thing was shrunken and she put it in a bowl of water. To her horror the frog instantly swelled up and burst. She hastily poured the mess into the lavatory and pulled the chain.

The next evening a small yellow bird lay stiff on the sofa. Could it have flown in the window? Later she heard from Eileen that old Mrs Finnegan, who lived on the ground floor, had lost her canary.

'She can't understand it. Chirpy was locked in his cage. Now the cage is empty.'

Sabrina opened her mouth to speak but shut it again.

It was her own fault, of course. She had left ajar a small high window in her bathroom to get rid of steam and unpleasant odours. The cat must somehow have climbed out that way, although she couldn't imagine how. Not with only three legs. Or else perhaps Chirpy, making a doomed bid for freedom, flew in that way. When Sabrina went back to her own apartment, she found Koshka entertaining himself by chasing a large, lazy wasp that had forgotten to hibernate. Absorbed in *Buffy the*

Vampire Slayer, Sabrina failed to notice, until the commercial break, that the buzzing had stopped. She looked at Koshka, who was licking his lips and staring at her through narrowed eyes.

She conscientiously gave him clean water. She fed him his gourmet meals, suspecting however that he also raided her bin for scraps during the day while she was out, since she regularly came across bits of chicken bone and skin in odd places on the floor, plastic pots of cream or yogurt licked clean. Once she left out the butter dish by mistake and later found nothing left of a quarter pound except a few whitish hairs. She wouldn't let him sleep on her bed, although she reckoned that he leapt up anyway when she was asleep. She tried once to clean his feet but he scratched her arm quite badly, so she gave up. Instead Eileen had come in to do it for her even though Sabrina didn't care to have her visit too often, she made such a mess.

'Isn't he a pet,' Eileen cooed, 'Isn't he a dote!'

Koshka arched his back and rubbed up against her. He even let her wash his three feet, although under protest.

'Poor love,' she soothed, 'who's got sore tootsies...?'

Sabrina told her that although Koshka had so far caught no mice, he somehow managed to bring in trophies (not mentioning the canary!) which he then deposited around the flat.

'That's natural. That's in your nature, isn't it, sweetie. They're hunters, after all, Sabrina. Never forget it.'

'I wish he'd hunt mice.'

'Maybe there aren't any. Maybe you got the only one in the entire building.'

Eileen took the last jaffa cake (crumbs all down her front) and broke it in half, giving one piece to the cat.

'Oh, you aren't supposed to!'

'Nonsense, he deserves it for being a good boy... So anyway Sabrina, you're going to keep him, aren't you.'

'Er...' The woman and the cat were looking at her.

'Ah, you must!'

'Hasn't Tomás found anyone to take him yet?'

'Not really. A fully grown three-legged moggie isn't exactly easy to place... And you're such a cat person. You know how Pablito absolutely adores you.'

Sabrina was finding it difficult to sleep. She was aware of the cat staring at her through the darkness, waiting for her to drop off so that he could jump up on to the bed. Sometimes she got a strong feeling that he considered it his bed, and her the usurper. She was already unnerved after returning from work to find a decapitated hamster on her pillow (having overslept for once, through lack of restful slumber over almost a week, she hadn't had time in the morning to turn the bed back into a sofa). She had to remove the pillowcase, sponge the pillow (her only one) with disinfectant and let it dry on the hot press before inserting it in a clean cover. Nor could she help wondering once more how Koshka got out (a locked room mystery), whom the hamster belonged to and above all where its head had gone. But her own head was throbbing and all explanations were beyond her.

Finally she got up and stumbled across the room in the dark to the bathroom. She switched on the light and opened the cabinet to take two paracetamol from a plastic tub. She swallowed them down with bathroom tap water, something she normally wouldn't have done in case there were dead pigeons in the tank. But she was so very very tired. She leaned against the basin and looked at her face in the mirror. Without her glasses, all she could see was a blur, mousey fur and a pink snout. Then she staggered back into the room.

Afterwards she was at a loss to explain it all. She must have been dreaming or at least half-asleep. For it seemed to her suddenly that the cat had grown and grown or she had shrunk like Alice in Wonderland after eating the mushroom. The now enormous creature, his mouth wide in a triumphant smile, pounced and caught her in his paw. She felt his fishy breath on her and saw the glint of his pointy teeth. Was he about to bite her head off too? Not yet. First, it seemed, he wanted to play. He tossed her to the ground and put his paw down on her but she wriggled and slipped away. He came after her but she was quick and scuttled under the bed, pulling her long tail after her just in time. She waited then, her nose twitching, her whiskers. She backed off even further.

It was then that she bumped into it, where it had rolled, the hamster's head. Its glassy eyes stared into hers out of the murk and it seemed to say 'You can't escape your fate, Sabrina.' In terror she almost rushed out again but realised just in time that under the bed was the only place she was safe.

Her heart was racing. At least three hundred beats per minute. At this rate it would give out before the cat caught her. She saw his white face, his glittering eye, as he pressed against the bed and reached his paw in as far as it would go towards her, she smelt the paralysing odour of the hunter...

In the morning, having woken up on the floor of her room with a crick in her neck and bruised ribs, she phoned into work sick. Then without a glance at the now normal-sized cat, who was stretched out in full possession of the bed, pretending to sleep, she went down to the hardware store where the gingery man was rubbing his raw neck.

'I'll take some of your poison,' she said. 'Against vermin.'

'Oh yes? Traps didn't work then?'

'I just want to be sure.'

He lifted down a packet marked with a skull.

'Now keep this away from husbands and boyfriends. I don't want to be an accessory. *C'est très dangereux.*'

She looked at him.

'I'm Guillaume, from the class,' he explained. 'Billy, actually.'

She remembered now. He sat at the back. Didn't say much.

'I'm Thérèse.'

'I know,' he said, smiling with his sparse teeth.

The autumn sunshine glinted on the glass of her spectacles, masking her eyes as she paid him.

'*Au revoir!*' he called after her. '*À bientôt!*'

Then Sabrina went to the fishmonger's and bought a quantity of whiting, as well as some smoked salmon. Possibly there would soon be something to celebrate and so she treated herself to a bottle of Chardonnay as well.

Back home, Koshka watched her as she boiled the white fish. He had caught no trophy that day as yet. Perhaps he reckoned he was stalking the next one. That it was only a matter of time. She emptied the fish into his bowl.

'It's too hot,' she told him. 'You'll burn your mouth. We'll wait for it to get cool.'

She took the bowl into the bathroom and locked the door. Then she opened the packet with the skull on it and read the instructions. She mixed five times the specified amount in with the fish, turning it bright blue. But cats are colour-blind, aren't they? She wrapped up the packet and washed her hands.

'Silly me,' she said brightly to the cat, 'taking your dinner into the toilet.'

She put the bowl down on the floor and then busied herself with other chores, emptying the rubbish bin, for instance and taking the plastic sack down to the wheelie bins. When she returns Koshka hadn't touched his dinner. He stared at her.

'You don't want it?' she asked. 'What a pity. I got it for you specially. As a treat.'

She lifted up the bowl and placed it on the counter, lightly covering it with a saucer. She puts her coat on again. The cat watched her every move.

'Just going for some milk. Silly me, I forgot to buy any.'

After she shut the door and locked it, she stood outside for a while listening. Soon she heard a smash as something, a saucer perhaps, fell to the floor.

She went to see a film. It was about a gangster who set his enemies on fire, and then inexplicably went to Austria where a ski chase ensued.

On her return, in the yard ghostly with nuns, she met Eileen just coming home from her waste disposal job.

'How's Koshka?'

'Grand.'

'Caught any mice yet?'

'He nearly did. Last night. It got away.'

'Pity... Have you decided about keeping him?'

'Tomás can stop looking for a new home.'

'Oh good. He will be really pleased.'

The light over the door glinted on Sabrina's glasses, masking her eyes. Eileen, her psychic powers alerted, suddenly felt uneasy. What was that smell, that effluvium? The paralysing odour of the hunter? And surely that couldn't be the tip of a twitching tail that she glimpsed under her neighbour's long skirt as she padded away?

'So,' she asked uncertainly, 'do you want me to come in later and help you do his feet?'

'No, that's all right,' said Sabrina, her squeaky voice unusually strong and firm. 'I don't think it'll be necessary any more.'

And as things turned out, it wasn't.

PRESSED POWDER

Following his aunt's slightly skewed directions, he arrived at last at a house that seemed to grow out of the granite boulders that tumbled down the mountain behind it. No ivy-covered cottage this, no roses round the cabin door. The facade scowled at him. There was no answer to his knock, but a path led round the house to a garden beyond, its scents and exploding colours drawing him on.

The sound of water attracted him. A stream gushed down the hillside into a pond covered with enormous lily pads, even a frog poised to leap. Another frog, this time huge, a lump of clay roughly moulded, sat at the side of the pond. Beside it, frog-faced too, a woman was pulling weed from the water and muttering to herself.

'Hi,' said David uneasily. He might be thought to be trespassing.

The woman frowned up at him.

'I'm David. Sheila Kavanagh's nephew. She rang...'

'Ah!'

The woman stood up with difficulty. She was heavy, in her late sixties, David reckoned. About his aunt's age, but fighting it. A thick pencil had drawn heavy eyebrows over grey bristles, hair hennaed to an unnatural red. The pale powder on her face was streaked with sweat.

'Didi!' she said, shooting out a hand towards him like a frog's tongue. 'Oh no,' withdrawing the hand, 'don't shake. It's wet.'

Actually, what she said was 'Is vet.' His aunt of course had neglected to mention that her neighbour was foreign. Not that it mattered. David just wondered what else she had forgotten to tell him.

'It's very difficult for me,' Didi was saying. 'Joe used to do all this,' indicating the pile of weeds.

'*Myriophyllum aquaticum*,' said David casting a knowing eye at the weed. 'Parrots' Feathers. Once in, it's very difficult to get rid of it.'

'You telling me something I don't know already?'

She took him round but the garden was huge. Several acres, David thought.

'Did you see the magazine article about us?' Didi asked. 'No? I will show you later.'

At a certain point, perhaps impatient with the way he lingered over every specimen, exclaiming with surprise and pleasure, Didi left him to go back to pulling out the Parrots' Feathers.

The garden was a delight in almost every way. Except for the lumpy sculptures scattered around that he kept tripping over or bumping into, rough forms, animal and human, some crumbling, some covered in a green mould, like gangrenous flesh.

Eventually, feeling that he could do no less, David offered to help with the pond-weed pulling.

'No,' Didi said. 'If you want to help you can spray the roses.'

And she gave him a gun to poison the greenfly.

The garden sloped down to the edge of a reed-fringed lake. A golden path led across gentle waves from the setting sun to a small jetty. The end of a perfect day, thought David, wielding the spray gun. A perfect place. He glanced down at the *nerine sarniensis*, a marvellous specimen, its crimson umbels seeming to curl with delight as he gazed. He envied the lucky people who lived surrounded by such loveliness.

But when he looked up again, he gasped aloud. Black against the gold, a hunched shape had materialised at the lake's edge, a troll risen from the reeds.

'There's Solange at last,' said Didi. And called out, 'Come up and meet David.'

He watched the figure clumping towards them, head bent. Concentrating on the stony path. Step by dragging step – she had a limp – becoming more defined. She was younger than he had first imagined, hardly more than a child, in a grey dress like an old-fashioned school tunic, a navy cardigan pulled out of shape by wear. Ankle socks and laced up shoes. Cropped mouse-brown hair dragged across her forehead and secured with a tight clip at the side.

'Hi,' said David.

Solange raised glittering eyes and looked at him.

The expedition had been his aunt's idea. He had turned up on his annual duty visit and when he told her for what had to be the nth time that he was studying botany at Trinity College in Dublin, she had smiled encouragingly without understanding anything except that it had to do with flowers. Probably she thought of him as some sort of over-educated florist.

'There's this most wonderful garden,' she'd said. 'You'd love it. And Didi's a real character. I'll ring her, see if you can drop round.'

He'd expected the usual flower beds of hardy annuals, perhaps a herbaceous border, a pond with goldfish and maybe even a fishing gnome, immaculately weed-free lawns edged with one or two of the palms that flourished unexpectedly in this south-western part of the country. So he could scarcely believe what he found. It was as if spring, summer and autumn had come together at once: flowers from the different seasons blooming together. Moreover, plants that shouldn't have been able to survive in the cold northern climate at all were flourishing here. Plants that he'd only ever seen in glasshouses: spiky *callistemon citrinus*, sweet golden *acacia dealbata*, fiery red *crocosmia*. Glorious fat blooms sucking in the rare sunshine, great ferns that wouldn't be out of place in a rain forest, even a flowering cactus. And beside all this, in a rock garden, alpine flowers so delicate you had to stoop right down to see them.

Solange had green eyes streaked with yellow, like exotic glinting stones. Otherwise her face was forgettable, wan and slightly flabby. Her hand, when he shook it, was clammy and seemed to stick to his. Close to, he could see that she wasn't the child he had taken her for after all. Her body was lumpy in the right and wrong places. Tired lines creased the skin around her eyes, her forehead. When she opened her mouth to speak, her teeth were yellow.

'Day-vid,' she intoned, as if making magic with the word.

'Solange is an artist,' said Didi, touching her daughter's shoulder. 'All the sculpture,' gesturing at the frog.

'Ah,' said David, not knowing what else to add. He smiled encouragingly. 'Well done.'

'We go to the house to drink tea,' said Didi in a way that made it sound like an order. 'I show you photographs.'

'Oh, good,' said David.

The large room was stifling, with an open fire blazing unseasonably. After two cups of some sort of herbal stuff, David felt dizzy. He was looking at the article in the magazine with its pictures of the garden and Didi with a scarf round her hair displaying a lily.

'Kiss Proof,' said Solange. Then when he looked puzzled, she laughed, displaying her yellow teeth. 'Call yourself a botanist, Day-vid! That's its name.'

Another picture showed an old man with a cap, digging.

'Joe,' said Didi.

Solange went over to the mantelpiece and took down a framed black and white photograph.

'This is him.'

David looked at the scrunched face, eyes glancing somewhere out of frame.

'This is the picture that we put on his coffin.'

'Ah.'

He wished he could go home. It wasn't just the heat that made him uncomfortable. These two women were seriously weird. Whatever had his aunt been thinking of, sending him to them?

'Do you like this room?' asked Didi, putting her face close to his. He caught the scent of the pressed powder she had freshly applied, paler than her own skin, ending at the red and crepey neck.

'It's very nice.'

In a way it was, but like a room out of an advertising brochure. Pale chintz furnishings, red velvet drapes, large vases full of dried flowers, woven rugs scattered over the carpets, prints of hunting scenes on the walls. Only the photograph of Joe gave a personal touch.

'I redecorated after my husband left.'

'Oh.'

'He went off with a childhood sweetheart,' Solange said.

Didi threw her head back and barked a laugh.

'How sweet is that?' she chortled.

'Er...'

'And the funniest thing,' Solange added, not smiling, 'is that he was ten years older than maman and the woman was his age. Sixty-five, then. He ran off with an older woman.'

'What can you expect?' Didi said. 'He made his money in pornography.'

'Dirty postcards.' Solange fixed her greeny-yellow eyes on David. 'Just think of those two geriatrics doing it!'

She offered him a slice of chocolate cake. 'Home made,' she said, 'by maman.'

'When I found out he was seeing her again, I put all his things into black plastic bags and drove round to her house while she was at her son's funeral, and left them in the porch.'

'Her son's funeral?'

'He died,' said Solange.

'Good God!' The cake was slippery with syrup. It slid down David's throat like some living creature.

'Show David the photographs,' Didi said suddenly.

Oh no, he thought. Would these be the dirty postcards or some incriminating evidence against the husband for whom, at that point, David felt a certain sympathy?

'I must wash my hands first,' David said to buy time. 'I'm all sticky.'

'As the bishop said to the actress,' said Solange. 'I'll show you where.'

She led him along a corridor lit by electric lamps in the form of flaming torches.

'I had sex with him,' she whispered.

'Who?' asked David as a reflex.

'The dead son. Not when he was dead, of course. That wouldn't have been much fun.'

'No.'

'I've had sex with fourteen men.'

'...Wow.'

'Mostly old men. They like me. Here's the bathroom.'

David locked the door and washed his hands. He washed his face. He had a pee and washed his hands again. He took out his mobile phone to ring his aunt but there was no signal. That damn mountain, he supposed. With trepidation he emerged from the bathroom.

'Do you want to have sex with me?' asked Solange matter-of-factly.

'Er... Thank you but I'm engaged. To be married.' It was almost true and he thought longingly of Aisling, athletic, tennis-playing, wholesome, adroit in bed, if a bit predictable.

'Oh,' Solange said, and led the way back. He noticed how, as she limped ahead of him, her buttocks rippled in a circular motion under the rough fabric of her gym slip. And had the sudden disturbing suspicion that she was wearing no underpants.

David was genuinely thrilled by the album, hundreds of exquisite shots of flowers, in close up. Didi's harsh face softened as she looked at them.

'These photographs are terrific,' David said. 'You should publish them.'

'Ah well...' Didi simpered. 'Who would care?'

'There are magazines... or maybe you could have them made into cards.'

'Do you think so?' She smiled, showing crooked teeth. 'What a nice boy.'

'Let's have a drink,' said Solange. 'Not tea. A liqueur.'

'Well, I'm driving...'

'One drink.'

'You can sleep here,' said Solange. 'If not with me or maman, then in one of our many spare beds. We keep them ready for visitors.'

Didi shook her head at her daughter as she left the room.

'My baby,' she said. 'She is so droll. Don't you think so, David?'

'Er... Yes, a bit.'

'So talented and clever. And in her own special way, you know, beautiful. A man could do worse.'

My God, was the woman match-making?

'Actually, you know, David,' Didi ruffled his hair, causing goosepimples to rise on his back. 'Solange is not my baby at all. I am infertile. I was raped by German soldiers as a child in the war and got a disease.'

Under her hand, David squirmed like an insect just landed in a spider's web.

'I bought Solange from a woman in Belarus. Her given name was Lacrimosa – tearful one. The mother said she was Chernobyl victim but I think this was an excuse. She was drunk all the time. Beat the baby. That's why, as you may have noticed, Solange has a limp.'

'Oh dear.'

'I gave the woman fifty dollars. Probably she drank herself to death. I hope.'

'Does Solange know?'

'Of course. I tell her everything. She tells me everything. And if we don't tell, we still know. We are very close. I would do anything for Solange. Anything.' She fixed David with an intense and angry look. 'If anyone else ever hurts her...'

'So poor Joe passed away, 'David changed the subject, quite effectively, he thought, since Didi shifted off. 'You must miss him a lot, with such a big garden and all.'

'Yes. I need new gardener. One who knows about flowers. One who does what he is told.' She looked hard into his eyes. He coughed and took a swallow of the cold and bitter tea.

'Yes, poor Joe. It was a tragedy,' Didi said.

'Was he sick?'

'No, not at all. Fit as a fiddle. Which he played, by the way. Irish jigs and reels. Sometimes we had a session here. Just the three of us. Joe played and we danced.'

Didi with her great weight, Solange with her limp.

Solange returned with a tray of glasses and a clay bottle.

'Balsam,' she said. 'Made of herbs. Good for you.'

She poured the thick brown liquid into the glasses and proposed a toast.

'To botany!'

'Aargh!' said David. The drink tasted like fermented grass. It was also very strong. He picked up the bottle: 51 per cent proof.

'From Latvia,' Solange said. 'Different, isn't it.'

'It certainly is.'

'Joe drank,' Didi said. 'No, not this. Guinness, of course. Whiskey. And poteen, which he made himself.'

'You think this is strong!' Solange laughed. 'You should try Joe's poteen.'

'And of course he smoked.'

'A disaster waiting to happen.'

'Fell asleep full of drink with a lighted cigarette. Poof!'

'There was nothing left to identify. Just sticky bones.'

The women were like a double act or a monologue in two voices.

'Poor Joe.' Didi refilled her glass and made to pour more for David, who hastily covered his. A brown drop fell on the back of his hand. Solange flicked out her tongue and licked her lips.

'Was this quite recent?'

'Oh yes. Just three weeks ago.'

'The day after the funeral,' Solange said, 'I was driving back from the city and mamma was in the village visiting a friend, so I called to pick her up.'

'The minute I got in the car, I could smell it,' Didi said.

'Poteen,' said Solange, giggling. 'Maman asked if I had been drinking.'

'Of course, she hadn't. I knew that. Solange is like you, David. She will not drink and drive.'

'I had smelt the poteen myself for the last few miles.'

They both looked at David, eyes bright, smiles on their lips.

'It was Joe.'

'He hadn't been able to say goodbye properly so he had come to find us.'

'Good God,' said David.

'We stopped the car and had a little goodbye ceremony there by the side of the road. We thanked him for his work and told him that despite everything we loved him.'

The word 'loved' enunciated, David thought, with a ravening kind of hunger.

'And when we got back in the car, the smell had gone.'

'Of course.' Didi smiled at David. 'But we have frightened you with our talk.' And she ruffled his hair again.

'Spirits are everywhere, David. Nothing strange about it.'

'You just need to tune in.'

'Sometimes we have meetings here and speak to the spirits. People come from a long way. We have the gift, you see.'

'We invited your aunt after your uncle died, but she refused.'

'Maybe you would like to talk to your uncle, David.'

'No,' David said. 'Not really.'

'Or someone else. Your fiancée, perhaps.'

'Aisling isn't dead.'

'Aisling,' said Solange. 'Ah.'

'She doesn't have to be dead. Our essences wander freely, but most of us don't know it.'

Solange grabbed David's hand.

'I think someone wants to talk to you, David.'

'Yes, yes. There is someone here,' Didi said. 'I can feel it.'

The fire flared and died. Suddenly the room turned chill. Or did David just imagine it. He shivered.

'I really don't think...'

'No... 'Solange had a voice like syrup, like her mother's chocolate cake, as it glided down his throat. 'Don't think. Just give in to it. Day-vid...'

'Give in to it, Day-vid.'

Solange pushed his hand against her tiny breast. Soft all the same through the thin fabric of her blouse.

'Day-vid,' she said.

My God, he was getting aroused! He pulled his hand away so hard that Solange fell from her chair to the floor. Didi looked at him with eyes like slug pellets.

'You are afraid,' she said. 'You are not ready.'

'No, I'm not. I have to go. I'm sorry. Solange. Are you OK?'

He helped her up. Her hand was rough, cold as a lizard.

'It was lovely,' he babbled, 'seeing your wonderful garden, the pictures and, and...'

'Come again, David...' said Didi.

'Yes, I will, I will...'

'Promise,' said Solange.

His aunt poured him a large whiskey.

'And did you promise?'

'I may have. Anything to get out of there.'

'Well, of course I knew they were odd. And that Solange has a reputation, believe it or not. But I thought you'd like the garden.'

'I did. It was great. Only...' thinking of the unseasonality of it all, those unnatural fleshy blooms, the over-abundance, the heavy mix of perfumes, masking what? A smell of death and putrefaction? David took a large gulp of whiskey, his hand trembling. He wasn't usually so fanciful.

'Poor Joe,' he said.

'Oh yes,' said his aunt, 'that was a terrible tragedy. Joe wasn't the full shilling, you know.'

'Ah.'

'A great worker, though. Didi must miss him a lot. Though seemingly she got into a terrific rage when he dug up her giant hogweed. He said it was dangerous but she said it was to keep out undesirables... So she hasn't found anyone else yet?'

'I think perhaps they were hoping to engage me. In more ways than one.' David laughed shakily and raised his glass. 'Cheers.'

'Slainte,' she replied.

What he hadn't told his aunt was how, as Solange was showing him out, she had suddenly grabbed his arm and pulled him with surprising strength.

'I just want to show you something in my studio. Please.'

He couldn't have resisted without flinging her to the ground again, so he let himself be led through to the side of the house, across a courtyard illuminated only by a sliver of moonlight, to a cabin apparently set into the mountainside itself.

Solange didn't let go of his arm until he was inside and the door closed behind him. It was pitch dark. She struck a match and lit several candles. Standing around were several of the same sort of lumpy sculptures he had seen in the garden, oddly deformed creatures, which in the trembling light seemed to shudder into life. David never wanted to leave anywhere more urgently, or felt more unable to do so.

'This is Joe,' Solange said, pointing at one of the shapes.

And indeed David thought he could discern a rough human form emerging from the clay. A face staring away from him.

'I did a bad thing,' she giggled. 'I kept one of his bones.'

'Oh...'

'It's in there.' She gestured at the sculpture.

'Ah...'

'I like to put something in each of my sculptures. Some part of the original or something associated with them.'

'Mm...'

'I'll put him back in the garden when he's finished. He'll enjoy that. It was his favourite place.'

David found his voice. 'A lovely place...'

'Except here. He liked coming here best of all. We did it in here loads of times.'

'Did what?'

'Fucked. Joe was a virgin till I had sex with him. Seventy-three and a virgin! He wanted to make up for lost time.' She giggled again. Then her voice went hard. 'But he shouldn't have told on me. That was bad... D'you know what he said, down in the pub? "I got me hole." That wasn't nice, was it.'

'No... Very crude.'

'Very crude. Yes... You aren't a virgin, are you, Day-vid?'

Her eyes were glittering in the candlelight and her tongue flicked. He stared at her hypnotised as she leaned against a wall and, staring back at him, took off her shoes and socks – the sight of her bare feet on the cold earth floor making him shiver. He couldn't move as she undid her skirt and let it drop. He looked at her one strong leg, her withered one, the slit of her hairless sex. She took off her cardigan and slowly, slowly unbuttoned her blouse. Naked now, she rubbed her hands over the nipples of her tiny breasts, throwing back her head in pleasure. Then dropped one hand and started masturbating.

'Day-vid,' she called. 'Day-vid.'

He hadn't done anything, had he? A gust of wind had surely banged the door open, and blown out one of the candles, bringing him to his senses and sending him careening out into the night, to his car, banging past Didi, standing motionless on the path.

He hadn't promised anything, as Solange flicked her tongue deep in his ear, as she tore the buttons off his shirt, pinched his flesh with her stubby fingers, as she bit his lip and drew blood. He hadn't promised anything, to prolong the intensity of the moment. Had he? He hadn't, had he, finally sunk into the musty cave of the girl's body, and, as she reared up screaming against him, emptied his very soul into her.

No, none of that had happened. It was just a fantasy, driving home fast through the dark night. Even though, as he found when he staggered to bed full of whiskey, some buttons on his shirt were missing. Even though bite marks tattooed his chest. Even though he could hear a voice – Didi's voice – hissing in his ear, 'Don't forget Solange. You promised...'

After a couple of days more with his aunt, he headed away from the village, driving back to Dublin past the turn to Didi's house with only a sideways shameful look. The mountain loured under a black cloud and there was nothing to show that anyone lived there.

David turned on his CD player, but it only jabbered at him. Something wrong with the disk. He tried another but it was the same. Strange. Suddenly he became aware of a strong scent that filled the car. He couldn't place it for a moment and thought for some reason of his grandmother. The road veered up, skirting the mountain and in his rear view mirror he caught a glimpse of the grey house blazing as if on fire, red and yellow blooms licking the walls like flames. And at last he recognised the scent in the car: pressed powder, dusted over a sweating face. He coughed as if smothered. As if a cloud of the stuff swirled round him.

He pressed on the accelerator, swerving round another car as he approached the brow of the hill and nearly crashing into an oncoming vehicle. He wondered briefly how the son of Didi's husband's lover had died. Then he swept down into the next valley, opening all the windows and singing loudly, accompanying the CD which had just righted itself, 'It's the end of the world as we know it, It's the end of the world as we know it, It's the end of the world as we know it, and I feel f...'

Which was the moment when he was hit head on by a truck.

Solange looked up briefly at the sudden sound. Then back down at the clay she was kneading into a certain shape, mixing into it as she worked a handful of little pearl buttons.

LETTING RIP

This wasn't the way I had wanted to travel. Not stuck in the back of my brother's state-of-the-art whatsit with its computerised direction finder and its digital country-and-western station; certainly not squashed among his three lardy children, who pinched and dribbled and guzzled and roared all the way down the country.

I had said I would get a bus but no, my brother wasn't having it. The way he put it was he wanted to save me inconvenience, but I reckon he thought it would look odd if I didn't go down with them. With mam away with the fairies and unable to attend the funeral, God knows the begrudgers already had plenty to go on. My brother never liked to be at a disadvantage, to give people grounds to bad-mouth him, so he phoned to explain in his special patient voice how remote the village was and so on. As if I didn't remember the way we used to come down all those years laden with our summer gear, to be picked up off the bus by Uncle Dinny in his van, mam sitting up front with him, us shoved in the back, bumping for dark ages to the farm. Smelly old thing it was, that van. Carried calves and piglets other times. Smelly old man, too, even then, Dinny was. Smelly and scary. Eyes like broken glass. Hands crusted with scabs. Filthy fingers you'd be afraid might touch you. Although he must have done something right, the same Dinny. My brother kept telling Eileen all the way down the country how it turned out he was worth a small fortune when he died.

'Minded the pennies, d'you see.'

Right enough, there was no state-of-the-art whatsit for Dinny. The old van served him till the end. Lived in the same primitive hovel all his life with no fancy gadgets, Aunty Mary doing all the washing by hand, pushing it after through an iron mangle.

It would be part of the fun of the funeral, my brother said, to see who might get what. But I knew what he was really thinking: an opportunity missed. How he should maybe have sent Eileen and the kids down to charm the old man into a legacy. With Celine's whiny voice in my ear, Natasha's elbow stabbing into my eye, and Shane's spit on my knee, I reckoned my brother stood more of a chance the way things were.

'I can't breath,' I said. It was true. My brother's state-of-the-art air-conditioning didn't seem to be working and Celine ponged. The inimitable stink of pubescence.

'Blast,' my brother said. 'Now the windows won't open.'

Panic set in among the lardy kids.

'We're trapped,' Celine screamed, thrashing thick bare thighs. 'We're going to die.'

Then Shane started to howl while Natasha flailed at the windows.

'Here,' my brother said, tipping a tray of fuses into Eileen's lap. 'See which one works, for God's sake.'

'They're all different colours.'

'Course they are.' He had put on his how stupid-can-you-get voice. 'They're colour differentiated... by function and power.'

'So what colour is the fuse for the windows, then?'

'God give me strength,' said my brother.

You have to understand, he was a bully and a prankster. Always had been. A bully who paradoxically still thought he deserved to be loved. While Eileen shrank, my defence was to go sullen and wait my opportunity. Not seeing him helped. They'd stopped inviting me ever since I said I wouldn't babysit any more, not after the incident with the piss in the cough bottle. My brother claimed I had no sense of humour.

'Piss is good for you,' he said. 'Actresses drink it.'

Wonder if he'd have laughed so much if he'd ever found out that the curry I made after for them was concocted from spiced-up doggy food. That's what I mean by waiting my opportunity.

Meek Eileen was certainly the recipient of the worst of my brother's bullying. But if you suppose that put me on her side, think again. Every woman for herself. And while I certainly wasn't enjoying the ride, squashed on the back seat between the kids, I kept myself going by thinking how much money I was saving. How much time. These things matter when you're strapped for both, like me.

We reached the village and my brother ran a competition to see who would be first to spot the funeral home. He'd always liked competitions: I spy with my little eye something beginning with R, changing the solution each time someone guessed right – road: no; river: no; runny nose: no no no – because he had to win. Anyway, I spotted the funeral home ages before anyone else but kept my gob shut. Actually we almost drove by it and I had to nudge Natasha hard in the ribs and wink.

'There it is,' she screeched.

'Good girl,' my brother smiled.

Uncle Dinny was all cleaned up and wearing a suit, the way I'd never seen him. My brother made a beeline for the widow. Maybe he thought he could make up for lost loot by shaking her energetically by the hand. I was surprised to see her push him away with some force. He actually staggered. Meanwhile, Natasha, Shane and Celine, on cue, all started howling with grief at the sight of the dear departed. Eileen tried to shut them up and got Shane's snot on her skirt for her trouble.

Suddenly something struck me.

'Did Dinny get a divorce and marry again?'

'What divorce!' he yelled loud enough to wake the dead. 'You mad or what?' He was still raging at the push.

'Only that's never Aunty Mary, not unless it grew back.'

Our poor aunt had lost a foot in a domestic accident no one talked about, and was fitted with a shiny pink plastic one that had fascinated us as kids. We were forever hanging around to see if we could get a hold of it when she took it off at night. We never did.

My brother started staring so hard at the widow's leg that I thought he was going to get clocked all over again.

Then Eileen came up.

'The deceased is a Mr Patsy Galoogley. That can't be right, can it?'

We hastily departed, my brother evidently still in some confusion.

'After all I did for that woman,' he complained.

Natasha got a slap on the head for identifying the wrong funeral parlour, which just goes to show how wise I was not making a bid for the prize.

'It's at the bottom of the town, seemingly,' Eileen said.

There was a long queue of people waiting to shake Aunty Mary's hand and despite my brother's attempts to jump to the front, we were pushed outside in the rain to take our turn.

Celine started it: she said that if she didn't have a burger at once, she'd starve to death. Then the other two said they'd starve to death too, and screamed at the prospect of being cut off so young. I commented that if they were planning to die, they were in the right place for it which made them scream even more. People looked over at us and my brother maintained that my remarks weren't helping.

But he was thoughtful as he said it. He was obviously amazed at the turn-out.

'People must have loved your man very much,' Eileen commented.

The short little fellow in front of us turned around at that and gave her a look. He had a crunched-up face with grime in the folds and a rats-tail hairpiece slapped on top of his baldy pate.

'Not at all,' he said. 'We're here to make sure he's truly dead.'

That shut Eileen up.

At last we got in out of the rain and shuffled over to Aunty Mary. My brother stared at her foot, just to be sure, but she knew him, well enough. Something about him made her chuckle. 'Dinny was always saying you'd inherit...' my brother perked up at that... 'the family conk.'

True enough, my brother had always had a big nose, and now it was permanently in bloom, as a consequence of the brandy he used as fertiliser.

Me however, she couldn't place at first. Then she clapped her hands. 'Oh yes, I remember. Sulky!'

Near enough, I thought, wondering all the same what she had to be so happy about.

There was a daughter, too, a lumpy woman, who answered to the name Crystal. The streak beside her was her husband, a creamery manager.

'Crystal married so well,' mam used to say. For years I thought that was his name. So Well. Then I found it was even sillier. He was a Mr Ball. Crystal Ball.

By now, the little man before us had reached the coffin. It was tight closed.

'Here,' he called to Aunty Mary. 'You sure he's in there?'

'Didn't I screw down the lid meself, Florrie.'

'Then wo-hoo!' sang he, and before you could say Biddie Mulligan, up he'd jumped on the coffin lid and proceeded to dance a jig.

It seemed we out-of-towners were the only ones gob-smacked. Even the priest tittered and the undertaker went so far as to get out his accordion and start to play The Mason's Apron. Next thing, everyone was reeling around. I even got caught up in the dance myself and Eileen started to beat time.

Suddenly three loud knocks sounded out, as if from the gates of hell. Then three more. Bang, bang, bang.

Everyone froze. Florrie on the coffin stopped short, one leg cocked in the air.

'Tis coming from inside the box!' someone said, and Florrie leapt to the ground as if scalded.

This was the moment my brother took control of the proceedings. He stepped forward and banged on the lid. Bang came the reply from inside. Once more and Bang echoed back again.

'Open up,' he instructed the undertaker in ominous tones. 'I'm afraid something bad has been perpetrated here,' he added self-righteously.

The undertaker found his screwdriver and with shaking hands tried to loosen the lid. Impatiently my brother grabbed the implement. At last – and no one had said a word during the entire time – he took a deep breath.

'Heave ho!' he said.

Some people leaned forward, more drew back. Aunty Mary alone sat placidly tapping her false foot as if she could still hear the melody of the accordion.

The lid was off.

'Holy God!' exclaimed my brother.

I peered in. Uncle Dinny, dirty in death as in life, lay there in his work clothes. A skinny mean-faced man with a blossoming nose. What was unusual was that some class of a wooden stake had been plunged deep into his chest. It must have been the top end of that had knocked against the lid of the coffin when Florrie danced and when my brother banged.

Now everyone turned to Aunty Mary.

'I had to make sure, you see. You all see that, don't you?'

The lid was replaced. The party resumed. My brother gloomily took his lardy children off to the chipper. He was clearly surprised when Eileen said that if I was staying on a bit she wouldn't mind keeping me company. He rubbed his red nose and looked preoccupied.

'OK, so,' he said.

Two things amazed me that night. First, how meekly my brother went off without us. And secondly, how well Aunty Mary could dance a reel, and her with a false foot.

'Fine girl you are,' said Florrie, as he twirled her round.

Acknowledgements

The Meadow, Blip and *For Ever and Ever* were first published in The Stinging Fly. *The Meadow* was subsequently included in the anthology *Irish Writers against War* and was performed on stage by actor Olwen Fouere as part of a showcase production entitled *About the Days*.

The Film World was first published in The Waterford Review, Vol. 4, 1994.

In 2009 *Shrine* was runner-up in a National Museum competition.

In 2008 *It's Hard to Die in Springtime* won the Molly Keane award at the IMRAMA festival in Lismore, Co Waterford.

In 2007 *Flowering Cherry* won the Brian McMahon prize at Listowel Writers' Week.

In 2004, *Letting RIP*, was winner of the prestigious James Plunkett Memorial Award.

In 2002, *Jealousy* came third in the Francis McManus RTE competition for a radio short story.

A huge thank-you to Phyl Herbert for her invaluable help and encouragement.